Apple Hair

A Boy Band Fantasy Novel

Airen Ho

Published by AppleHairStory
www.applehairstory.com

ISBN-13: 9798991919418 (paperback)
ISBN-13: 9798991919425 (hardcover)
ISBN-13: 9798991919401 (digital)

Cover design and illustration by hastapena.
Edited by Raven Quill Editing, LLC.
Proofread by Brandee Paschall Books LLC.
Formatting by Polgarus Studio.

First edition.

Follow Apple Hair, the boy band, at www.applehairstory.com

For my family.
I would never want a universe without you.

Prologue

Van

Day one. Crisp. Nothing goes wrong.

Day two. Seiya makes an *extremely* dirty joke and only Corrin laughs.

Day three. David almost throws up when Corrin attempts to make a tuna melt on his wok. It's from both the smell and the actual first bite. Kaden almost fares the same.

Day four. I *finally* get to play a game of *League of Legends*. I only die once, but my team loses after forty-seven minutes.

Day five. I forget to journal.

Day six. The team and I look at our scores on the leaderboards. It's not looking good, with me in the bottom half of the trainees. I pick up a Spam musubi from 7-Eleven and eat it in shame.

Day seven. I give up journaling.

Okay, maybe the first month consists of more than these... little mishaps. But it was my first attempt at journaling, okay? But if I can describe the first month of being in a group in AWE Entertainment... I guess I could say that there's a *bit* of magic. I'm not just saying that because I'm a fantasy fan. I'm saying it because, well, this is my dream. To be part of a group, or a band, rather.

Merlin Kim, CEO and superstar in his own right, chose us. Five of us, to be one of the first groups with a potential to debut in AWE. Highlighting the word *potential*, because there's nothing really certain about us—we have to score high, compete against the other groups, and just be fighters every single day.

I remember the day he put us together. I also remember the chaos of the first thirty days together, learning how to confront, sacrifice, and compromise in little ways. Sure, I have an older brother. But I've never lived with four other guys before. *If only you could see the absolute mess after only seven days in the dorm…*

"Can you, I don't know, clean this up?" Kaden asks in the middle of our first month together.

Seiya chews on his gum and pops a bubble obnoxiously loud. "I don't think that's mine."

"I've never seen that before…" David offers.

I share a glance with Corrin. He shrugs. "Me neither."

Even though *I too* have never seen that particular gray t-shirt, I throw it into the hamper along with a bunch of other crumpled articles of clothing. I sit down on the couch and nurse a headache.

I think about K-pop and music in general. How much do I love it? How much do I want to be a part of it? I never thought training would be easy, but I thought it would be *easier*.

A second after calming myself down, our manager sends us our schedule for tomorrow. Its ring sends a bolt of panic through me. *Great, another twelve-hour day.*

We can't exactly say that we chose each other. After all, Merlin and his team calculated how likely we are to succeed in the music industry. But we *did* feel a connection when the five of us were gathered in Merlin Kim's office. We had a choice. A chance, rather.

And we took it.

Chapter 1

Van

Being alone means being comfortable.

I'm serious. Unfortunately, that's not possible when you're in AWE Entertainment. AWE, a phenomenon that erupted thanks to the K-pop scene. They aim to emulate the K-pop model, producing groups that can tackle the global stage. With their first international headquarters being built on Oʻahu, Hawaiʻi, I had a chance. To create a dream. And if you didn't know about AWE before, now you know…

Back to the moment. A *very* chaotic moment. Living with four other guys means chaos at every turn. And I mean *every* turn. All I want is to curl up with a good book, or to lose myself in a PC game. Girl, what I'd do right now to enter the *Grishaverse* or queue up for a game of *League*. But what I want even more?

That's to debut.

Tasked with waking up the other members, at least on Mondays and Tuesdays, I head into the bedroom. One futon spreads out between two bunks, making our lucky number—five. My morning vitamins and energy drink haven't quite kicked in yet. I breathe in deep, wondering whether I have the strength to yell.

"Wake—"

David groans, kicking his pillow away from his body. It ends up falling on Seiya, who's sprawled across the futon like a spider. In reaction, he rolls completely across the floor and slaps Kaden on the face. Kaden shoots up and smacks his head against the bunk's frame.

Corrin wakes up and almost falls out of the top bunk with a start. I leap forward, holding out my arms to catch him.

He ends up saving himself, barely holding on to high ground with his left leg and arm.

I accidentally bite my tongue. Freezing in place, I taste iron and watch as Seiya sits up into the morning sun. He scowls at nothing, rubbing his eyes. Corrin wiggles around and tries to save himself from teetering.

"It's Monday," David says with a scratchy and soft voice. "Can't believe our only day off passed so fast."

Kaden's the first to get up. He stretches his arms high above his head, showing off some of his corded muscle. "Life's fast. We don't want to get left behind."

David probably wants to roll his eyes, but he simply hums and readies himself to jump to the floor.

Seiya and Corrin race to use the bathroom first. The latter groans when he loses his chance to a slamming door. I reflect on the additional chaos of sharing a bathroom among five people. The dorm's best friend? By far, it's been Febreze. The next best thing has been our Swiffer. Ah. Can you tell that I'm the one in charge of cleaning?

I munch on a Stroopwafel from Costco even though a very persistent lady on YouTube has been warning me not to eat sweets for breakfast. Miraculously, nothing breaks in the mad rush to get ready. Something pops up into my mind—last night, Corrin persistently argued to adopt a pet for the dorm. *Seriously, Corrin? I can't imagine something jumping on our feet while we get ready. Not to mention the added smell.* Corrin's probably still mad at me for shutting him down. I feel a little bit bad.

In record time, our group readies to pile into the van. At eight-forty-five sharp, I say, "I hate to say this, because I don't want to sound like a field trip chauffeur. But please, put on your seatbelts. Let's not fly out the window." Now, usually I'm more shy around people, but these guys have successfully brought out my sassy side. "We're ready, Shar!" Shar—our guardian angel who somehow manages to keep us alive and well. Oh, and on schedule. She swerves out of the parking lot, and we speed toward Ala Moana.

The clouds seem brighter today, blinding me when I look up at them. I keep my eyes on the sky as the guys all try to catch a ten-minute nap. Everyone except Seiya, who's scrolling through his social media—which we're all technically not supposed to have. I warned him about this too. *I see how it is, Seiya…* No hard feelings, though. My gaming Discord technically counts as social media, even though my name is *goldfishhero2* and is impossible to find by the AWE team.

When we arrive at the AWE building, I yawn into my hand and close my eyes for a total of one second. Then, Shar tells us our schedule for the day—another five-hour dance practice, then a two-hour vocal lesson. After lunch, it's another four-hour dance session, ending with a language class.

"Feeling okay?" I ask Corrin, one of the youngest in the group—eighteen, like David and Kaden. He looks like he's going to fall over.

"Oh!" He straightens up. "Just fine."

Considering we've only been a team for one month, the awkwardness is still there. Since I was voted as the leader of the group, I do my best to break the ice. Being a major introvert doesn't help on that aspect. If I had a choice, I could go through a whole day without saying a word.

Shar leads us into the company, but before I enter, I look over my shoulder at Ala Moana, the largest open-air shopping mall in the world. In the heart of Honolulu, we're near the beach and if I *really* focus in, I can smell the salt in the air.

AWE Entertainment, a thirty-story building that was once a luxury high-rise, welcomes me with a cold kiss of air conditioning. The lobby sparkles with cream and brown undertones, all picked out by our billionaire CEO, Merlin Kim. Merlin is the mastermind who personally handpicked this building on O'ahu, even though there were tons of other cities he could've set up his headquarters. Whispers are going around that he has a secret lover here. But really, I just think he fell in love with the island when he visited a decade ago on vacation.

A rush of trainees gather in the lobby, sipping iced coffee from the company's cafe. I stay with my members. Sad to say, we've been isolated ever since we were chosen as a group to potentially debut. "Um…" I say. I hope someone will rescue me. I have flashbacks of being alone in school, when my best friend Nick was sick at home, and James and Kainoa were stuck in another class. I *never* want to experience something like that again, even though I'm usually comfortable being a loner, keeping myself company.

"I heard we're picking our name today," Seiya says.

Seiya's my age at nineteen, and even though I *should* see us as equals, I can't help but be jealous. Seiya's always chill. Of course he'd not sweat about the name of our group. On my end, I can't help but think about how many times I'll stutter in front of CEO Kim. At least I have four other guys to hide behind.

"I'm sure Kaden can come up with something good," Corrin says, reaching out to pat Kaden on the back.

Kaden gives a tight smile. "I think it's something we should all agree on. If it sticks with us for the rest of our careers…"

I quiet at that, and David also respects the silence. He's more on the quiet side too, so I feel an affinity with him. Either he or I will end up listening to one of Corrin's stories at the end of the day, nodding along.

I wonder whether we're all thinking the same thing, how our careers have yet to begin. How they may never begin.

The trainees file into the elevator, and we head inside after a group of four. One girl and three boys. Most of the trainees are around sixteen or seventeen, with a few being thirteen to fifteen. So, our group's on the older side. The high-school-like situation makes things… *interesting* at times. One boy with a topknot sneers as I share his space, as if he can't stand to be around us. I think his name is Jason.

"Here are Merlin's favorites," he says.

At first, the five of us stay still and try to ignore the way poison leaks into the air. But I can sense it coming, the air shifting around our most confrontational member—Kaden. And then he takes the bait. With a measured voice that could probably kill you. Girl, I would *not* want to be on the other end of that voice. "We all had the same chances to make an impression. You don't have to be bitter about it."

As someone who hates confrontation, I wait for something to happen—maybe for the entire elevator to implode. Instead, the door opens to our floor. I rush out and try to be the leader by example. Hopefully, my four teammates will file out without another word. They do… which earns my sigh of relief.

As we make our way to the dance studio, David fills the hall with his thoughts. "It's not like we're the only group that's been formed so far," he says. "There're two other boy groups and four girl groups."

"Maybe it's because we're different?" Corrin says, jamming his finger onto his chin. "I mean, we're the only all-Asian American group. That could be weird for some people."

"I…" I open a door on my left to an empty studio. I wait until we're all inside. "I don't think it's that. There are tons of Asians on the island. I think it's just that we're easy targets."

"For what reason?" Kaden asks.

"It's…" I lose my words, wishing that our dance instructor would barge in so I'll have time to think of a better explanation later.

"We don't look like the fighter types," Seiya says, flexing his arm. "We need to build some muscle so all the other trainees will be damn scared."

David laughs, his cheeks turning a bit pink. "So, we need to follow Kaden's routine. If we all could gain enough mass in the next few months—"

The door opens, and Shar peeks her head in. "Hey, boys! So, I have news. As your training gets more serious, your instructors will change. It's natural, and even though it's scary, I know you guys are up for it. Say hello to your new instructor for dance."

I immediately stand, watching the door, waiting for whoever it is to make their first step. The boys follow. We're ready to face the music. Or whatever it's called when your heart feels like it's going to overflow with anticipation.

I may be imagining it, but the air feels heavier. Something shimmers when the door opens wider, clouding my vision with the feeling of something big about to happen.

Chapter 2

Corrin

I'm not *crazy*. Just excited.

When our new dance instructor walks in, I can't keep still. I shake, rubbing my palms against my thighs, like that will calm me down. I remind myself of an anxious schoolboy. Even though I'm eighteen, people say that I don't read eighteen. I'd like to say that I take that as a compliment, since I'll probably look thirty when I'm forty. Maybe I won't even have to wear a sunhat and massive sunglasses like my mom always does to prevent wrinkles. Or maybe that should be even more important for me? I glance at everyone—Kaden, David, Van, and Seiya.

I'm never good at hiding my feelings. My mom calls me an open book, but really, I hate keeping things to myself. Sharing things with my group mates should be a bit easy for me, but I have to admit, it's been hard. Being a trainee takes a *lot* of energy already. I don't want to give them more to worry about. Is that weird?

"Are you guys ready?" she says. She wears a purplish pink tracksuit, looking vibrant against her deeper skin tone. "I'm Armani Bera."

For a few seconds, the room quiets down. The boys probably don't know what to say—and for a rare moment, me neither. I grin and try to think about what she'd want to hear. "I'm Corrin." I point to the members beside me. "Seiya, Van, Kaden, and David! Um… and by the way, your hair looks great."

She laughs, combing through some of her loose curls. "Thank you, it took me hours." When it's clear we don't have much more to say, she continues. "I already know you boys, of course! Making all sorts of waves in the company. So much potential. Feel free to just call me Armani—I don't really care about formalities, and we're all adults here, right? I can't be more than ten years older than you guys."

David gives a nervous laugh, and the rest of the boys just nod. I try to smile big. My cheeks hurt a bit from doing so. My fingers feel like nothing can stop them from fidgeting. I don't really know when I inherited the scatterbrain qualities of the cats that I take care of. (Cat after cat. And other animals too.) Until I started to act like them, just a little bit? Or maybe some sort of bug got into my stomach, making me act a bit different than the rest. Not that different is bad, but I do stand out a bit compared to the other, more laid-back guys.

Armani introduces herself further. She grew up in California, after her parents immigrated from Delhi. She talks about finding a passion for dance at an early age, competing in many televised competitions until she settled on teaching it for a living. She, of course, worked with so many pop stars that I lose track after the fifth one she mentions. The word "qualified" flashes in my brain, and I wonder once again just how genius the wizard Merlin is.

"I'm ready to make you guys into superstars," she says, winking.

By the time I try to wink back, she has already turned toward the full-size mirror, twisting her body into our first stretching position. I follow along with the boys.

As she reaches down to touch her toes, the mirror twinkles. I *can't* be imagining it. A black cat runs across the surface, perpendicular to the floor.

"What—" I say. But everyone turns toward me, looking at me weirdly. Sweat crawls down my neck.

Armani twirls her hands above her head, moving into the next stretching position. I continue, following along, but the cat still runs rampant in my brain. It's like it's in there, running around. Leaving paw prints all over. Even though the mirror looks glossy and empty, the cat's black fur crosses my mind over and over.

"You okay?" David says, after we finish our first run-through of the new choreography.

"Yes!" I wipe off the sweat on my forehead, trying to smile.

"You sure?" he says.

I nod my head adamantly, even as Van peers over from where he's sitting down, chugging a bottle of water.

I don't want them to feel like they need to check up on me. Sometimes I feel like I'm the youngest in the group, even though David and Kaden beat me by a few months. (It's not a good feeling, especially with the added pressure of not coming across as weird.) I know the guys will accept me either way. But.

I *need* to be strong. Not only do I want to debut, I want to go further. I want to release many EPs and albums, perform on world stages that I could once only dream of. And when I retire, I would like to start my own cat cafe that all my own fans can come to and enjoy. The scratches on my legs, which all turned to light scars, begin to itch. I've taken care of *a lot* of cats in my lifetime.

After the five-hour practice, I completely forget about the mirage. I collapse onto the floor of one of the trainee common rooms, rolling over to a comfortable position on the rug. A breath suctions out of me, as if pulled by an invisible force. Tired doesn't even begin to describe the feeling, though I'm slowly and surely getting used to the feeling of my lungs almost collapsing.

"Chee! Great minds think alike," Seiya says. Chee is a word that comes from Hawaiian slang! It's actually Samoan, and the full phrase is "cheehoo!" as in woo-hoo or that something is very exciting or worthy of exclamation.

Seiya settles down next to me. In ten minutes, we'll have to head over to our vocal class.

"Mm-hmm," I say, closing my eyes.

It feels like a second, but soon Seiya shakes me awake with a panicked look in his eyes. "Dude. We're late!"

I groan, forcing myself up to a sitting position. I press my wrists against my eyes, trying to understand how ten minutes passed so quickly. Did that weird cat mess up my sense of time or something? "How long did we knock out for?"

"Thirty minutes," Seiya says. "Shit. Sorry, I should've set an alarm or something."

"No worries, me too." I take a deep breath and stand, wobbly on my legs from the five-hour dance practice.

Ten seconds later, we race to the elevator. Thankfully, no weird trainees this time. I begin to hum one of the melodies that got stuck in my head yesterday.

"You're really something else," Seiya says. "How can you sing at a time like this?"

"Well, we are heading to *singing* class," I say.

He scoffs. "You're lucky I'm older. More mature and shit. Or I would've bopped you on the head."

"You would never," I say.

Then, the door opens, and I race with Seiya to the vocal practice room. I *do not* look forward to what I'm about to see.

Diane White, the notorious vocal instructor of AWE Entertainment, stares at us like she's trying to split us apart into tiny pieces. It feels like she can do so if she really tries. I try for a smile and then stop. I don't think Diane White likes smiles very much.

Even though Seiya's older, I feel responsible for the whole nap turning into a mini siesta. "Mrs. White! So sorry for missing the first… twenty minutes."

"Twenty-two minutes," she says. "You and Seiya, meet me at the end of the day. You know where to find me. I'll make sure those twenty-two minutes come back to bite you."

I shiver. Next to me, Seiya tries to show no reaction—probably because the other guys are looking. Then he surprises me. He gives Mrs. White a small bow. "Will do, Mrs. White."

I follow along and almost stumble over myself. Then I take my spot between Kaden and David. When Diane's distracted (a very rare moment), Kaden nudges my stomach. "Sorry. We got stuck with Diane and realized that you guys didn't wake up. But it was too late. Couldn't go and look for you."

I nudge him back. "It's fine." Kaden always speaks his mind, but I'm glad he isn't afraid of apologizing (about anything, really).

We work on our harmonies, trying our best to sound pleasing to the ear. My voice, scratchy at times, got me through the auditions. I played the guitar as well that day, but now I can't hide behind its body. I remember the day as Mrs. White corrects us so many times it begins to feel like a time loop.

It was a sunny day in Mililani. I begged my mom to take me to the AWE Entertainment auditions, thinking it would change our lives. Maybe I was right. Maybe I *am* right.

I want to change my mom's life. As a single mom and a nurse, she works so many hours that I want her to get those back in the future. ("She will!" I constantly tell myself). I used to think that I'd change her life through coding or inventing something. When I went busking for the first time, I knew I wanted to take the risky route, no matter the cost.

"Are you even thinking of the lyrics?" Mrs. White says. Seconds pass before I realize she's talking to me.

I straighten my spine. "Oh… did I sing the wrong words?"

"Wrong words?" Mrs. White leans back and gives a bitter laugh to the ceiling. "You might as well have been singing an entirely different song."

"Sorry," I say, trying to ignore the way my chest heaves.

Kaden opens his mouth. I know he wants to say something to defend me, but I shake my head, hoping he can hear my thoughts. *Not now.*

By the end of vocal practice, my throat doesn't hurt. That has to mean something good, right?

"Did you guys see anything, like… when Armani was teaching us?" I say. Am I spewing bullshit unintentionally? Am I being suspicious?

The guys all say no, except Van, who stares ahead as we walk to the cafeteria. "No. But I did see something weird in the air when she first walked in."

"Okay, I didn't see *that.*"

"I think we're just sleep deprived," Kaden says, rubbing his chin with his pointer finger. "We're seeing things because we need to be sleeping more than five hours a day."

"I guess that makes sense," I say.

At lunch, I grab all the crispy ends of the pizza, and I ignore the other trainees staring at me like I have a problem. I can't help what kind of piece I like! That's just me. I skip to the table with the rest of the guys, finally feeling like maybe, by the end of the day, we'll have our name, and our dream won't feel so far away anymore.

I'm so, so ready for that.

A hush settles throughout the cafeteria. I turn towards the handsome guy walking through the doors. (Very handsome, by the way.) I can probably cut my hair with his jaw, and his eyes can probably set the BBQ grill on fire. "OH!" Then I quiet myself, using my whisper. "Who's that?"

Chapter 3

Kaden

I pride myself on being smarter than average. And being smart sometimes means showing little reaction. I train my face to still as the most handsome guy I've ever seen walks through the door.

I would say the f-word, my favorite curse word and the most efficient of the bunch. But I don't—my little sister is always in my mind, as if she's sitting by my side. Somehow, my finicky mind thinks she might catch me.

It seems every trainee notices him at the same time. He gives off an air of importance, and the space around him almost wavers. Like he has power radiating off his skin. I blink quickly and think about the science of being grounded, of breathing. I often tell my little sister that all it takes to train and quiet your mind is a few steady breaths. One. Two.

I turn my attention toward my food as he looks our way. "I don't get starstruck easily," I tell my team members. "But he looks like he owns the company."

"He kind of does," David whispers back. "He's the new producer. He'll be overseeing the development of all the groups."

Seiya breathes through puckered lips. "Damn. That's crazy."

The two boys look at each other, as if sharing a thought. Then, they look away and pick up their pizza at the same time. I've observed too much about the world to miss the clues those two give off all the time.

"It's a good thing he's here, right?" Corrin says, shaking in his seat. "That has to be a good thing! It means that we really are going to make some progress."

Corrin reminds me of my little sister, Lora. Corrin and I are around the same age—I'm actually younger by one month and eight days—but his energy radiates pureness, just like my sister who I've tried to protect my whole life.

I nod, trying not to burst his bubble. I do remember the guy. Leo Pak. I've seen him in several interviews, and he quit the idol scene to take up a managerial position. I remember his lyrics to one of his most famous songs. My memory, which rarely fails me, gives me the melody alongside.

Opening up to you.
A new parallel
Ah, ah, lead me down the stairwell.

His voice makes me heady. I visualize myself spitting out my pizza, as if that would get rid of the sour taste in my mind. Actually, I'm a small eater. But spitting out my food? I might as well regress to the Dark Ages. I swallow, deciding I've eaten enough for the day. Like a seasoned office worker, I eliminate lunch off my to-do list. I eat simply because I need to fuel my body. Lora would scoff if I said that aloud.

Then I turn and Leo's completely gone. But the trainees don't notice. They already turn back to their meals, oblivious.

"Where did he go?" I say, my voice matching some of my confusion.

"What?" Van turns his head like an owl. "No idea."

I shake my head, wondering whether the air in the company

makes me nauseous. Not likely. I practically live here. I watch Seiya take ten massive bites. Then I tell my team that I'm going to head off to take a nap before we have to attend our last dance practice.

Leo Pak stands in the hallway.

"Oh." I take in his sharp jaw and the way his eyes swirl with wonder. "Hi. Welcome to Hawai'i."

He mutters something in Korean, but I haven't taken enough language classes to discern the meaning. I think he says something about the weather, but I'm not completely sure.

"Well…" I press my lips together, reminding myself of my disapproving grandmother. "Nice to meet you."

I shift around him, but he grabs my shoulder. An icy wave travels into my joints, and I stifle a gasp. His English sounds unnatural, but still clear. "Be careful."

"I will," I say, trying not to overthink things. My sister often says I get stuck in my head, going over hypothesis over hypothesis.

But as I head up the elevator to the dance room's floor, I pore over Leo Pak's words. What do I have to be careful about?

I often sleep in the dance studio so that the boys will wake me up when the instructor comes. As I close my eyes, I think about our group—five Asian American guys with a dream of setting foot on the world stage.

The probabilities of actually setting foot on the world stage? The chances may be slim, but I chose to take the risk.

I rub my arms and turn, opening my eyes and studying myself in the mirror. I see what the world would see—an eighteen-year-old Filipino guy who looks like he could use three naps in a row. I turn, closing my eyes again, using my forearm to block out the light.

I dream of snorkeling, even though I've never been. My parents died snorkeling when I was five. My little sister was two.

I wonder what they were thinking when they were carried out to sea by a rogue current. The officials said it was impossible. The bay was supposed to be completely safe. They were supposed to come home to add a new vibrant shell to their collection. I guess no one can account for all the logistics, all the tiny risks of life.

They would've loved seeing me audition for AWE. My grandparents hated the idea, just like they hated taking care of me.

"Time to get up!" Corrin slaps my arm, and I groan, wondering how the minutes could feel like seconds.

Armani Bera arrives, looking exactly the same as she did a few hours ago. Maybe even better, if that's possible. I try not to admire her too much. She shows us a new song, one that we'll use for our monthly evaluation.

"Now, guys," she says, smiling like the idea of an evaluation is the equivalent of discovering a new fossil. "You'll be graded on multiple things in this evaluation. Dance is a *huge* part of it. Let's try to prepare something that the execs will *love*."

Armani launches into a sequence that lasts a full minute, twisting and hitting every beat as if punching someone in the face. She flips her hair like a pro, using each of her limbs as if she merely presses a button to control them.

"We'll go slowly," she says after finishing—not even breathing hard.

I take the center position, following Armani as she counts to eight and shows us each step with clarity. As she increases the speed, I lose myself in a time loop as we repeat section after section. I think about solving the same simple math problem over and over again, except this equation runs far from simple. I think about how the repetition is necessary, how I'll move in the same way millions of more times.

Sweat runs down my back, and the lights of the studio imprint into my eyes and the mirror. Armani cheers us on and corrects us when necessary, shouting with so much energy I would be surprised if she didn't have more than one coffee today.

"I want to get to know you guys better," Armani says, once we sit down for a break. "I think we've had enough dancing for today, so I want to ask why you guys were put into a group."

I exchange glances with the members. I speak up. "It was CEO Kim's decision ultimately. I wish we could say that we chose each other, but we didn't."

"That's not completely true," Armani says. "You chose each other by sticking together, by spending this month making sure you all have the same dream. That counts for something."

"I guess…" I turn to other guys.

Seiya, the second oldest, clears his throat. "I like looking at it that way, Armani. That's a sick mind you got there."

Armani dazzles me with her smile. "How do you guys like it so far?"

"Besides being formed as a group early on," I start. "It's been hard. The other trainees seem to target us, and our training schedules all got more intense."

It'll only get harder, a voice says. I look around, wondering who said it. The boys also look confused, their eyes darting left and right. I look at Van and see a bead of sweat form at his throat. Am I hearing things? A lack of sleep will do that to you.

Armani seems oblivious. She takes out a hair band, reaching forward. "Sorry to be unprofessional, but may I?"

I realize she's talking to David. He gives a little nod.

Armani makes a part in David's hair. She ties a lock of it with the band, so that it sticks upward. I heard of this unconventional style before. But the name escapes me. "I always wanted to do that," she says.

Waiting for the voice to come back, I don't dare bring it up. Maybe bringing it up would make it come back in full force. Today definitely was the weirdest day, one that I could never even dare to plan for. I come up with one conclusion—more sleep will be our definite cure.

"I heard you guys are getting a new language instructor too," Armani says. "He's a polyglot, and he can teach you guys multiple languages that you'll need to tour the world."

"That would be helpful," I say.

"Exciting!" Corrin says.

The clock strikes nine p.m., and Armani takes her leave. I glance at David, who still has the tie in his hair. He looks ridiculous. "Are you going to take that out?"

"You know I look pretty great," David says. "I should keep this thing in all the time. It could be my signature look, and everyone will copy me."

"That's odd," I say, and everyone laughs. David pouts.

"You guys heard that weird voice too, right?" Seiya says. "That shit was crazy. I just want to make sure we aren't hallucinating."

"I definitely heard it," I say. "If these weird happenings continue until tomorrow, we'll do something about it."

"Agreed," Van says. "But it's time to meet the polyglot."

I wonder how this new instructor will look at us, whether he'll also contribute to the strangeness of the day. Whoever it may be, CEO Kim only hires geniuses—I know I won't be disappointed.

Chapter 4

Seiya

B ro. The polyglot instructor could *kill* with his razor-sharp looks.

With dreadlocks tied up into a ponytail, a fancy blue dress shirt, and black slacks, he first introduces himself as Cory Matthews and comments about being AWE's first Black language instructor. He speaks with pride, like he really owns his position. That's fire.

David sits next to me as we read our vocabulary for the day. Our language classes are going to rotate once we get a handle on things, but the first language we're focusing on is Korean. Probably because our company was founded because of K-pop. And we're planning to visit for training in the future.

David's Korean and the only one who could probably read the text in front of him. I scoot my chair closer to him and lower my voice. "Dude. How do you read this again?"

He gives me a little smile, tilting his head from left to right. I've always found him cute, and he gives me butterflies. Just saying.

He *still* has that tie in his hair that Armani gave him. Is it crazy that I want to reach out and flick it? Probably.

After David helps me with the first few sentences on my

worksheet, Cory shows off his mad skills by reading a Korean poem. His pronunciation sounds like water, completely smooth. So cool.

"I've been thinking," Cory says in English. "Each group has their own concept. I know this isn't exactly related to language, but why don't you guys begin to think about your story?"

The room quiets as everyone begins to think. Corrin raises his hand. "I love that idea! In fact, why don't we start now?"

"Now?" I look toward my worksheet, filled with indecipherable marks. God. Maybe I do need a distraction.

"How about we come up with the first line?" Cory Matthews says. "The first line sets the tone for the whole story."

David lets out a sweet laugh. "Why don't we write it on the whiteboard?"

Because David's mad cute, I raise my hand and agree. Cory passes me the Expo marker and asks me to stand. I head over with a weird buzz in my hands and feet, like I'm about to do something big.

I place the marker, dark blue, on the board. Even though writing's not my thing, I know what to write. I want my group to be one thing—interesting. The guys and I all decided we want to create our own universe. Cory's right. Why not start now?

The marker lets out a squeak on the board. Bruh. I shiver from the sound, and Cory Matthews says, "Go on."

I think. Maybe I should write in pidgin?

Hawaiian pidgin—a creole language spoken on the island. Ami— my older sister—and I used to speak it to each other. We challenged each other to learn more words. We went a bit cray with that. But it's one of my sickest memories with her.

Now? My favorites stand out to me.

Da kine—a placeholder that can mean almost anything. Like da kine lunch plate—to refer to the lunch plate you might wanna have.

Braddah—meaning bro. I often call the members this.

Choke—meaning a lot.

And one of my personal favorites, shoots, which you can say in enthusiastic agreement.

I write, *It was the dead of night, with choke shadows.*

As soon as I poke the board to make the period, the lights in the room completely go out. Everything's blank. Silence descends upon us. What did David write in his notes app the other day? Like a pall or something? A cold wind rushes into the classroom. Damn. I think Corrin squeals, and someone else—either Van or Kaden, bangs their desk with their knee.

"What's going on?" I say, half expecting Cory to answer and make everything right and cool again.

"Um." Cory doesn't sound surprised. "I'll go check the electricity. Wait here."

If you dare.

The voice is creepy as hell, and it's my second time hearing it. I tug at my stud earring and flip my hair back as our teacher heads outside.

"This day is *not* normal," Kaden says. "Could it really be because of sleep deprivation?"

"Hm." David taps his fingers on the desk—at least, I think. "I don't think so. I think this is happening because we're about to choose our name. Weird things always happen when people are about to do something big."

"Mm-hmm." But Van doesn't say anything else.

I set the marker on something solid. I think it's the desk. Suddenly, the chill feels crazy.

"I think we should go outside," I say. "What if there's a fire or something?"

"The alarm would've gone off," Kaden says. "But I think you're right. Let's head outside and try to find some help."

"Shoots," I say. I squint. I can barely see anything. The single window lets in some moonlight and streetlight, but otherwise I see zip. I stumble over a chair and recover just as a rumbling sounds in the hallway. Damn. Must be the other trainees.

"Anyone want to lead the way?" Corrin says, his voice small.

Van speaks up. "I'll lead the way. You guys just follow close. We should put our hands on our shoulders."

"Good idea," I say. I take the rear and put my hands on David's shoulders. He stiffens just for a second, and I mutter an apology that sounds all hamajang to me—or all messed up.

"Let's try not to panic," Kaden says. "There's no way a building as modern as this one doesn't have a generator. Or a way to restart the power in some way."

"Big brain things," I say.

But no one finds me funny. Except David, who laughs with a hint of nerves.

As we walk in a miniature train-like thing, I keep thinking about what it would feel like for another pair of arms to grab me by the shoulders. I'd scream. Seriously. I may be the oldest along with Van, but I'll turn into a child if I come across zombie hands.

I love watching movies, even horror ones. I like the feeling of losing myself in a dope, new world. For some reason, I imagine someone filming us. Not in a creepy way, but just because our adventure as a boy group just began.

The guys walk like snails. It seems it takes forever before we trudge out into the hallway. The darkness thickens here. I hear other trainees. They seem far away and close at the same time. They seem to whisper the same things. But each time they speak, I forget what they said.

"Let's head to the staircase?" I say, when Van pauses in the middle. Or at least, I think we're in the middle.

"Good thinking," Kaden says. "We maybe need to exit the building. Finding the staircase is a good first step."

"This is scary," David says.

I can tell he's trying to say it nonchalantly, but fear emanates out from him. A nasty buggah, or fellow, is anxiety. I hate how it could be affecting one of my bros. I squeeze his shoulders. "Don't worry, bro," I say. "We'll make it out of here. I guarantee it."

"I trust you," David says, softly.

When we finally make it to the staircase, the light above the door flickers in green and white. I squint to make out Van pushing the door open. We saw other trainees on the way here, but they ran off in the opposite direction. Some may have gotten to the staircase already.

We head through the door and find total darkness this time. Kaden takes out his phone flashlight, illuminating the concrete steps. Why didn't I think of that?

We head down several floors. I half expect to see a zombie in Kaden's light, but thankfully, we're alone.

"Door to the lobby's locked," Van says, twisting the knob in vain.

"Weird," I say. "Let's try the second? I think the main electrical room's on that floor anyway, my man."

As soon as Van opens the door to the second floor, I squint from the brightness. At least twenty trainees stand around, pointing their flashlights all over. Like a crap ton of stars.

"What's happening?" one says.

"I don't know."

"This is like, the perfect setting for a crime."

"Let's just wait, I'm sure the janitor or something will fix it."

I push through with the four guys in front of me. Each time we pass someone, they seem to sneer at us. A boy with a gray sweater. A girl with a tattoo on her neck. This rad looking guy in a tracksuit rolls his eyes as we pass.

Soon, we come face-to-face with a human wall. Ten or more trainees gathered by the main control room. Some look shitfaced when they turn back. Others look like statues. I'm pretty sure they begin to wobble? I'm reminded of my favorite game, *MapleStory*. How the NPCs, or non-player characters, wobbled like friendly robots. Man, I do miss that game. It was often the highlight of my day. Of my summers. Ami called me addicted. I got mad about that, but I guess 'dat's kinda true? I could still play, but the free time issue is maddening.

"What's going on?" I say.

No one answers, but Van turns around and shrugs.

"Let's try to push through or something," I say. I nudge David a bit, and from there we enter into the fray.

Dangit. The trainees squeeze all around us, breathing hot air into my ears. I can't help but think they want to trap us here. Like hamsters in a cage or something.

"You're going to regret this," one trainee says. He sounds like he speaks from above me.

"No turning back after this," a girl says, pressing her thin red lips together.

Okay. Maybe I'm not as good with horror as I thought. Man. I picture Ami and I huddling together as we watched a movie about a doll turned ghost turned goblin. That had nothing on this. Maybe Kaden's theory was right? We need sleep. Twenty hours or more would be cherry. Or cherreh. Good. Beautiful. Awesome.

We make it to the control room. When Van touches the door, the lights flicker back on. All of a sudden. The trainees sigh and clap as they realize the blackout was just a fluke. They scatter, heading off into their choke—a lot of, remember?—practice rooms and studios.

And the door has a plaque that says "CEO Kim's office" on it. Isn't his office on the penthouse floor?

What the hell just happened?

Chapter 5

David

CEO Kim looks at us like we hold the secrets to the universe. The five of us face him, and our various postures speak of our nerves, and the fact that we almost died in a blackout. The blackout, covering us in mystery, felt like trying to swim through a mud pit, all limbs and no clear direction. I sweep the bangs out of my eyes, grounding myself in Seiya being beside me.

Strange things are happening in AWE Entertainment, and all I can do is ask God to protect us.

The rubber band on my hair seems to tighten on its own, and I wonder if leaving this hairstyle on was a mistake, whether my lock of hair jumpstarted all the anomalies of today. I wait for our CEO to speak, trying not to daydream—my biggest weakness of all.

Maybe my biggest strength too.

"I don't want to hold you guys for too long," CEO Kim says. "Have you all thought of a name? I came up with several options. But I don't want to choose on my own."

"How about…" Corrin stammers. "I don't know. Apple Hair?"

"Apple Hair!" CEO Kim turns to stare at my hairstyle. "And how did you stumble upon that name?"

"Um." I clear my throat. "Maybe it's not a coincidence that I'm wearing apple hair on the day that we're deciding our name. Maybe it's fate."

"Maybe." CEO Kim strokes his imaginary goatee. "I need at least one other reason besides you wearing it today."

I scramble for the first thing that comes to mind. Grasping hold of it, the words fall out naturally, like dropping pieces of glitter into the mud pit. "Well—A for Apple. It can also stand for Asian. Hair for H, which means that we're all from Hawai'i. Asian Americans from Hawai'i, all in a group together."

"Simple yet profound," CEO Kim says. "Interesting. Very interesting. I don't even need to give you the list of names on my end. I love it so much that we'll make it official."

"Really?" I say.

"Really," he says. "Well, you guys can go. I'll be updating the team on your name and getting started on branding. Boring CEO stuff."

I take one last glance at the middle-aged Korean man, who rocks the silver of his hair which matches with his tie. His black suit hugs his medium-sized frame, giving him the illusion of an uptight businessman, even though he's anything but—more like a savvy creative, one that's willing to take risks. He looks straight at me, or maybe at my hair. He captures my disposition and probably compares me to the dozens of recent trainees he hired, and I wonder what I need to do to stand out. Maybe I need to wear a more convincing costume next time, in addition to apple hair. Again, the rubber band tightens.

Outside, Van rubs the back of his head. "Well. This day was… interesting. How about we all head back home and catch some sleep?"

Much to the unfiltered joy of Corrin and Seiya, Mrs. White messages that their punishment has been canceled, as if banished along with the earlier blackout. On the way to the elevator, I notice a dark oak door that says "Library" in cursive, carved into the surface.

A thought comes to me, as if carried in rushing wind into my ear. "Guys. We always said we wanted to make our own universe for our fans. How about we write a few things down in the library? I brought my notebook with me."

"Good idea, hammah," Seiya says. He taps me on the back, which brings a spark that travels down my tailbone and throughout my shoulders. His touch, like unfiltered sunlight, beckons me to put up some kind of protection—a defense, no matter how vain.

The other guys don't object, even if they do nod very sleepily. Kaden opens the door to the library, and we all head inside. The darkness in the room vanishes as I switch on the light, as if retreating, as if shifting into another plane of reality, somewhere that the guys and I don't belong. Three bookshelves stand in an open triangle, and three glass windows overlook Ala Moana Beach Park.

I take out my notebook, sitting around the only table in the room, which just so happens to have five chairs. As the guys join me, I will my imagination to put away the fear of another blackout. It feels safe here, though, and maybe the five of us hold the power to make any place feel safe—like owners of a sacred talisman.

I would probably be killed by my parents if I believed in talismans, since they raised me to be a Christian. I'm pretty devout as a believer in that regard, so they have nothing to worry about, except a little bit of guilt eats at me, as if wanting to expose the tissue under my outer skin, making me into a fake—a pretender and a flatterer.

"Where's the librarian?" Corrin says. He knocks me out of my daydreaming—another fault of mine; I often get lost in my imagination, and I'm pretty sure it reaches a maladaptive point on most days. It's something I can't control, like falling in love or nursing butterflies in your stomach when your eyes lock with the person you've been crushing on for eight hours in a day in high school.

"It's late," Van replies. "She's probably sleeping in the closet."

Kaden grins, then laughs. "I always thought that my teachers never left school. That they just slept there all throughout the night and the weekends."

"Same, bro." Seiya swivels in his chair. I notice that his gaze catches on me, as he seemingly watches my neckline. "What did you want to write, David?"

"Just, like, a one liner or something," I say. "Something that will completely capture the goal of Apple Hair."

"I think that's easy," Van says. "You talk about it all the time, David. Our own little universe."

I smile, finding comfort in those words. "In the past, I always felt like having my own universe wasn't possible." *Toxic—my life at home with my parents.* I don't know how to describe them in any other way, and the one word often brings me comfort, like I could make sense of my first eighteen years of life. "Because of you guys, I now feel like we can do that together."

As I write in my notebook, which has an image of cartoon rockets flying across the cover and back page, I feel powerful. The words flow out of me, dyeing everything in my vision a light purple. They brush against the invisible hairs of my face, singing me a lullaby in a foreign yet familiar language.

Apple Hair is a boy band that will create their own little universe for them and their fans.

I look up after writing the last word, expecting something else weird to happen—but all that happens is Seiya yawning and Kaden staring off into space, probably making a calculation in his head.

I stand after showing all the boys our mission statement. As a Christian, I went on various missions trips with my church. My favorite was going to Korea, attending a summer camp in Gapyeong. I know no one else is a believer in our group, maybe Seiya to some extent. Writing this mission statement reminds me of the times I did my best to share God's word.

Before we all fall asleep in the library, I stand up and check my phone. "Shar's waiting for us in the lobby. How about picking up some dinner from 7-Eleven?"

"Oh my *God*!" Seiya says. "That sounds amazing. I'm starving."

Despite him using God's name in vain, I can't help but grin. I've only known Seiya for a month, but... there's something about him. When he talks to me, he makes me see color.

Nothing weird happens as we walk down the hall and take the elevator to the first floor. I think about how my parents wouldn't care less if I called them up and told them how my day went. I might as well be Kaden—he has no parents to talk to at all. I know it's harsh to compare. I squeeze my toes and imagine the tension slowly siphoning out from me.

Seiya offers to drive, as he always does even though it's Shar's job to chauffeur us after we finish a rough and draining day of practice. Shar refuses and tells him to take shotgun if he wants to.

As we drive to 7-Eleven, Kaden turns to me. Behind me, Corrin and Van catch some Zs like seasoned pros. "Why do I feel like this isn't the end of weird days in AWE?" Kaden asks softly.

Light jazz, Seiya's choice of music, plays dreamily from the speakers. "Probably because it isn't. Maybe this is... the universe telling us how hard it is to debut."

"I don't think so," Kaden says. "There has to be some scientific explanation. I won't believe in ghosts so easily."

"You think so?" I lean my head back, watching as we make our way to Kaka'ako, where our apartment lies.

"I know so," Kaden replies.

And because nothing weird happens in the van or on the road, I trust him. It's a bit hard to trust these four boys fully, knowing that

I couldn't trust my own family for so long. How can I treat these four guys like family? Or should I just comfort myself in the fact that we're all chasing the same goal?

Debut. I've never wanted anything more. Debut will be like stepping into the sunshine after a decade of being stuck in a dark room. It will cure everything, this God-given dream of mine. I *know* with certainty that God gave me this dream. I should do everything I can to make sure it comes to pass.

7-Eleven comes into view. "You guys can pick up your things," Shar says. "Are you fine with walking back home after?"

"Yeah," Seiya says. "We're only a few minutes away anyways."

I get out with the boys. The rubber band on my hair finally snaps, disappearing somewhere on the dark pavement. A sense of loss courses through me, but also the feeling of a new era arriving, coming over me like a fresh wind, a breath from a sleeping giant. I fix my hair and walk into the 7-Eleven, thinking about how my mom always criticized me whenever I ate something even close to junk food. It was a balance of trying to please my parents, while easing myself of the guilt and criticism, but the stains on my conscience were often too permanent.

I pick the blue raspberry Slurpee and begin to fill up a medium-sized cup. A girl, maybe in middle school, comes up to me. She wears a pleated skirt, white blouse, and a giant bow in her pigtails. "Are you guys Apple Hair?" she says.

I try not to show my shock. "Um. Yes?"

"I'm *so* excited for you guys," she says. Then she turns and leaves the store without another word. The jingle on the door rings out louder than usual, almost stinging my eardrums like a lamentation. Or is that just my imagination?

To me, praying means constant conversation with God. I tell him about a dozen different fears as I pick up various snacks with the guys.

I used to want to be an astronaut. I picture myself blasting off to the moon, living on its surface for a day or two before launching back to earth with a defiance of gravity. That's what it feels like to be starting this group—Apple Hair.

"I got it," I say, taking out my credit card. The other guys don't object like they've tried to before. They know about my family being almost filthy rich. I'll gladly treat the guys until we one day become artists who can afford anything they want.

Seiya hugs me with one arm as he retrieves his Spam musubi. "Thanks bro," he says sweetly, probably unaware of the sparks he creates that spider down my arms.

Kaden raises his eyebrows, probably picking up and analyzing the gesture with his razor-sharp brain. I shrug as he begins to open his mouth in my direction.

Outside, the streetlights turn blinding. I almost drop my Slurpee. A voice interrupts me from turning in the direction of our apartment.

Apple Hair. You better watch out. I won't make your path to debut so easy.

That's definitely not the voice of God. The sinister breath in it makes me believe that someone, something, really doesn't want Apple Hair to exist. In fact, they want us to fall into a dark pit, never to see the starlight again, never to hear a voice of comfort, nor to feel warm hands that are like clouds folded into an angel's touch.

Sleep tight tonight, the voice says. *Tomorrow, the real fun begins.*

Chapter 6

Van

I don't believe in God. I know... that's hardly offensive these days.

But after devouring my food from 7-Eleven, which always hits by the way, I watch David as he prays at the threshold to our bedroom. I think about the voice we all heard, the one that seemed to come from an evil power. Maybe David's doing the right thing.

"Do you think we'll get attacked or anything?" Corrin says.

"I don't think so," I say, partly for myself to believe. "This... thing could just be a fluke."

Even as I say the words, I know they aren't true. Apple Hair forming into an official group caused this ghost to come out of nowhere, like some sort of flying fish. A flying fish... *Am I thinking right?*

Anyway, as the leader, I should be doing my part to find the cause, or at least the remedy.

I guess I'm not a good leader. I end up burying my nose into one of my favorite novels. I lose myself in a world of dragons and knights, staying up later than any of the other guys as they turn in one by one. I squint to see the words from a tiny light attachment that my best friend Nick gave me.

And when no mysterious voice comes to disturb me, I let myself believe—we're safe. There's no way something or someone can break apart Apple Hair so easily.

The next day, I wake up the boys after downing my vitamins. I put in my contacts carefully. Last time, I shredded the inside with my nail. Girl, that was *not* a fun day for my eyes. Shar picks us up on time, and we go straight into dance practice with Armani Bera.

"As you all know, the monthly evaluation is coming up soon," she says. "It'll be your first monthly evaluation as a group. I want you guys to *kill* it!"

As she says "kill," I expect something strange to happen, but nothing does. Too soon, I guess? Armani grins at me and then begins to talk about the song we're dancing to for the evaluation. She executes another dance sequence flawlessly, and then begins to help us follow along.

Since AWE Entertainment was inspired by K-pop companies, we follow their blueprint pretty closely. That means lots of practice— hours and hours dedicated to the perfect movement and vocal run. If I knew what I was signing up for, I would've probably tried to negotiate less dancing for me. Hah—I think I may be the worst dancer out of the five of us.

Be confident, Van. I hear the voice of my older brother, Ryan. He was always one to encourage me. Even when I thought I failed my audition at AWE and ate three donuts from the convenience store to comfort myself. *You're better than you think. Puff your chest out a little bit and tell yourself that you're "the best." Even if you don't feel like it.*

Ryan always knows what to say when I'm feeling down about myself. Or... even when I'm *actually* bad. When I hit an off pitch note. Which happened... but which now happens less and less.

After my left leg feels like it's going to break, Armani ends the dance practice. She tells us that Merlin Kim reserved the cafeteria for an executive from Tokyo. So, we have to have lunch elsewhere. Shar picks us up and drives us to the mall. On the way there, the boys try to catch some rest and Shar hums a tune that's soothing and comforting.

The drive is short. Since I'm shotgun, I turn to Shar and use a voice only for our ears. I'd say I succeed. Seiya would fail this type of whisper immediately, *no offense to you, Seiya.* I whisper, "What do I do if it seems like something bad is out to get me and the guys?"

Shar raises an eyebrow. With black and gray hair and a strong brow, she turns and gives me one of her kind stares. Her eyes, dark brown with a hint of hazel, seem to sparkle. "You're going to have to be more specific than that, Van."

Shar's half Native Hawaiian and half black, and she was chosen as our manager one month ago. Shar's always made me feel safe. That's not exactly her job… well, she makes sure we're always on track. But has a steady quality about her. We can always count on her, especially when more than one fish goes flying.

Why do I keep mentioning fish, you ask? Good question. It may be because I have a goldfish named Hero. I miss the little guy, but I know he's in good hands. Ryan treats him like a second brother, and my parents are always making sure the fish swims with a little pep.

As we drive, Shar hums when I don't answer. Then, while turning the wheel toward Ala Moana's parking garage, she says, "Don't worry about anything, Van. I'll keep you guys safe. I know you guys can go far. You're all smart and capable. But I'll lend my hand when needed, so you don't have to worry."

She says it with such certainty that I believe her. With Shar, maybe the guys and I don't have to face the voices alone. Or the *voice*—not entirely sure how to describe everything that happened yesterday.

"What do you guys want?" Shar says, raising her voice to wake up the four guys behind me. "Jollibee? Sandwiches, bentos? I'll pick them all up so you can sleep."

"Lifesaver!" Seiya says. He votes for Jollibee, and we all confirm that fried chicken and spaghetti sounds marvelous. Kaden comments, *again*, about how Filipino food is the best to ever exist. *We heard you the first time, Kaden.* No qualms though, 'cause I'm already salivating.

"We're all good," I say, as Shar leaves us in a parking stall in the back of the garage. Thankfully, lots of light pierces through the surrounding greenery and illuminates the vehicle. I don't feel like that voice will come back. "We're good because Shar says she's going to protect us. Done deal."

David tilts his head back and forth in the backseat. "Shar does seem like the type of manager who would risk it all for us." His soft voice mellows me out, and when I smile, I turn back and see that Shar left a journal on the driver's seat.

For Apple Hair, it says in loopy letters. "Hey," I say. "Shar got us a present."

"I bet she bought it when we told her about writing our own story," Corrin says, shaking his knees. "Amazing. Why don't we open it!"

"She probably wanted to surprise us," Kaden says, a bit weakly.

"Well…" I stare at the book, drawn to it. The cream, suede cover reflects the light and places an ember of comfort in my chest. Is it wrong that I feel this kinda way? About a *notebook*?

Seiya reaches over and grabs it. "It's just a notebook, dudes," he says. He opens it to the first page, then begins to flip through it. "It's just a normal book. No lines though. How am I supposed to write in straight rows?"

David tries to look the other way, but he continues to glance at Seiya's neck, most definitely checking the guy out. I save my comment about that for later.

"We should continue to write our story," David says. "In that book. It could be like our… dream diary."

"I love that!" Corrin says. He takes out a pen from his pocket. "Luckily, I'm always prepared."

"We should at least wait for Shar to give it to us," Kaden says. "Officially."

As we stare each other down, the guys eventually start to look at me. Right—I'm the leader. I bob my head and think about the way Shar said she'd protect us. "Let's write something that'll make her happy," I say. "That way, there's no way she could be mad at us."

"Sounds fire," Seiya says. He takes Corrin's pen and writes something on the first page. Reading upside down, I make out the line David wrote yesterday—the one that sums up everything we want to be.

Apple Hair is a boy band that will create their own little universe for them and their fans.

We all stare at the blank page. David looks lost while Kaden glances out the window, probably wondering whether Shar will catch us writing in her mystery journal.

"Something that will make her happy," I say. "What could that be?"

"Let's start with describing our universe," David suggests. "Let's start with Shar. What makes her a magical person in our lives?"

"She makes sure we're everywhere on time…" Kaden grunts. "I guess that's pretty boring. Necessary, but not story material."

"How about, a line about Apple Hair relying on their fearless manager, Shar Keawe?" David says.

"I didn't know we had a writer in the group," Seiya says.

David blushes while Corrin and Kaden exchange a judging look. I nod and glance over my shoulder, wondering how fast someone can fry a chicken.

"Go ahead," I say.

Seiya reads as he writes. As he does so, his voice takes on a tender sort of mystery. Am I turning into David now? My heart just fluttered a little bit. *With the support of Shar, Apple Hair begins their journey to debut.*

The car shakes an inch to the right and left. Then, it begins to blare. The alarm rings seemingly ten times its usual volume. I cover my ears, grimacing. I close my eyes.

This is it. This is where the story ends. *It was good to know you, members. I hope we can meet in another life...* Preferably one without voices and ghosts. Perhaps there is also chicken in the place we're heading to now?

Then I open my eyes to see Shar. She runs, two bags from Jollibee in either arm. Her arms pump like a champion's. A look of pure determination crosses her face, and in her baggy jeans and hoodie, she appears as more than just a manager.

With food in both hands, she runs and runs. I wonder what she'll say when she gets here and finds the car completely freaking out. Kaden messes with the controls with flying fingers, and Seiya tries to open the doors unsuccessfully while his biceps flex. At least the members in my team don't freeze up. I cover my ears more tightly and watch Shar cover ground like a track star.

Chapter 7

Corrin

"I thought someone broke into the car or something," Shar says as she drives back to the company.

I take a bite of the steaming fried chicken. "Nope! Only the weirdness of the week continuing. Sorry to make you panic, though. You almost fell with the lunch."

"Well, count on me, you guys." Shar turns into the company parking lot. "I won't let anything hurt you."

I dip my chicken into the gravy and try not to devour it too quickly. I *have* thought about going vegan quite a bit, since I love animals so much. But I can't give up cheese. (Vegan cheese makes me want to eat just about anything else.) And meals like these with the boys excite me too much. Who can really give up late night pizza with the guys? Won't that make me, like, a solitary tortoise or something? I can't help but laugh to myself at the visual.

I mean, I *have* taken care of a tortoise before. I used to feed him hibiscus, veggies, and all types of fruit. I almost lost the memory of him, thanks to my menagerie of other animals. I liked him though! His name was Marvin. (This was before I started listening to Marvin Gaye.) We ended up giving him away to one of my school friends, but I believe he's doing very well.

"I see you guys found the book I wanted to give you," Shar says. "I got it for you guys since I want your story to continue and last for a long time. Keep writing in it—and don't stop dreaming."

"We won't," I say immediately. "I mean, we won't stop dreaming and we'll keep writing."

"It's thoughtful of you," Kaden says. "We will make use of every page."

Van responds after licking the gravy from his lips. "Yeah, Shar… Who knows, we might just become the next big universe besides *The Hunger Games*."

"No one's gonna be wanting to write fanfiction about you, bro," Seiya says.

David lets out a bright laugh, stifled a bit by his spoon of mashed potatoes. "We should prepare for that, though. The fanfics and stuff. I can't imagine all the different worlds we'll be a part of…"

Per usual, David gets lost in a daydream. I don't blame him, since I'm also in my head whenever I think of my favorite topics—animal rescues and music (particularly the guitar).

"Good," Shar says. "Now time for the rest of today's schedule. We have two hours of vocal practice, another four hours of dance, and then language class."

Before I let out a groan, I lean back and try not to think about how I only got a few hours of sleep last night. I stared at the ceiling for the longest time, trying to count sheep or tortoises or whatever I could think of. Eventually, I settled on dolphins. I kept seeing their eyes as I drifted in and out of restlessness.

Have I experienced anything like that before? Ugh… probably not! But I just need to adjust. Soon enough, I'll sleep like a baby kitten. Or maybe even an adult kitten, as my orange tabby Zora used to do—before she ran away. (In terms of tragic days, that takes a spot wayyy up there.)

So weird. But after today, I'll catch up on rest. I kind of have to if I want to avoid dying.

Practice goes as usual. (It's still weird, though—since there's nothing usual about practice.) It always feels like a dream that we're all chasing after this goal together. The boys and I, running and running and running.

Was dancing hard for me at first? Yes, of course. But I joined the company at around the same time as Seiya. I saw how hard he danced, even before we were put into a group. That inspired me (I wouldn't tell him this too often), and soon enough I learned the eight counts and the basic moves of hip hop. Like today, where I successfully spin around without leaning to the left or right.

Leo Pak sends us a group message after language practice wraps up. David reads out the Hangul slowly, and I try to make sense of it.

"He wants to talk about our vision," David says. "I don't exactly know what he means, but he wants to have us in the conference room first thing tomorrow morning."

"Dude, you scared me," Seiya says. "I thought he would want a midnight meeting or something."

"AWE cares about our sleep," Kaden says. "Somewhat."

As we wait for Shar to pull around the corner of the road, Van says, "We didn't hear any voice or anything today."

As I open my mouth to reply, I catch movement out of the corner of my eye. Some of the other trainees approach us, carrying soft drinks from the nearest convenience store. "Look who's here," one of them says. "The *special group* Apple Hair. Who even came up with that dumbass name? Probably comes with an ass concept."

I think his name's Allen. (Have I been transported back to high school? Hasn't he graduated recently too?) I *hate* fighting, so I just stand and wait for him to walk past. He stays right in front of us though, along with his groupies. Eventually, Seiya steps forward. "Well, we hope that when you get put into a group, you can pick a better name." Seiya puffs out his chest, probably without realizing. "We just want to train in peace, bro."

"Well, *bro*," Allen says, sneering. "I have a prediction. Your group will fall apart before the year ends."

Kaden takes the bait. Well, I know Kaden can absolutely destroy this guy. He reminds me of a tiger, one lick and your skin will come off. He keeps calm and points to the door. "Go practice more so you can get chosen. Then we'll take you more seriously."

Allen pushes past us and strides toward the company, like some kind of leader of the pack. Weirdo. His groupies follow him, and I try to laugh it off while they're gone. "Maybe this is what the voice meant?" I say. "Everything seems to be getting a bit tougher for us."

"Let's just focus on what we need to do," Van says. "Focusing on the people who hate us won't do us any good."

"Amen," I say. "As David would say."

David puckers his lips, his eyes still stormy from facing Allen. "Yeah…"

That night, I lie on the top bunk. My mind races with all sorts of things I could've said to Allen.

At least we're all decent looking, unlike you.

I wish we could debut at the same time. That way, we can outsell you. You'll cry after taking a look at the charts.

Okay—maybe the last one's a BIT petty.

Even though my limbs ache and I feel as though I could pass out, I can't sleep. I shake my legs like crazy even though I try not to wake Kaden on the bunk below me. At the same time, my mind races.

I think about taking care of my many animals back at home. I've two iguanas, a cat (which didn't run away—thank the big cat in the sky), and a dog. (All my pets have human names, from common to rare.) I've taken care of countless animals in my lifetime, and each one gave me comfort. I hope Mom's doing a good job at taking care of them, along with the stray cats outside.

More thoughts come. My brain! I can almost sense the synapses firing off. I think about my whole time at AWE Entertainment. My happy moment of being put into the debut group, Apple Hair. *Of course we had no idea of our name at the time.*

Soon, morning light enters the apartment. I shuffle on my bed and drag a hand through my hair. I can't explain the feeling that settles into my head, like a rush of adrenaline with a small dose of unease. Well, there's always time to catch up on sleep later.

Wednesday means it's my turn to wake up everyone. Jumping on the floor from the ladder of the top bunk, I raise my voice, "Guys, time to wake up. We don't wanna miss our uber important meeting."

David groans, which sets off the other boys' mumbling and turning in their sheets. I smile and repeat myself one more time. Outside, I see the book Shar gave us. I'm tempted to write something else, but I don't want to do that without all the guys with me—it's *our* story, after all.

After we all get ready, it feels like déjà vu when Shar picks us up. But instead of heading straight to practice, we find ourselves in the office of Leo Pak.

He appraises us as we walk in. I can't help but grin, and Van glances at me like something's off with me. Leo Pak says something in Korean. From the rudimentary Korean lessons that we've had, I think he's introducing himself.

He gestures toward the book Kaden's holding. Reluctantly, Kaden hands it over.

Leo flips through the pages, stopping somewhere in the middle. With deft hands, he *tears* a page right out of the book. I gasp, almost swallowing a knuckle when I cover my mouth. Outside, the sky seems to flicker as the sound of ripping repeats over and over against my eardrums.

He says something else, with only a hint of remorse in his voice. David translates, "He says that he wants to keep a page so that he'll be able to write some things too."

And then he dismisses us. Outside, Seiya leans against the wall. "That was extremely weird, damn."

As we head off to our first practice session of the day, Kaden hangs back with me. We lag behind like we actually can take our time. "Corrin," he says, softly. "Are you feeling okay?"

"Yeah," I say, taming my bangs on both sides. "I just couldn't sleep well. But I feel fine. It feels like I actually got to sleep. It feels like a good day—that it will be one, since I can't look into the future. That would be extremely strange of me."

Kaden eyes me like I said something a bit weird. In the end, he taps me on my back and tells me, "You're allowed to take the day off."

"Oh, never," I say. "It doesn't feel fair. This is all our dream, and I don't want to miss out. Not even one day, or one second even."

As Armani Bera goes over the second verse of our dance for the monthly evaluation, I put a hundred fifty percent of my effort into my movements. Even though my legs feel like they're going to break, I keep at it. I keep striding, keep running. And I think I look good doing it.

Chapter 8

Kaden

There are 86,400 seconds in a day.

I waste about five hundred of them, trying to tell Seiya that Corrin needs to take a week or two off. His uncaring boyishness really shines through when he assures me that things are fine, even though Corrin hasn't slept a wink in three days. "He's a strong little guy. He'll be fine. You don't need to keep worrying about him, so just stay in your lane."

He says the last part lightly, but my nerves bristle. "Stay in my lane?"

He chews a piece of gum, scrolling on his phone while lying in bed. "Yeah. I mean, I know he'll get through it. Trust."

I abandon him to peek out at the three other guys in the living room. They're fitting in a game of *Super Smash Bros.* Van and David get close to swearing at each other. Corrin fidgets with an expression I can't read. Nervous? Overly excited?

Tomorrow's Sunday. I'll have ample time to figure this out. Another set of more than eighty thousand seconds.

On Sunday, our only off day, I abandon Seiya as he shops for a new basketball online. I head to the doctor, one bus stop away. On the bus, I study the buildings and the other passengers. No sign of the anomaly in my life. The voice along with its strange tricks on the mind.

What could it be?

I have long tried to rule out anything supernatural. But no other explanation makes sense. The collective hallucination theory still takes precedence over anything else.

I clutch my hands tightly. If he were alive, my dad would know what to do. He was a professor. He studied the brain, particularly how medicine interacted with it. My mother stayed at home, but it was only because she gave up her job as a professor to take care of me. And later, Lora.

I have a very thin memory of them. But somehow, I remember them talking about the brain. One of my father's published articles that bolstered his reputation in the field.

My fingernails dig into my palms. I know what I need is a good stress relief. That will funnel good chemicals into my brain and body. Possibly, it would break me out of seeing things. I always turned to exercise and sports as my outlets. I rarely put my nose into a book like Van.

My steps almost weigh me down as I climb the steps to the doctor's office. I know I've been a bad patient. An uncooperative one.

"Are you still considering surgery?" The doctor hits me in the face—candor probably his best medicine.

"No, I can't," I say.

"Your scoliosis is pretty severe," he says. "If you don't get surgery, it could affect your lungs. Long term."

The doctor's little stubble on his chin annoys me.

"Is there another option?" I ask, trying to hold my ground.

The doctor rubs his stubble. "No. There was, but you refused to wear the back brace that we gave you. In turn, your scoliosis was not kept at bay. With such a large bend, you need this operation."

I hold his gaze. Then, I ball my fists even harder. "Thanks. I will let you know my decision."

I end up leaving the office feeling worse than when I came in. I don't have a strong relationship with this doctor. Actually, the fact that he's been trying to convince me of this surgery for a few months now prevents me from seeing him in a positive light. It's annoying. My little sister agrees with him, but they both aren't set on debuting—there's no such thing as recovering while my other four members chase their dreams full force.

When I return home, Seiya has finished shopping, and he wants to drive down to the beach. My back aches, either from the scoliosis or the thought of the scoliosis—I don't know. The brain is surely powerful. I snuff out the thought before it can catch onto me any further.

While Corrin tries to take a nap, Van is spending time with family and David's with a few friends. I know maybe I should talk to my sister—who lives with my grandparents. But Seiya insists. I relent. He drives us down to Lanikai Beach, one of his favorites.

Has he forgotten about our little argument? Maybe it doesn't matter as much to him. He probably pushed it away in his sleep. I envy that, a little bit.

He brings his old basketball, and after walking on the sand for about an hour, he challenges me to a game at the nearest basketball court. "I need your advice on something," he says, stopping in the middle of dribbling.

"What is it?" I say, already knowing what he's going to say.

"David," he says. "I don't know what to feel about him. It's like, my brain always fires off when I'm near him. I can't focus or think shit."

"Just talk to him instead of me," I say. I stride forward, stealing his basketball. As I go to shoot, my back tenses up. I stumble. My shoulder hits the pavement, and I think it'll bleed.

"Dude!" Seiya leans down beside me, trying to help me up. Maybe it's the first time he's admitting liking David. Maybe it's time for me to let out a secret too.

"I have scoliosis," I say, sitting on a nearby bench. Seiya has his arm out, supporting me in case I magically fall to the floor like a spinning top.

"Isn't that for, like, old people?" Seiya says, squinting against the sun.

I'd scoff if the cut didn't hurt so bad. "No. It could be for anyone. I just have a pretty severe case. The bend is more than fifty degrees. Nothing I could've done would've prevented it. It's genetic. I didn't even get to ask my parents if it runs in our genes. And if I did the calculations correctly—"

"Don't do the calculations, dude," Seiya sighs, hitting our shoulders together—my good one, thankfully. "It's best not to think too hard. But hey… thanks for telling me. We can trust each other. I won't say I never noticed your spine and shit, but I didn't wanna bother you about it."

Seiya reaches into his backpack and magically produces a first aid kit. He takes out some antiseptic and bandages, torturing me like he's using everything for the first time. "Does it really sting that bad?" he says, cringing as I tense my jaw so tightly that it might strain.

"Of course," I say. "You should know, being so sporty and all."

"Dude, you're the sporty one," he says after he finishes with the bandage after a beat of silence. "I brought the book with me. Wanna write something in it?"

"You just left our most prized possession in your backpack while we played basketball?" I say.

"Yeah! Why not?" He holds the book and runs his hand over the suede cover.

"Why don't we draw a picture?" I suggest. "Something that will represent us. We might as well try something different."

He opens the cover, clicking his gel pen until the sound annoys me. "Yeah. Let's draw an apple with some planets around it. It can become our logo later. Sick."

"Sick is right," I say, trying not to infuse too much sarcasm into it. I'm beginning to sound like Van after we all test his nerves after a long day of practice. I voted for him to be the leader, though there were talks of me taking the lead too.

Seiya opens the notebook and begins to draw. As I look up, the air shimmers around the basketball hoop. I shake my head and ascribe it to imagination. There has to be an explanation on why Apple Hair is experiencing so many anomalies.

If David's right, about there being a God, could there also be other powers? I shake my head. No.

"I'll draw the planets," I say, taking the notebook from Seiya when he freezes.

I draw quickly, not caring that my artisticness only adds up to stick figures, one-lined birds, and in this case, loops that can only dream of being symmetrical. David would draw it better, I'm certain. I once caught him doodling what looked suspiciously like Seiya's profile.

I look at the drawing when it's done—Seiya salvaged the piece, I must say.

"Okay," I say. "Let's head to Longs and pick up something for Corrin."

"Yeah, like melatonin or some crap," Seiya says.

I think about my and Seiya's first meeting. We didn't mix at first—he thought I was too serious. I didn't blame him. But now… he's starting to trust me. I don't know how to process that. It's not predictable. Nothing like counting the seconds of the day.

As we walk back to the car, my focus lies on the pavement in front of us. I look up after hearing a gasp.

"Boys!" Armani Bera stands with a surfboard in hand. She's dressed in a sky-blue two-piece bikini with a dab of sunscreen not yet rubbed into her nose. Gorgeous as ever, and I immediately feel myself try to correct my posture. A move that goes in vain.

"Armani!" Seiya does a double take. "I didn't know you were the… ugh, surfer type. Cool stuff tho'."

"I love to dance, swim, play tennis—and of course surf." She gives us a little wink and turns her board.

On the white surface, something flashes and catches my eye. It's my turn to do a double take. A medium sized sticker, a large apple with planets around it, joins a bunch of other equally random stickers.

I turn toward Seiya. His eyes widen—I know he saw it too.

Armani seems blissfully unaware as she waves at us with her left hand. She skips down toward the beach, her bare feet not caring about the pebbles and twigs.

"You saw that too?" Seiya says, huffing a bit.

Breath escapes me too, and not because of the basketball session. "Um. Yeah."

"We're talking about this at dinner, man," Seiya says, heading off toward the car.

I follow. My back aches. Of course it would rebel against me, after I saw the doctor and a surgery in my timeline became all the more real. I look up, realizing I slowed down. Maybe it's my spine, slowing me. My spine needs a lesson in being cooperative. "Wait up!" I call out.

Chapter 9

Seiya

"It's just da kine," I say to David in the cafeteria.

Da kine—like I said, it's one of my favorite pidgin expressions that can mean almost anything. David hates it, and he shows it by scrunching up his face. "It's not *da kine*," he says. "I saw the logo too. Some person on television was advertising his telescope with it. A telescope that can apparently see farther than anything that came before it."

The other boys study their phones, reviewing the dance routine that Armani's been teaching us for a month now. We should have it down. But I guess they want to really make sure.

Man. Is it really time for our first evaluation as a group?

"Maybe it's best to not be so serious about it," I say. "It's happening. Let's just let it play out and go with the flow."

David sets his fork down on his plate, creating a clattering noise. "I don't think so. This is bigger than a little mistake or superstition. This is *bigger than us.*"

He looks pretty damn cute when he gets angry. I shake my head and try to ignore the way my pulse goes all crazy when I'm next to him. It's distracting. But kind of a vibe.

I wonder if he feels it too. I shake my head, not able to accept that

I actually like one of the guys.

I almost do this unconsciously. But I guess it's conscious 'cause I'm telling you. I rub my tattoo of a ramen bowl on my left wrist. The bowl is small. Almost like a wimp. But it has all the details it needs. Even a little hint of noodles visible from the top. One of my favorite foods. Also, a tie to my culture. Man, I wish I could have a bowl right now.

But I focus on the food right now. The croissant with chocolate kind of smacks. I cut it in half even though I never use knives. Guess I just want to impress David.

"Talked to your parents lately?" David asks, a hint of softness in his voice.

I keep my voice down even though I know all the guys know about me and my parents. "I don't talk to them," I say. "It's always been like that." I pause. "Or laddat."

David nods. Maybe he wants to roll his eyes. Who knows? All I know is that a lot of the trainees do speak pidgin, but David always sensed that I used it to be different—since none of the members of Apple Hair speak it that often. But, mad thing is, I did catch David speaking pidgin in his sleep once.

"And your sister?" he asks.

He always knows what to say. "Oh, I talk to her every day. You always see me FaceTiming her."

David gives me his little smile. "I wish I had a sister."

"You have pretty great parents though," I say, remembering the time they visited him in the company. They were all over him.

He smiles again, but his face darkens a bit. "Yeah…"

"Are you guys nervous too?" Corrin says, putting his phone down. It kind of shakes on the table, and Corrin's eyes dart around.

I think Kaden was right. Corrin doesn't sleep much these days. He's kind of jittery. The medicine we got him worked only a little bit. I know if things continue like this, he'll have to go to the doctor.

"I think everyone's nervous to various degrees," Kaden says. "Maybe we need a word from our leader?"

Van gulps. He's been quiet these days, which is usual, but kind of on the bad side since we need him more than ever. He makes a weird gesture with his hands. Funny guy—this Van. "We practiced a lot." He sticks his spoon into his rice. "I think we've got this."

"He's right," Kaden says. "Statistically, there's no way we can fail this."

David hums. Under his breath, he says, "But things don't always work out the way we expect."

After lunch, we head straight for the top floor of the company, where evaluations take place most of the time. We enter a room with floor-to-ceiling glass windows on three sides, and a judge's table sits opposite the door. Sure—I've been here before. Never as a group, though. Never as Apple Hair. That's a mad thought.

I rub my lil' ramen bowl again. What did Kaden call it? Some sort of grounding? Weird how a ramen bowl can do that for me.

All our instructors are here, including Leo Pak and CEO Kim. They appraise us as we walk in and stand in a straight line. Here it is. What we've worked for. If we screw this up, we could confirm or deny our chance at debuting. I don't want to act uptight and everything, but I gotta be a little bit serious about evaluations.

First up—dance.

With one hand outstretched, I get myself into position, a crouch that reminds me of a bear. Here we go. *Remember all your time freestyling, Seiya. Remember your passion for dance.*

The music starts from the speakers. Crackling at first. I begin the eight count. I force my legs to move. To remember all the times I did this already. I just need to rely on muscle memory.

Then, after relying on the memory, I gotta go crazy on it. Infuse all my moves with a hundred percent strength. Not going overboard tho'. That would be called overdancing.

Hands moving to the beat, I fall in line with the members. Our legs follow the beat and the lyrics. As one. Like an actual, certified band.

We go through the routine, a bit heavily at first, then we really go ham on it. Just like I wanted. I almost knock into Van, but we speed through with all the angles, formations, and little gestures that we practiced.

A part in the lyrics goes, *We gotta run, escape and just love.* At that part, I twist around and lock arms with Corrin. We launch into a sequence of steps. Like a little army of ants. Dancing ants?

When we finish, the song still rings in my ears. I think I see Armani in the corner of my eye, nodding. Not smiling or anything, but I think she's proud.

Diane can seriously kill with her stare as we gear up for the vocal evaluation portion. We're singing an English cover of BTS' "Not Today."

Sweat sticks to my neck. Funny, how the evaluation makes you look at things. 'Cause I don't care one bit. My heavy breathing? Not even an issue. I gotta make it through the vocal portion. I gotta absolutely kill this.

The music begins again. I lock eyes with all four members. We give each other a little nod. Almost to say, *we've got this.*

And now, I see ourselves as a boy band. As Apple Hair. Man, when did I get so sentimental?

I ruin a few harmonies on the first verse, where we changed the rap to a simple melody. But when it comes to my rap in the second verse, I really go hard and tear it up. The members flash me a smile when we finish the song, and I actually get the harmony right this time.

We belt out the last note. The music ends, and then it's pure agony of waiting. Choke nerves ripple through me.

The judges scribble into their notepads. Merlin Kim and Leo Pak share a look that's totally unreadable. I swallow and prepare for the third part of the test—language.

Cory asks us a few questions in Korean. We each take turns answering, and I know we're being recorded so they can watch it back later and see how bad our pronunciation is. I get a question about my favorite restaurant.

"Um," I say. "I like this restaurant because it's spacious and has good food."

Bruh. I hope that's good enough.

"All right," CEO Kim says. "That wraps up your first group evaluation. We'll be adding a bigger variety of tests later. Give us some time to discuss."

The hush of their voices makes me crazy nervous. Are we just expected to stand here? Eventually, Van leads us to shift back a bit. We give each other nods again, like little figurines who can't stop doing their signature moves.

Failing this? I can't even let my brain go there. It won't mean we'll be thrown out of the company or that crap. But it will definitely make the executives question whether we can debut.

After a minute or two, CEO Kim breaks apart from the group and stands before us. "You already know that seventy and above is a passing score. We were impressed by your dance, but your vocals do need a lot of polishing. And the language section… needs a whole lot of work.

"We're giving you a seventy on the dot. Next time, I want to see you all achieve a better score."

A rush of relief goes through my chest. I almost explode. Brah, I cannot do this every single month. This stress? I've never felt anything like it before.

We all thank the CEO and wave goodbye to the instructors. Leo Pak sits on his chair with his arms crossed, his eyes darting about the room like he's bored. He acts like he got one puka—hole—in his underwear or something. Also, that's "one puka" as a complete phrase. I can't explain it fully, but "one" is sometimes used to replace "a."

Another word I can teach you? Chicken skin. That means I have goosebumps. They probably came up sometime during the evaluation. My lil' ramen bowl almost tingles.

"Wow," I say outside as we walk toward the elevator. "We barely passed. 'Grats, guys."

"We should've done a lot better," Kaden says. "But a seventy is a start."

Corrin shakes his fists in the air. "Good job, guys. Maybe I should've sang with a bit more oomph."

Van nods. "Good job."

David glances at his phone. "Yeah… Oh. We have a gap in our schedule—a one hour break. How about we head to the cafe and really start writing our story in Shar's book?"

Chapter 10

David

A la Moana's nicest cafe happens to be within walking distance of AWE Entertainment. I walk there with wispy clouds in my stomach and the rainbow shining between my ribs. I try to manage the strangest mixture of relief, pride, and disappointment. We could've done a lot better than a flat seventy, but with the weight of everything that's been happening to us, a seventy might be a sign from above.

I squint against the sunlight, watching Corrin as he chases away some pigeons.

I think about what Seiya said about my parents, the assumption that they love me greatly—the facade they put up for everyone. I think about our conversation before I first became a trainee.

I'd settled on the loveseat in the middle of our mansion, head spinning about the fact that I was accepted. I was *accepted* to AWE Entertainment, and my dream suddenly felt like it wasn't so far away. In fact, it hovered in reach, almost taunting me with its shiny wings and its enchanting yet slightly terrifying face, which blinked at me with every passing second.

"And college?" my mother had said. She flipped her luscious curls over her shoulder, turning to my dad.

Dad added, with a quip that felt personal, "This is what we talked about when we said that you weren't headed toward success, David. We don't know if this is what God wants for you."

"In fact, we *know* that this isn't what God wants for you," my mom added.

After a few minutes more of arguing, I knew that they would never accept what I wanted. I should've expected it. I mumbled a bit to myself, trying not to fidget, as if they would see how much it affected me that I didn't have their approval—that I didn't earn their approval.

"Being a singer means that you'll be more subject to the devil's ways," my dad had said.

"Amen," my mom said, squeezing a lemon into her pitcher of water. "And we already *accepted* quite a big part of you. Do we really need to stretch ourselves more?"

I stormed to my room, trying to ignore the buzzing heat of my forehead. It overwhelmed me, covering me in an icy yet suffocatingly warm pall. I blinked away the tears, leaning so hard against the door that my back ached from the top of my spine to the bottom, and I thought I would never recover.

"Earth to David," Seiya says.

I turn around, realizing I walked a few paces past the cafe. I shake my head, looking up at the sign, Coffee Storm. I try not to flush. I'll tell Seiya, along with the other members, more about my parents one day. I know God wants me to tell them, about my toxic life at home that felt like trying to swim in mud with a full suit of armor, and I will, maybe when the thought of my parents doesn't lodge a knife between my ribs.

It's a relief to be with the guys, to soak in the sunshine without fear of being criticized or put down again. As I enter the cafe, I wave my black card in the air, and Corrin cheers. After we order, we sit down at our favorite table in the corner, facing the ocean, which draws me in with its foamy waves like some sort of living fluffy dessert. Inside, the hanging bulbs remind me of stars—all different distances from the ceiling.

Van sips his iced macadamia nut latte. With a quiet voice that reminds me of the whispering wind, he says, "So, we're really going to flesh out our story."

"Right," I say, forgetting my toxic parents if only for a moment. "We want an expansive universe, something that all our fans can enjoy. We don't want to put a limit on our narrative arc."

The boys nod and take sips, and I imagine all the different kinds of bitter, all the different shades we enjoy as a group. The lights above us grow brighter—maybe the employees adjusted it, or maybe my imagination acts up again, changing my view on the world every time I'm with the boys.

"That's a sick idea," Seiya says, placing Shar's notebook in the middle of the table.

"We can have multiple storylines," Kaden suggests. "How about we have a canon story—our main one. And then alternative universes. And maybe even fanfiction if we can fit that in."

"Fanfiction?" Corrin squints, stirring his caramel macchiato too hard. A bit of coffee spills out from the rim. "Isn't that for fans?"

"Yeah, but we can still guess what fans would like to write about," Kaden says.

Van pouts, looking like he's chewing on something in his mind. "I'm on board."

I came prepared with five pens. I click and unclick mine, meditating on the meaning of gel pens, whether they've any sort of connection to the gel that Kaden uses on his hair. As I stare at the blank page, I bite the inside of my lip and think about what story I'd like to write.

Corrin scribbles frantically on the page, while Van and Kaden find themselves stuck like me. Seiya begins to write slowly, as if outlining a masterpiece. I could be just lovestruck—Seiya could write scribbles, and I'd still find the delicateness of the way he holds his pen and leans back in his chair, pausing as if finding the words in his next breath.

After the first twenty minutes, I put the pen to the page and write in smooth cursive, watching how the words begin to string together and form their own story. The story that comes may not have started quickly, but once it begins in my mind, the waves of the arc pound relentlessly against my soul.

Apple Hair discovers their dream world. The place that always gives them hope—their constant escape. In this world, creativity is currency. The universe is run by imagination.

"What are you writing?" Seiya says, pausing in the middle of writing a sentence.

"Our canon," I respond. "And hopefully something that will help guide us. To make a universe that our fans will really love to be a part of."

Van nods, likely chewing on something in his mind. Kaden starts to put ink on the page first, and Van follows. The scent of magic lingers in the air, reminding me of incense, but my imagination often whispers strange things to me, coloring my senses with things that aren't there. I decide that this is one of those times my imagination will work in my favor.

At first, they don't have control of their world. It scares them to find a world that they cannot control.

The air in the cafe whizzes past my ears, and my forearms heat up, hairs standing on end. I hear Seiya say something about *chicken skin,* but only in my head. There goes my imagination again, running rampant, like a child, or some sort of pixie that can't stop floating around and making me look in every direction.

"Do you guys feel anything strange?" I say.

"Stranger than Corrin's fanfiction about us being magical squirrels?" Van quips.

Seiya snickers, and Kaden cracks a smile. Corrin fakes offense before continuing his story—he almost has a full page right now. When I realize I forgot to add a period, I add the dab of gel ink and watch as I accidently smear it with my left hand.

The whizzing increases, and I close my eyes when lighting strikes our table. Our drinks go flying, and I don't know who's screaming or squealing. When I blink, I expect fire to spread outwards and engulf us. Instead, I find the cafe again. Or… kind of.

The cafe spins around once in my vision. Then, it comes to life with the buzz of a choir in the distance. As they sing a song about the Lord's kingdom, I watch as the cafe bursts to life with new color— pastels and rainbow-like tones, muting everything but making normal items a dozen times more beautiful.

The comfort that enters my soul reminds me of candy, sugar sweet that sticks to my teeth but with the ickiness that comes after, all bundled up into one.

This place gives the atmosphere of a place I never want to leave. The tantalizing aspect of it grabs me, pulling me in. The images of the other guys turn hazy, but I grab onto them, pulling them close with all the power in my conscience.

"Hey," I say. "Guys."

"This place feels weird," Corrin says.

I nod, watching as the other guys assess the strange colors, as if a peacock had a role in decorating the place. Besides the other guys, the other customers and the workers in the cafe fade away to ghosts— and then nothing at all.

"This is *not* the kind of universe I had in mind," Kaden says.

I look at him and gulp. With all the sincerity within me, I can't agree any more. But something tugs at my heart, a voice whispering in my ear telling me to stay, telling me that I belong here and that the world I'm used to doesn't deserve me.

"I think we should get out of here," I say, my voice sounding far away to my own ears. I take my pen and cross out my last sentence.

Immediately, the color sucks away into an invisible vacuum. The other patrons and workers appear, laughing and gabbing, unaware of the blissful yet terrifying story I just wrote.

Van reaches for his drink and takes a sip. Looks like the cups didn't actually go flying? I glance at my clock and wonder how motivated I have to be to think about practice after *that.*

"What was that?" Kaden asks. "What did you write?"

I show them the few sentences I wrote, along with the one I crossed out.

"Maybe we should stop writing," Corrin says, swallowing guilt as he looks at his page filled with ink.

"I don't think so," I say. "I heard the voice—or at least part of it. This voice or whatever it is doesn't want us to debut. That's why we need to keep writing. It doesn't like when we have control over our lives."

"Good thinking," Seiya says. "Bros. Are we just going to sit here and give up? We need to show whatever this force is who's boss."

I nod, even as fear lodges in my throat. I know I'll enter that place again, the place that felt like temptation, like the sweetest piece of fruit wanting to dance on my tongue. Will I muster the strength to cross out my own words again? Will Seiya, Kaden, Van, and Corrin find the same strength?

I can only pray to God. He's the one who placed me in Apple Hair. And he can surely defeat whatever voice decided to haunt us since last Monday.

This time, and the next time.

"Let's head back to practice," I say, wondering with a bit too much intensity about the next time when we'll be sucked in, placed into the unknown where the waves crash above us and the leaves quiver as if whispering.

Chapter 11

Van

pple Hair's second month as a team begins with a literal bang as Kaden falls to the floor in the dance practice room. I reach out too late, and the clatter of his body against the wooden floor shocks me. It's like staring at a book and watching the letters rearrange themselves. I must look like one of those cartoon characters with their eyes bulging out of their heads. Earth to Van? *Universe* to Van?

"What happened?" I say, when I finally find my voice. Girl, I could really be better at leader-ing. Leader-ing? I can't even get my role right...

Armani runs over and kneels. She grasps his shoulder. "You've been pushing yourself too hard. It's obvious your back is bothering you."

Kaden scrunches up his face, and I know he's about to deny it—like he has the past month. But this time, he stays quiet. I want to tell him it's okay not to be so strong all the time, but I decide to save that for when we're back at the dorm.

"We're almost done anyways," Armani says. She moves her hips back and forth, as if weighing something. "Let's end a few minutes early. It's been a long practice. Plus, you have your very first etiquette practice today!"

The sighs of relief from the other guys makes me breathe my own. I help Kaden up, and we head to the corner of the room. David passes out our water bottles, and the sip I take almost makes me believe in God like he does. David would give me a look if I said that out loud…

"Time to take your meds," Seiya says, nudging Corrin against the shoulder.

Corrin scowls. The newest development? Corrin's been prescribed with medication to help his sleep. Now you know, and now we have so much more to think about, with both Corrin's and Kaden's conditions.

With bated breath, I have to lead with confidence. The water sloshing around my mouth distracts me a bit. Is this what my goldfish Hero feels?

Ever since Corrin was prescribed the meds by the doctor, he balks every time he needs to take them. Either Seiya or I will be the ones to remind him.

"It's been helping you bit by bit," I say.

Corrin rips out a packet of meds and takes them in one big gulp. His grooming needs some help sometimes too, and I reach out to brush his growing bangs out of his eyes. "You guys are seeing weird things all the time too. Why am I the one who needs to be on meds?"

It's true that we're still writing our stories, coming across the ghost who sometimes speaks or the dream worlds that try to suck us in. But Corrin's case is… different. He sees things even outside of those shared events. He listens to the birds and comes up with sentences that instruct him to do strange things. He talks to shadows and expects them to answer back to him. And his energy normally takes him all over the place.

"I'll make us a soup when we get home," I say. "That'll make us all feel better about… everything." My Vietnamese parents told me that a good dish can cure almost anything—and my older brother and I experienced it many times before.

Corrin perks up a bit. "Well, that won't fix *everything*," he says. "But it's a good start. Thanks, Van!"

"Yeah, mahalos," Seiya says, flashing me a peace sign.

Kaden crunches the water bottle with his fist. "Make sure to add something good for bones."

"I will," I say, not sure if I have the superpower to cure scoliosis.

"Damnit!" David draws me out of my thoughts about beef tendon. "I mean, danggit. I think I left our book back in the library."

"I'll get it," I say, thinking about how good it will be to be alone for a few seconds. My introvert ways perk up at the chance to even walk down the halls alone. Sure, it's no *book* or *video game*, but it'll have to do.

I leave as the boys try to catch a few Zs before etiquette class, using yoga mats for pillows. If the ghost doesn't get us first, it'll definitely be the sleep deprivation.

I hum the new song Mrs. White is teaching us, while Mr. Matthews' story about how he got lost on the Korea metro distracts me from remembering the right notes for the harmony. When I open the door to the library, I don't realize the edges of my vision are blurring until it's too late.

The library comes to life with shadow that furls into tendrils of smoke. I blink a few times, then focus in on Shar's book. The book's open to the last page we were writing on. I think it was a fanfiction work about a girl fan who was obsessed with Kaden. David got particularly invested in it, his creative side putting us all to shame.

"Not this again," I mutter to myself, like it's some sort of spell that will make our dream world go away. The dream world usually attaches itself to one of the members. And since I'm the only one here…

I close the door behind me before someone sees me freaking out in the library. The library comes to life in that old-book smell, just magnified by a hundred. I mean, I love that smell, but not to this level.

The books all wiggle on their shelves, like little puppies. I wait and breathe, knowing that a choice will arise for me to stay or leave. Sometimes, the other guys like to write in the book or cross something out to make everything go away. I just like to wait it out, using my will to get me back out again.

The voice I've learned to fear comes out, almost leaking from the spaces between the shelves. *What if I invented something to weigh you down too?*

A tingle starts at my throat. It turns into a heat, and suddenly I remember my days at school. I barely talked back then, and I only had one very close friend, Nick. And two other kind of close friends, James and Kainoa. Ah, they would probably scoff at me for calling them kind of close.

My parents said that I might've had selective mutism, but I refused to go to the counselor. I wish I did, if only to make my experience at school less like a warzone and more like, well… *school.*

I stride up to the notebook, taking out the gel pen that I always keep in my pocket these days. Before I write, the dream world calls to me with a soft warmth that I always felt when I got home from school—when my brother and I would play a video game, or I'd vent about my day to my parents. It calls for me to stay, to linger here forever instead of going back to practice.

Screw that—um, excuse my language—I'm the leader of Apple Hair, not a kid who needs a wonderland. I write something random on the page, only to counteract this weird as hell ghost.

Apple Hair learned how to control their dream world after overcoming their first month as trainees.

The dream world draws back, the shadows turning back to normal and the draw to stay fading all the way back. Girl, my brother Ryan would probably be proud. I want to call him, but I know he's busy at college. The memories rise, how we'd always be together after school. Just me and my best friend.

I grab the book and head out, walking straight to etiquette class on the twelfth floor. All the guys are there, along with about ten other trainees—all in their own groups for debut. I flash the guys the book, trying not to be too proud about it. That was a *ridiculous* few minutes that I just spent in the library.

I heard a lot about Nancy Gomez, AWE's first trans instructor and the first solidified *pop star* to grace the company. She's an absolute badass with multiple number one hits. How Merlin Kim got her to join is *beyond me.*

The tingle on my throat's still there. It stays as Nancy walks in, right when I take my seat between Kaden and Corrin.

Her platinum blonde hair catches the light of the classroom. Her beautiful hazel eyes make me feel things, and her casual long dress flows like waves on the beach. I glance at Kaden and see him swallowing. I can't really blame him at all.

"All right," she says, in a voice like dripping honey. "Why don't we all introduce ourselves?"

She somehow calls on me first. She tells me to stand, which I do in a second. Then, I open my mouth.

The tingle constricts my throat. And I—can't speak. I'm back in third grade, refusing to make friends because of how scary it was to talk. I fiddle with my hands, trying to will my vocal cords to move. I try to visualize myself as a character from an anime, who needs to act before something freakishly bad happens to his allies.

But, nothing.

I feel my members' eyes on me. Still, I'm a sitting duck—is that the right term for this? I don't know, all I know is that the voice that haunts us yanked me back to my school days. I make some weird gesture with my hands, pointing to my mouth as if that would explain everything.

"You can go last," Nancy offers, somehow getting the hint.

Kaden goes next, speaking in his measured and intellectual tone. Besides making a complete embarrassment of myself, I know I let my teammates down. They need someone to lead them, not a failure who gets a little scared all because of the ghost of the AWE company building.

Corrin goes right before I try again, and a quiver sticks to his hands. I know he's barely holding it together. Well, one day at a time, as my parents always say. As Ryan would say too. I watch Corrin go on a tangent about candy apples. *Really, Corrin? Candy apples?*

And he says how much he's looking forward to tomorrow's vocal lesson, when Mrs. White will teach us the new song for our next monthly evaluation.

Sorry to be a downer. But I wonder if we will even be able to sing tomorrow.

Chapter 12

Corrin

Mrs. White stares at me as I *go off* on a high note, reaching farther than I ever had with my voice.

The other guys stare at me like I growled instead. (It has a place in some songs, but I swore I hit a decent note?) I stifle a laugh and try to play it off—like I was actually just messing around.

Diane squints. "Are you… okay, Corrin?"

That's weird. Mrs. White never asks me whether I'm okay. I must've done something really horrible. Or did I? "Yeah! I'm okay. I'm completely sure that I'm okay."

I start to laugh fully now. I try to cover my mouth with my hand, and then my arm. I think about the medication I'm taking, a white pill that should have a different effect than the one stated. (It's actual effect: making you loopy and a bit dumb.) The other guys don't take anything—except maybe Kaden who just got started on some supplements. But that's different. The doctors can actually *see* that something's wrong with his back.

"I'll take you to the hospital," Van says. I can tell it's hard for him—it seems that he can't talk in front of others as easily as before. He says he met the ghost in the library. It's crazy how fast we believed him, how it could happen to any of us now. More than suspicious.

We're all suspicious now. We're criminals? No! Suspects.

"Your manager can," Diane says, turning the page on her music stand.

Really? "I'm just a little off, but not bad enough to go to the hospital," I say.

"You can't see what we see," Kaden says, bluntly.

I look to the other members for help. Seiya seems uncharacteristically solemn, and David bites his cuticle with a bit too much care. Fine. Even though I think my symptoms are bullshit and that they'll go away (just like this ghost will), I can't go against *five* people at once.

Shar meets me outside, and we ride toward the hospital in mostly silence. The sun reflects off everything and feels hotter than ever. I imagine all the guys sunbathing instead of practicing, and I try hard not to giggle. "Do you think something's wrong with me too?" I ask Shar. "Like actually? You can be serious, no need to bullshit me. Sorry, maybe that was the wrong thing to say?"

She changes the radio channel, and all that comes through is worship music—something about God accepting you and your flaws. David would love it—he has that connection with Shar. "I don't think there's anything wrong with you," she says.

And we leave it at that.

As we approach Queen's Medical Center, I start to panic. I think someone might have implanted a chip in my brain, controlling me to do weird things. To take control of every nerve in my body. Do I really have control over my own life? Did I join AWE Entertainment out of my own free will?

Despite myself, I start humming. I hum one of the options Diane gave us for our monthly evaluation, but it turns into about a hundred different things as I forget notes and replace lyrics with random phrases that pop into my head.

Shar turns the radio down. "I don't know everything, but I do know this. You're gonna be okay. And you still belong in Apple Hair."

I kind of want to write down a whole new page in the book she gave us. Creating our story, the world that we want our fans to be a part of, gives me so much comfort. I want to let her know this in some way, but we're already reaching the hospital.

As Shar pulls into the parking lot for emergency, I think about the other guys and how they're probably killing it in practice. I know that we're meant to be five. I know that I belong, even though I've no idea how long I have to stay in the hospital.

Now that I'm an adult, I don't have to tell anyone that I'm going through stuff like this. But my mom—she would want to know. Even with my swirling thoughts, I decide against calling her up. I don't want to worry her. As a single mom, she already went through a ton. (Perhaps I will tell her later? I can't imagine I would ever find a good time to talk about my slow yet kinda rapid descent.)

"Do I have to stay overnight?" I ask Shar. I'm trying not to treat her as a parent either.

She just ties her hair up into a bun. "We'll see what the doctor says."

As we pass through security, Shar hums a comforting song— almost a lullaby. By the time we're waiting for my turn to get checked out, I've calmed down a lot.

"Thanks for being here," I say.

Shar simply nods. "I'd say it's my job. But it feels like more than that. I know you guys have been going through a ton. Is the ghost still talking to you guys?"

"Sometimes…" I think back to the last time, when it told us that we would never debut. It had a little criminal laugh to it, like a little seasoning of sarcasm, maybe even a dark humor. "You're the only one we can trust to tell. That really gives us some peace."

"I've experienced something like that before," Shar says. "When I first joined AWE. I thought something was haunting me from saying yes to the contract. Eventually, I got through it. And now I get to manage such an amazing group. Apple Hair."

My panic fluctuates as the seconds pass. I definitely don't see a black cat again, but a smog rises from within the hospital. It surrounds me, making me want to shout out or worse. Just when I think my heart will actually explode, Shar stands up as a nurse comes over with a clipboard.

She asks me a few questions, most of which I answer easily. Like my name—Corrin. It means spear. My mom and dad had a huge argument about my name before I was born. My dad joked that they should settle it with a joust. Eventually, the topic of spears came up. When I answer the nurse, I think about all the times people have mistaken it for "corn," either intentionally or not.

The nurse also asks my religion—agnostic, kind of. When it comes to the questions about mood though, I stumble. I don't know what to say besides how I keep fluctuating. Hot one second and cold the next. Have any of my pets felt like this before? Like their mind was tricking them?

Maybe after this whole thing, I'll be able to help various animals going through mental distress!

Shar waves at me a bit sadly when I have to go into a different room for further assessment. I hear her words. *You'll be okay, Corrin.*

The doctor inside smiles at me. He tilts his head, and his gray hair catches the light. He looks a bit like my old math teacher. They're both hapa. It means mixed race, but this doctor looks more specifically hapa haole—half white. After I've really screwed up with all the questions, he asks me, "Do you think you need to stay? At least for a night?"

I bite the inside of my cheek. Gosh… what would the guys want me to say?

I think about calling my mom and just staying the night at the house. I suck it up—I'm eighteen now, not a baby. "I think I'll stay for a night."

"Okay," the doctor says, and I stare at his goatee for the rest of the time we're together. "From my assessment, it would be a good idea to monitor you for a little while. You don't seem like you'll hurt anyone or yourself, so we'll give you a normal room in the emergency ward."

"Thanks!" I say, a bit too brightly.

The doctor grins even though I think he's finding a thousand things that are wrong with me. "We'll monitor and see how you're doing. You can keep your phone and everything."

Does he think I'm a phone addict? He is not wrong, though I'm not at David's or Seiya's level. Anyway, I can't complain!

Ten minutes later, I'm in a dark room with no one to talk to. I guess I have my phone, but it feels wrong to text the guys. The hospital bed scratches my skin, so I stand up and stretch. A burst of energy rises within me, overflowing like I'm standing right under a waterfall.

Dancing and singing. That's all I have, and all I've been doing for months now. I scroll through my phone and find "Honeymoon Avenue" by Ariana Grande. A beast of a song, but maybe I can finally hit the notes after so much practice? Maybe? I clear my throat by coughing even though I know it's horrible for my vocal cords.

After I get through the song, which I think I screamed through after the halfway point, I change to a different song, a hip-hop instrumental called "When the Leaves Turned Gray" made by some producer in AWE. I bounce and try to do all the complicated moves we practice in the studio.

Hours pass, of me repeating the same move over and over, trying to perfect it. I probably fail, but I think about Shar and the guys—how hard they're working to make sure Apple Hair succeeds. I dance until I sweat buckets. I sing until my throat goes sore.

A nurse knocks on my door about a dozen times and tells me to quiet down. After the tenth time, her voice turns shrill.

Fearing that the ghost will come on the thirteenth time, I sit and think about the world the boys and I have created. Our universe includes everything from magical powers to libraries that play movies at night. The main thing we want is our fans to feel comfortable. To know that they are creatives with brilliant imaginations (even more brilliant than ours). So, we want our universe to be accepting of everyone. I think all of us agreed to that in half a second.

I don't have anything to write with, so I use my phone to jot down notes. I wonder if we could have a fanfiction crossover with my favorite book series, *Dune*. I've been wondering a lot of things lately. A lot of those thoughts end with a fire in the dorm, or verbal abuse by Allen, or another page ripped out of our book from Leo Pak.

I feel a sense of loss, like he stole our story. Whatever. I turn up my songs to the max volume. I sing and dance at the same time, imagining that I'm performing at the Blaisdell. Who's to say that I won't do that one day?

I'll be out of here by tomorrow. Ghost, I promise.

Chapter 13

Kaden

A variable I many times refuse to account for? It's an embarrassing fact about me—my addiction to porn. There are multiple studies about it, how it can alter the brain and its matter.

Somehow, I've ruled out the hypothesis that it could affect me.

Each time I search up some adult content on my phone, I deal with the guilt that comes with it. This morning, I don't want to think about it too long. I walk out to the living room and find Shar who walks around and tidies up various little things in the living room. She definitely doesn't have to do that. I volunteer to go with her to pick up Corrin from the hospital.

My addiction started when I was young, when the stress of losing my parents ate at me and I needed an escape. It pummeled into me, the fact that they weren't here anymore, a fresh wound like a shocking revelation. It was not that I remembered so much about them. In fact, the opposite was true. But the longing gnawed at the soulish half of me.

I never told Lora about it, wanting to protect her from everything. In fact, I always keep a cool and collected facade in front of her. I just don't want her to lose faith in me.

I can't lose faith in Corrin either. So, when Shar takes me in the van early in the morning, I don't pop in my headphones like usual. I tense parts of my body, starting from my head down. I tense my thighs, trying to focus on the predictable ache of my muscles. I let the muscle quiver a little. At the same time, I take measured breaths that do not match the cacophony of thoughts. Next up, I ready my hamstrings.

I watch as Shar lowers the volume of the radio. Her careful hand hovers over the control. A hidden memory pops up within me, taking me off guard. I once slept in the backseat, without a worry or care, while my parents hummed along to their favorite song on the 80s channel. All my muscles relax as if on instinct.

I think Shar wants to talk.

"How was taking him yesterday?" I ask.

She hums. "He's still there. He just needs some support. These sorts of things take a lot of time to heal."

"I know," I say, not adding that I wrote about mental health for my senior thesis. I click my tongue. "This is just really bad timing."

I realize I sound like an ass, but Shar doesn't call me out for it. "Yeah, it is."

We pull into the parking lot. I put a hand on the door handle, squeezing. I lean forward, like a track athlete ready to begin a race.

Corrin's standing to be discharged outside of the emergency room. He meddles with his shirt and pants, even though their wrinkled state is unsalvageable. He gives me a wave, which is subdued when compared to his manic state yesterday.

His hair sticks up in a wayward mess. He gives me a little smile, and from his eyebags, I know he didn't sleep a wink. "Hey," I say. "Was it okay in there? What did they say?"

"I just need sleep," he says. "They also gave me new meds. To help with the so-called psychotic and manic symptoms. They'll have some effect soon—or at least that's what they *say*."

"Good, good," I say, even as Corrin glances around suspiciously.

I place my arm around his shoulder. Even though we've only been together for around a month, I've started to care for him. Maybe a bit too much. He's like my little sister, in a lot of ways actually.

He rests his head on mine, and I wonder what's going through his mind. Probably a thousand different things.

I want him to know one thing, though. I say it with as much conviction as I can muster. "You'll be okay."

He doesn't answer, and I think I see Shar wipe at the corner of her eye.

Back at the dorm, I wait until Corrin's idle in his bed—sleeping, or at least pretending to? I make sure the curtains are fully closed before I join everyone else in the van.

"He's alive," I announce.

The boys give me varying levels of stares, suspicion and relief all mixed into one.

"That's good," Seiya says. "I mean, he's not *dead*."

"Seiya!" David says.

Van crosses his arms, staring out the window of the front seat. He's probably the most affected about "losing" Corrin. They've always had a soft spot for each other. Maybe not to the degree of Seiya and David, but still.

I lean back. "It'll be the four of us for a while," I say. I don't bother mentioning that manic episodes could take months to "go away," if you could even call it that. I watch as David shuts his eyes. He probably offers a prayer. For once, my thoughts don't challenge him.

I'm on autopilot as we reach the company and head to the first class of the day—language with Cory Matthews.

"Now, we're gonna start with our presentations," Mr. Matthews says, calling up the first group. "And the following group is Apple Hair."

The first group does a role play in Korean, something about going to the beach and losing your boogie board. It irks me a little bit, as talking about the ocean always does with me. By the time it's our turn, I have to force myself to stand. My legs feel weighed down with bags of flour. The tensing and relaxing should've helped with that.

"I'm Kaden from Apple Hair," I say in Korean. I tell myself to keep it loose. Confidence—the key in mastering a language. I just need to speak it out.

"And I'm David."

"Seiya."

"And Van." He struggles to get out the words.

As I begin, I follow our plan to stick to our storytelling theme. We recount the tale of Alice as she stumbled upon wonderland, except we make it our own with very simple descriptions. Going to the store and finding that it's a whole new place—someplace beautiful where people are so friendly that everyone introduces themselves. I go ahead and introduce myself and my hobby—sports.

Halfway through the presentation, Mr. Matthews raises his hands. "I think we've heard enough. I think—maybe you guys just need more practice."

The tips of my ears burn. Maybe if Corrin were here…

"And I think you're struggling because Corrin isn't here." Mr. Matthews laughs, actually laughs with a good amount of gusto, and it feels like it's at our expense.

I clench my fists at my sides, thinking about how hard we worked in studying the Korean language. Sure, we focus mainly on dance and vocals, but I don't read from our textbook every night to be mocked.

"Can I be excused?" I say.

"What?" Cory Matthews raises his eyebrows at me. "Unless it's the bathroom, I don't think you can be excused."

When we first met, I thought this guy was decent. Now, it seems that no one is for our group except our members and Shar.

Some of our classmates begin to whisper. I constantly forget that a lot of them are younger. I keep my gaze ahead on our teacher. He adds, "Man, I just wanted to give some constructive criticism. No shade at all."

My fingernails dig into my palm. I want to argue, but I think our whole team will suffer if I say something harsh to our teacher. I turn around and walk toward the exit, ignoring the way everyone stares like I have a big spike on my back.

Cory gives a little sigh as I open the door. I want to be respectful, but the other part of me wants to turn back and say something real and honest. Instead, I listen to the logical part of me. I won't gain anything by starting an argument with someone in the company. Especially not one of our key instructors.

It definitely read like an argument though, even though we only exchanged a few blows.

With about thirty minutes left of language class, I decide to head to the gym and let off some steam. Studies say that exercise can be just as effective as medicine in some cases. For cooling off a hot head? I'll take all the help I can get.

I run on the treadmill at the highest speed I can manage for about ten minutes. I ignore my protesting spine, so fickle like a little kid. Jumping off, I feel both invigorated and totally exhausted. I decide to go toward the dumbbells. I'll do some arm curls and hopefully feel better about the whole Cory Matthews situation.

As I pick up the thirty-pound one, I feel my senses begin to tingle. It's our dream world coming to haunt us, I know.

Maybe I should be scared, especially since I'm alone. Instead, I clench my right arm around the dumbbell. *Come at me. I don't even believe in ghosts.*

The world that comes alive around me shimmers and makes the whole gym like an oasis in the clouds. I feel lighter. My back doesn't hurt. I feel the draw to stay in this in-between state and float out here forever. I will really be like the Alice who never returned.

But even though the relief comes to life in here, I feel the darkness underneath. The sweetness of the dream world sucks me in, but it will take from me too. I need to break it in some way.

I throw my dumbbell on the floor. It bounces off the vinyl and hits me on the knee. I cry out and flail around, looking at the frozen trainees in the gym like they could help me. When nothing significant happens, I bend down and pick up the dumbbell again. This time, I launch it hard on the floor, with an estimated twice the force. I calculate the angle in my mind, so it has plenty of room to bounce away. I don't need an injury to add to my back problems.

This time, it bounces in the other direction. It looks like a lob of matter, blurry and indistinguishable. It reminds me about how I used to want to be a professional athlete or a professor in sports science. And although a dumbbell is probably no match for this unexplainable phenomenon, I know it can break me out of it.

Can a thirty-pound dumbbell do more than just build my muscle?

The air wavers around me. I suppose we'll find out.

Chapter 14

Seiya

Sunday's our off day and my favorite day of the week. Yeah. *Sunday.* Who woulda thought?

I wake up strangely early and get a call in with my older sister—probably my favorite person in the world. Ami.

"Well, why don't you just do something nice for the other guys?"

I squint, looking at her through FaceTime. "Genius, sistah. Why didn't I think of that?"

"That's what I'd do. If weird things were happening." Ami repeats herself in pidgin, and I sigh. I wish I were four again and dressing up with her in something weird, yet pretty. Man, those were the days. I can still remember her getting her fairy queen costume. Her loud-ass scream that could wake up all the neighbors. My eardrums ache a little.

She scratches her brow, adjusting her phone. I catch our similar eyes, which often remind people of a mischievous cat. Our lips and nose are the same too, full and slightly crooked. She has a tiny scar on her chin. I remember the day when we were running around in the kitchen. She slipped and screamed when her chin clipped the kitchen counter. What a crazy day.

"Hey," I say. "You're finishing up your senior year, right? Shouldn't you be crazy smart by now? Why don't you tell me why these things are happening? The guys and I are debating on whether it's supernatural. Or just a trick of the mind."

"I don't know…" Ami tilts her head and accuses me with a squint. "And I'm studying graphic design, Seiya. Do you seriously think I would know?"

"Pfft." I wave at her, almost raising my voice before realizing the guys are in dreamland. "Ami, if I die, you know what to do."

"Huh?" She glares at me while flipping through a textbook.

"My things. All my precious collectables."

"Your basketballs?"

"Yeah! I got so many signed ones. And don't forget about the limited edition *MapleStory* playing cards."

"Don't remind me of your obsession," Ami says. "I will try to visit you soon. Anyway, I have a good feeling about you guys. Apple Hair. Your debut will be epic."

"Something laddat," I say.

She smiles, her annoyance disappearing. "Seiya, remember. Do something good for the guys."

When I end the call, I get a bad case of missing my sister. She's on the island, but we don't see each other every day like we used to. Some days, she would drive to our favorite boba place. She's the whole reason my nasty boba addiction started.

I take a deep breath that would stun Kaden, with all his talk about the science of our breathing. Peeking into our bedroom, I glance at all four guys. They seem pretty knocked out. Like something hit 'em on the head with a rock. Corrin quivers. David turns in his sleep, and I turn back before I get too caught up or something.

I dig through our pantry. Man. It's not looking too good for us. But I find something I bought before moving in here. A ramen kit.

Because I'm very Japanese, I thought it would be fitting to always have a ramen kit on hand. It was crazy expensive at Don Quijote, but

I think today's a good day to use it. I open the package and read the instructions. I'm not a very good cook, but I don't think I can screw this up. I could probably use Van's help tho'. He's our resident chef and he always makes a mad pasta.

I boil everything and think about how we already passed the two-month mark as trainees. We have another evaluation coming up soon. Crazy. I purposely don't watch the pot. I don't talk to my parents anymore, but I remember my mom saying, *You shouldn't watch it, or it will be scared of you. It won't boil that way.*

I throw the noodles in after the water boils. Stirring every once in a while, I prepare the soup packets. I pour the hot water into the bowl then arrange the noodles on top. Yessah! Yessah's used when you want to agree with someone. Or just to say yes in an excited way.

Assembling five bowls takes a while. But once it's ready, I call the boys out.

Everyone has panda eyes. I nuzzle Corrin's head as he sits down next to me and takes his first bite. "Seiya… this is, *amazing*."

"Really?" I say. "I know."

As I eat with my teammates, I notice that everyone's small kine half dead. Small kine—it means a little bit. Such as small kine spicy, or small kine difficult. Honestly, I need another term to describe us. I think about how I can cheer up the team even more.

We eat pretty quickly. I guess everyone wants to have more time to sleep. I'm right. My bros, after slurping down the ramen like animals, set the bowls in the kitchen. At least we aren't that comfortable to be leaving dishes everywhere.

They all head back to the bedroom one by one. David's last. He gives me a little smile—I guess we're all too pooped to even talk. "Thanks," he says before wiping his lips.

The salt makes my tongue feel dry. I down half a cup of water and sit in the living room for a lil' bit. We barely had time to decorate.

But Kaden did hang up a photo of a rocket in outer space. Our clothes hang everywhere, which is pretty wild.

The Hawai'i heat gets to me, because we don't like to run the aircon for too long. David's pretty sensitive to the cold. I hum a J. Cole song and try to do some cleaning outside. I get through half the pile of crap before an idea comes to me. Something sweet. Something to go against all the bitter shit we had to face recently.

I get dressed in sweatpants and a white T. Before I go, I sneak into the bedroom and find four snoring puppies. Puppies—that's what Van likes to call us. God, I wish I could join to catch some Zs. But my idea is much too good. I'm a genius.

Before I go, I open Shar's book that we set on the dining table. We all agreed to write things that are true to us. Whatever that means.

I think for a second before scribbling, *Apple Hair worked so hard, that they got their first fan.*

I continue my humming. Outside, the sun bares down on my shoulders. Shit, the Hawai'i sun could probably bake me alive.

The convenience store, a ten-minute walk, has some killer macarons. My teammates all obsess over them. I think about how many boxes to get. Well, each one has four. I should probably get at least five boxes.

As the sweat starts to travel to weird places, I take in Kaka'ako—the little shops and the hipsters, mostly. The blueness of today makes me feel a bit lighter about everything. Entering the 7-Eleven, I head straight for the dessert section.

Yessir. The macarons are here. And exactly five boxes! I grab them up quickly and pay at the register. The aunty gives me a little smile, like she knows how much of a sweet tooth I got.

"Seiya!" I turn around just when I'm about to go.

Nancy Gomez wears baby pink. Her blouse, skirt, all the way down to her sandals. Her platinum hair looks too bright and star-like to be in a convenience store. She changed her contacts? To a bright gray, almost like a marble statue. She holds herself like a member of a royal family, which is pretty rad in my books.

I'm surprised she's without a bodyguard. I think about half of Hawai'i wants a picture with her.

I get a bit nervous. "Ms. Gomez! Funny seeing you here."

"Oh." Nancy almost acts a bit shy. "Well, I'm here! And I'm a fan, Seiya."

Crap. I think about what I wrote in our book. Nancy is Apple Hair's first fan, I guess?

She looks down at my boxes of macarons. Then she licks her lips. "Great choice. Anyway, something popped into my head recently."

"Oh yeah?" I take a step back, just to get out of the sunlight.

She follows. "I wanted to give you a word of wisdom from my pop star days."

She's still a pop star, but I play along. "Cool."

"I know in Korea, they call them *sasaengs*." She grimaces a bit. "Or obsessed fans. They're the ones who will trail you everywhere and maybe even invade your personal space. There was this one time when a dude was hiding in a rubbish can for me. He just popped out like a weasel. I can still remember his face…"

I watch as she adjusts her pair of fuchsia sunglasses sitting on her head. She takes them off eventually. "Okay…" I say.

"I just wanted to warn you," she says. "Anyway, I'm a fan. A big fan. I can see your face advertising luxury brands and getting those deals left and right."

"Oh, that'd be good," I say. "Since we're getting so much debt from the company. Ha-ha."

She puts on the glasses. But I know she's squinting even though she blocks her face. "Very interesting."

Interesting? I think what's interesting is that I'm beginning to see pink everywhere. An aura surrounds the pop star. I think my dream world's about to bite me in the ass.

I say bye and run back to the dorm. That's right. I run back, balancing the macarons like a magician. Our instructors are a bunch of weird-asses. Maybe they weren't *always* weird, but something changed when we started our stories.

At the dorm, I take off my shoes and set the macarons in the kitchen. One of them crumbled on the way back. I open the box up and stuff it into my mouth. Green tea—my favorite. It's so sweet, my teeth hurt.

I think about our second major evaluation, coming up real soon. The boys are still sleeping. I don't know if they fainted or what. I close the door to the bedroom and pass out on the futon. I think I dream about pink pasta and a very feminine shark that won't stop rapping.

Chapter 15

David

The dream world wants me to stay. Why don't I stay?

The night before our second major evaluation, I sneak out into the dorm living room. The light from the moon carves out the little things we changed. It gets stuffy when I think about how the five of us share this space, revolving around the same moon, blasting across the universe at the same speed together. I glance at our book on the dining table, the key to our success and maybe also the first thing to cause our downfall.

Our imaginations run wild when we think about the Apple Hair world. A world where anything is possible and everyone can go for their creative pursuits—in fact, their imagination emboldens them and makes them powerful. I think we're all in that imaginary phase where our universe hasn't yet been filled in with the glittering details.

In the night, I imagine my five teammates breathing and regaining their energy as if siphoning it out from the starlight. They deserve the rest, when the training has been pushing us all to the cliff of exhaustion. I exit the house knowing full well that the ghost that haunts us can pop up at any time, cursing me or trying to single us out and break us apart.

Outside, I feel the tingling sensation that tells me the dream world will call to me soon or tug at the threads around my fingers. I need to be alone, so I tiptoe around the apartment building to the little garden outside, which is barely a garden. In the middle of two apartment buildings, it reminds me more of an attempt to save a little greenery and display it so the residents won't complain about the lack of life. Still, it brings me comfort to stand around here, like I'm searching for something that can't be found without a little nature.

Like before, church bells ring, drawing me in with ghostly hands. But instead of resisting, I decide to let it take me in. I work quickly, or rather, I imagine with all the strength I have. I know we change our lives in tiny ways by writing our stories, so why can't I change my dream world too?

"I want a perfect destination for a getaway," I whisper into the shadows. "Somewhere… that maybe Seiya and I could enjoy."

Even though I think I'm just whispering sweet nothings, I channel everything I have into making something beautiful, something that will glitter just like the stars. It takes a massive amount of energy to grow some flowers on the grass, changing a little square of green to a sandy area for a picnic, or maybe even a true getaway that two people can lose themselves in.

But after toiling, seeing my sweat and losing myself in fantasies, I have to drag myself back to the real world. The dead of night feels wrong now, like I just lost something deep within me as if it spiraled away without me knowing.

I go back to the apartment and fall asleep, listening to the metronome of my members' snoring and breathing. In the little seconds before I actually travel to dreamland, I reflect on the garden and the delicate, iridescent threads that held it together.

In the morning, I wake up everyone a bit earlier. "I worked on something," I say. "Last night. And I want to show you all."

At the miniature garden, I gather the members who probably

want nothing more than to grab hold of a few more minutes of sleep, a reprieve from our harsh schedule. I close my eyes, remembering the feeling of creating, like writing down something in my mind.

When I open my eyes, the flowers show translucently, along with the stretch of sand. I almost yell out in triumph, but I settle for turning to the boys with hesitance. I bare a part of my soul to these teammates, and even though it doesn't exactly reveal a secret, it certainly feels like something just as intimate.

"What does this mean?" Kaden says. "We can make things in our heads now? I don't know if I want that kind of superpower."

"I think this is *revolutionary*," Corrin says.

"It's sick," Seiya says, nudging my arm with his elbow. I think I see stars in my vision, and that has nothing to do with the dream world.

"Yeah…" Van says. I can tell he wants to say more, but it was the slithering ghost who stole his ability to speak like before, dragging him back to his shy past.

On the drive to the company, Shar plays the track we'll be performing for our second major evaluation. Its blaring chorus, almost a battle cry, invigorates me and motivates me not to only memorize the lyrics, but to study the delivery of a triumphant dance with your tongue. We'll be singing and dancing at the same time, so it'll take all our concentration, like channeling the sun with a magnifying glass to start a spark in the grass.

I close my eyes and pray, wondering if God can see the ghost. I know he does, but it feels like he gave us Shar and the book so that we can fight against it ourselves, whatever it is. I think about the pastor at my church and his wife, who took me in when I needed to escape from my parents. I long for a word of advice from them, something to color the world which has turned a bit muddy and gray.

"Are we ready for this?" Kaden says as we wait outside the evaluation room—same one as before.

Van nods. "We are."

I clench my hands at my sides, thinking of all the forces holding us back from debut, like an anchor used in the wrong way. I think about our instructors, who treat us differently now that we began to write. I think about Allen and the other trainees, who don't care about us—or worse. I think about the old ghosts in our pasts that have risen, threatening to choke us all, to snuff out the tiny lights that we hold.

I think about the five of us, what these two months have brought. The strength we share rising like a fog—an uplifting one, drawing me out of the mood of heartbreak and apathy.

"We can definitely do this," I say. *We have to.*

Inside, our instructors, Leo Pak, and CEO Kim face us with blank faces. I know we have something to prove, especially to the one who tore a page from our book, splitting our destinies with a rip that probably hasn't fully affected us just yet.

The sunlight sparks across my irises, and the hum of something around us, maybe the air conditioner, almost distracts me from what we've come to do. The energy we have to channel, and the mountain we must conquer.

I get into position at the center of the group. The song we're performing was actually written by a producer at AWE, given to a famous pop duo. It was almost custom tailored to match our voices, made to fit to the contours of our dance. It's perfect.

Van starts off the song, his shyness forgotten like a shadow that sinks back into the far corner, as he changes into a siren with the most powerful song—the one they would reserve for luring its most valuable prey. Seiya's next, enchanting me and everyone in the room with his rap. He hits every beat and gathers his syllables in the offbeat like little hits against the drum. Kaden and Corrin pair together for a harmony, and then I pierce through the chorus with the force of the sun.

I let out my anger for my toxic parents and the instructors who might turn just as toxic. For a second, it's Apple Hair versus the world, our universe colliding with all the stars in the galaxy.

I grip my microphone and phrase the lyrics like I'm cutting something with a knife, doing something so brave and brilliant. I don't try to read the expressions of the instructors, knowing that they're impressed. They have to be.

As the song wraps up, I think about one of my earliest memories at church. Standing still, letting the emotions of worship enter my heart and make me feel at peace, like the ocean was buoying me up with it. I finish the song with a belt that tests my voice more than ever, but I hit it with my full chest.

We've done it.

For a second, the room quiets to a stillness that's very rare in the company. Then, Armani Bera begins to clap. Cory Matthews, Diane White, Nancy Gomez, and even Leo Pak joins her. They fill the room with the enthusiasm our performance deserved.

I can hardly believe it.

CEO Kim stands up, clasping his hands in one loud pop and giving us a look that can only be described as *proud*. "Wow. Apple Hair. I didn't know you guys had it in you. I didn't know you would have this so soon, at least."

We did it. We really did it. I could grab a handful of opalescent paint and throw it at the wall, and it still wouldn't change what I'm seeing right now in the marvelous brilliance of the moment—because what we just put out on the imaginary stage can weave a future for all five of us.

I exchange glances with the boys. We go into one tight huddle, hugging each other while shaking in joy. I think Corrin may be close to screeching at the glass windows.

"By this, you boys definitely stunned us with an A." CEO Kim touches his jaw with his finger. "However, this was only the first part of your evaluation."

First part? No one told us anything about a second part. But I guess with AWE, we can't have it so easy. Ever since Apple Hair was formed, something evil stirred into the air, trying to snuff out everything good within us.

I expect CEO Kim to tell us what we need to do next. In a turn that smacks me across the face with hot metal, Leo Pak stands.

Our page-ripper, the one that may have caused a rift in our destinies forever.

Cory Matthews stands to translate for him. Even before Leo Pak speaks, I feel the fissure forming in my chest. With a hard shell made of diamond forming on my soul, I know I won't like at all what he has to say.

Chapter 16

Van

L eo Pak speaks, and Cory Matthews translates.

"We know you did a great job with this first part."

I can't help but get the creeps. The tightness in my throat gets even *tighter*, which I didn't think was possible. Even if I wanted to cough, I probably couldn't. I would spin around like a sick goldfish. Sorry for using your likeness again, Hero…

So, I just stand still and try to breathe. Key word is *try* here, because that performance took everything out of me.

"You guys have been a group for two months now. And your singing and dancing are already so great. But we want to take things to the next level. We want you to establish your *presence*."

Ever since Leo ripped a page out of our book, I've been doing my best to avoid him. I know that's basically impossible when he has such a big presence in AWE Entertainment. Right now, I channel my cool and *collected* face—my mindful face that Ryan would see through immediately.

At the same time, a little part of me is pissed off. I know I can't be like Kaden and confront anyone, but maybe my shoulder can be a bit colder. I need to be an emperor penguin.

"By that I mean, you guys need to establish yourselves. Who is

Apple Hair? What makes you guys so different?

"We'll give you one month for the second part of your evaluation. By the last day of your third month together, we want you to create a song and dance that is completely yours. You'll have limited help from producers. What's important is to create a *story* with this. Every lyric and every move has to have a meaning."

I exchange glances with the guys and realize the instructors are probably waiting for me to speak. I open my mouth and battle the tightness—which, gosh, got even tighter? I don't want to be a drama queen like Corrin, but this is probably the worst my selective mutism has ever been. And girl, I thought I beat it a long time ago.

"We'll do our best," I manage to say.

An aura surrounds Leo at this moment, reminding me of the darkness of a storm cloud. I wonder if the guys are seeing what I'm seeing. I wonder if the ghost can hear this challenge too.

And can we really do this? Does Apple Hair really have a strong presence?

On my gaming computer, one of my probably most precious possessions, I stay up late playing a game of *League of Legends.* I tap my fingers roughly on the worn-out keyboard. At the same time, I drum my wrists on the edge of the keyboard, as if providing a beat to my life in-game.

David was supposed to join me, but he passed out. Seiya sits on the living room couch watching a basketball game on his phone. While I click away. A normal night like this? Exactly what I needed. And I don't need to talk to my toxic *League* teammates, not when I can just type out all my feelings. The euphoria I feel while playing one of my favorite games? Don't even get me started…

Taking a sip out of some sparkling water David bought a few days ago, I cough after the shock of cold enters my throat. Seiya takes it as an invitation.

"Bro. Do you really think we can do this?"

I'm too busy trying to kill an enemy champion, and I only half heard him. "Huh?"

He sighs. "Finish your game first, bro."

After the enemy Nexus explodes, I turn back toward the only other nineteen-year-old on the team. "Hey. You sleeping?"

"Nah." He sits up, setting his phone face down. "You think we can do this?"

"We have to," I say.

He tilts his head a bit, but he doesn't answer. And then he really does go to sleep. His snores fill the house, giving me a bit of comfort. Our dorm's like a safe haven, because the ghost avoids haunting us here. I guess the ghost has a tiny bit of stage fright here? How ridiculous.

But how comforting is it that we have one place where the ghost won't steal from us? Just a little bit.

Month three of Apple Hair starts with Jason and Allen stabbing us in front of the company. Well, maybe there's a better metaphor for that. But when a poster saying, "Stop the favoritism for Apple Hair," pops up in the lobby of AWE, we know who's behind it.

"This is messed up," Seiya says.

In a rare moment where I actually want to be seen, I tear the poster from the wall and crumple it in my hands.

"Nice one," Kaden says. He looks over his shoulder, and I follow his gaze.

Allen. He looks at us with a raised brow and an amused grin. Girl, have we reverted to the toxic environment of a middle school? The paper rubs against my callused gaming fingertips.

"Wow. At least show some remorse or something," David whispers.

I clench my teeth and feel the lock around my throat subside a bit. I only let one word out, "Hey," before another poster appears. It *appears* in Allen's hands, like he cast some sort of spell. The cat, the ghost, the devil—whatever you want to call it, is definitely behind this.

I wish I could escape to the dream world right now—maybe then I'd be distracted. I think about all the words we wrote in Shar's book, the stories we are so ambitious about. Gosh, I'd do anything to make one of those happen.

I imagine shooting a music video and sharing a story of hope. I can't let Ryan or my parents down. All the things they invested into me led up to this, where I'll debut with them watching.

In the elevator ride to the practice room, Armani's voice replaces the person announcing the floors. "Welcome to level eleven!"

For some reason, her voice sounds a little bit too bubbly.

"Weird," Kaden says.

In the practice room, the ghost stays away for the most part, except when the bass drops and the whole room goes dark for half a second. Corrin wavers and almost falls. I have to steady him by the arm.

"Why don't we take a little break?" Armani says, not mentioning the blackout at all.

Five hours of practice later, we find ourselves with Diane White, who sings a call that resembles an eagle and asks us to recreate it. Halfway through finding my falsetto register, she says, "I wonder if you can incorporate a similar sound in your original song."

Original song. We barely got started, and we have less than four weeks to prepare. The thought makes me a tiny bit nauseous… Okay, for real though, how are we going to turn into choreographers and producers? *Vantastic*, my brother used to describe me as sometimes, and we'll need that same sort of enthusiasm about what we create.

As Diane corrects the rising and falling of my scales, I think about what it means to be Apple Hair's leader. It must mean that I'm responsible to stop these weird happenings. It also means that I need to offer some sort of stability for my members.

Why was I voted the leader again?

The fact that the ghost stole something directly from me, my voice, must mean something. And it means something creepy and bad. I wish I was back in school to talk to my old friends—Nick and James and Kainoa. Maybe they'd make some sort of joke out of this. To make everything seem a bit better.

After our practice finishes, I get the boys together. My throat feels more loose than ever. "Hey. Let's stay for a few hours to work on our original stuff."

Kaden raises his brows. Probably surprised that I spoke so much. "Agreed."

"Yeah, sleep is for the weak," Corrin says.

David squints. "For you, sleep is more important than ever."

"Yeah, yeah," Corrin says. I can tell his medication is working a bit.

As we walk through the hallway, letters swirl on the walls—all evidence of the stories that we wrote in Shar's notebook. For some reason, they comfort me. A battle with five knights. A rescue of a prince in a frozen castle.

"You guys can see that too, right?" Corrin half whispers.

I take one stride forward as Kaden takes my side. "At this point, I'm used to it. Come at me, Leo's best friend!"

"Hey," I say, *maybe not a good idea.*

"Do we really want to make this force of nature angry at us?" David adds.

"Five against one," Seiya says. "We got this, bros."

Thankfully, Leo's bestie leaves us alone. We gather inside a medium-sized studio. Seiya orders us pizza for later.

And in an act of magic or whatever, we manage to get *a lot* done. David hums the melody that we're considering for the chorus. Seiya busts several moves that we think look great for the choreo. Corrin adds harmonies and Kaden plays with a synthesizer. We move as one. Like a true team.

When the pizza comes, one a.m. strikes on the clock. David yawns, and Seiya burps at the same time. Somehow, that's more funny than everything we said or did today. Corrin and I burst out laughing, and Kaden chuckles.

I take a bite of the supreme pizza with a thick yet delicate crust. In the middle of my first piece, with a slice of pepperoni literally hanging off the crust, I watch the pizza box.

Dark letters form on top, crossing out the name of the cheap pizza joint and replacing it with a huge apple. An apple with a bite taken out of the center.

It spells: *Apple Hair, on the road to failure, with stories that resonate with no one.*

Before I can get properly freaked out, Kaden kicks the box. He juts his leg out like a hockey stick, and the thing goes flying across the room. The dark letters disappear once the box hits the mirror.

"That's one way to deal with it," Corrin says, taking a bite out of his second slice a little too nonchalantly.

Miraculously, the pizza stayed in the box. I go to retrieve it. In my hands, the box looks completely normal. Not a thing to be concerned about. *Okay, ghost. Do what you gotta do, I guess.*

"I bet it wasn't expecting a drop kick," David says, scrunching his nose up as if about to laugh.

I smile, bringing back our dinner. Two hours later, we tell Shar we'll sleep in the company despite her protests. Grabbing pillows from the break room, along with some blankets, we arrange five beds.

Sleeping in the company isn't so bad. When I have four other guys to face the evil force with me. Wow, that sounds a bit intense.

Chapter 17

Corrin

Halfway through month three, it feels like my feet are going to explode (and I'm trying not to dramatize).

Maybe it's the dancing. No, it's *definitely* the dancing. I've never busted so many moves before. I never pumped my fist so hard. Gosh. I wonder if the guys are feeling the same thing?

I guess I can ask. But with my new *condition,* I'm tending to keep a lot of things to myself.

I lean my head back in Seiya's car, clutching my phone so hard I might crack the glass. Then, I jolt forward when we stop at a red light. "Hey, this might be our first major performance or something."

"Singing in the church choir?" Kaden says, a bit skeptical.

I don't know *why* he's skeptical, but I'm about to say something that I hope is witty. Then it escapes me. (I think my meds sleepy-tize my brain. Is that a word?)

"Thanks for coming along," David says. "But church is really important to me. I'm glad we can sing together on stage."

"Worship songs," Van says, probably wanting to say more. And he does after a second of him finding his voice again. "It's new for me."

"Same." Seiya, in the driver's seat, slaps on his shades after squinting at the sun. "I mean, I believe in God and da kine, but I never go. To church."

I try to calm myself down in the passenger seat. From behind, Van reminds me to take my meds. I look back at the three members squashed together. Laughter bubbles in my throat, but I keep it there. I don't need any more accusations about my sanity!

I bob my head while walking to the church. Sunday—our off day. The day we get to crush the stage of the place where David grew up. The church, a large two-story building, rises up in the middle of Honolulu. Or to be more exact, by the Bishop Museum in Kalihi.

"We should go to the museum after!" I say.

"Nah," Seiya says. "That place is haunted."

"There's no such thing as ghosts," Kaden says.

And then we all get quiet at that. Of course, we all saw the spooky things that have been happening lately.

"I think the existence of Apple Hair proved that ghosts exist," David says, leading the way.

We had to wake up extra early. The service starts at seven, which is pretty crazy for someone who likes to sleep until eleven. We'll be singing in the choir for the service at nine and eleven too. (I lowkey can't wait.)

I hum to myself—the worship songs David made us memorize last night. I put a bit too much power in my steps, because Van grabs my arm and makes a suppressing motion with his hands. Maybe the superpower of having this condition means that I can have *lots* of energy on a Sunday. I still need to meet with psychiatrists of course! I'm a bit scared about the official diagnosis.

Inside, I'm surprised at how nice it is. The floors and walls are almost sparkly, the lobby filled with Christmas decorations since it's the middle of December. Who doesn't love Christmas? It was even my rabbit's favorite time of year, with all the leftover carrot scraps from my mom and I baking loads of carrot cake. Lilo passed when I was ten, but I can still see his beady eyes at times.

But *the middle of December*? Already?

I'm busy looking around like a lost deer. Seiya has to lead me backstage, where the rest of the choir is warming up their voices. They wave their hands, placing one hand on their diaphragms while trilling. Looks like we'll be singing with about ten other people. They all look like they got up at five and had about ten coffees.

I warm up my voice with trills too. I must be way too loud, because David whispers into my ear, "I think the people in their seats can hear you already."

I give him a wink and quiet down.

The worship team greets us, a group of five who look like they had eleven coffees. They gather us into a huddle, where we pray and ask God to lead the time. As a person who doesn't really know whether God is real or not, it's still pretty nice. Could David be onto something? I always considered myself a "kind of" agnostic, because is there really a label for someone-could-be-out-there-and-maybe-I-wish-someone-was?

My mom and I had a lot of discussions about this. She always said that there are just some things that we won't know. And I think she's seen so many lives leave the earth that maybe she doesn't want to talk about it any further. It always ended up with us getting sidetracked about the newest animals I found on Petfinder.

I study the dust motes swirling around the spotlight, breathing in the smell of fresh linen. I don't think we'll be attacked here in any way. This feels safe. David's church feels really safe, actually.

A hit of adrenaline attacks me when we walk out on stage and get into the stands. Wow. This might not be a performance, but we're giving the world a sneak peak of Apple Hair. (Are they ready for what they're about to see?)

I can hear David's voice though. *Really, this is about God, not you.*

I sing the songs like we practiced. The medicine works, because I don't explode or start screaming the words.

Right after the seven a.m. service—I admit I kind of fell asleep in the seats in the back during the middle of the message—the pastor and his wife give David a big hug. They squeeze him tight. If I didn't know better, I would think David's their adopted kid!

"My parents go to Saturday night service," David once told us before. "So we won't be seeing them."

Was it a little bit of relief in his voice? I might be reading it wrong, like I've been reading everything wrong lately.

I wake from my slumber to sing for the nine a.m. service again, shouting the lyrics loud when I realize the mics for the choir aren't turned up that much. I breathe in, listening to the others as they sing to the Lord they believe in. I really admire how one of the leaders hits a high note and lifts her hands like she scored a touchdown. The church members sound like one. Like actually living out the word *together.*

This time, I actually feel a bit less sleepy. The message from the pastor is about forgiveness. I snicker after he shares a funny story. Something about a rat and New York pizza.

"One more," David says. He glows when he leads us out on stage, as we ascend the choir stands.

And when we sing, we really do become one. It feels normal. It feels like the days before we came up with the name Apple Hair.

"Woo-hoo!" I shout out after we finish our last song. I guess my teammates weren't expecting it, because we're still not quite off-stage. They quickly grab me and lead me off.

"Let's go to the cafe," David suggests. "We already listened to the message twice."

"Memorized it like a good church boy?" Seiya jokes.

David turns a bit pink. I reach out to smack his arm, but Kaden intercepts me. I end up following them quietly out the back.

I look up in a blur of light, as the line to the cashier spins away. "Huh?" I don't know if everyone in the cafe heard me, or whether I spoke only for me.

Nancy Gomez orders an iced honey latte.

Her beauty makes her a standout, and she wears a teal dress that hugs her hips and tapers down to her ankles. But similar to Van, I would probably date someone based off personality. I know that's what everyone says. Anyway, I *do* want a girlfriend one day. But now's probably not the best time to be thinking of that. (Kaden, and maybe David, might be completely charmed right now, though.)

"I just started coming here," Nancy says.

I'm surprised there aren't a dozen cameras trailing her.

David takes the lead. It's his church, so I definitely get it. "I never thought I'd see you here..."

In, like, ten seconds or something, her drink comes out on the bar. She waltzes over to grab it. "My treat! Order anything you'd like."

I order the sweetest thing on the menu, some sort of caramel mocha. The other guys go for more boring drinks, and I make a face when they order a second iced Americano. My first sip tastes like what it was like to sing in the choir today.

"You know, I heard something interesting the other day," Nancy says, when we sit around a table for six.

"Yeah?" I say. She looks at me, so I guess she wanted me to answer. I get a rumbling in my stomach. Too much caramel?

"I heard something about medicine," she says, looking up to the ceiling. Her gold eyeliner may look extra to some people, but I think she really slays it.

"Medicine?" I say.

Van gets this guarded look. I'm not like him though—I can't guess people's next words, not even their very next one.

"I heard that chemically made medicine is of the devil," she says. "People who take stuff like that are actually listening to the devil's lies."

I process the words. Kind of. Somehow, I don't really listen. I continue to take sips of coffee, wondering how it interacts with my own medicine.

With my own medicine. I know I'm Corrin-level slow. But is Nancy Gomez trying to call me out here?

Kaden gets this hard look in his eyes. "I don't think that's true. At all."

"Really?" Nancy swirls her drink around. Some golden honey sticks to the sides of the plastic cup. "Just something I heard. Doesn't mean that *I* think it's true."

When she leaves, after telling us something about a new etiquette book she's reading, I look down at my cup. Is medicine really that bad?

Van looks strained. Like he wants to tell me something.

I shift my thoughts to the upcoming second part of our evaluation. Who cares if medicine isn't godly? I just gotta hit the right beats.

C'mon. Tomorrow couldn't come any faster.

Chapter 18

Kaden

I once talked to a flute-player at my high school, Punahou School. Punahou has quite the reputation in Oʻahu, mainly for being expensive. But there are also a ton of extracurriculars, an annual carnival, and very bright people. But this flute player seemed to think something, very strong actually. *Didn't the asteroid, like, hit the dinosaurs? That's why they went extinct.*

I guess she thought that the dinosaurs were wiped out from the earth by getting hit by the asteroid. Actually getting hit—like the asteroid could collide against so many places and things at once. I have since found out that a lot of people believe the same thing.

What they don't know is that the asteroid didn't immediately kill the dinosaurs. It took time. The asteroid changed the atmosphere, with dust levels rising and blocking the sun, effectively altering the entire ecosystem of the earth. With plant life affected, every other species soon paid the price.

It feels like Apple Hair forming was the asteroid. The boys and I are the dinosaurs, slowly succumbing to our opposition.

That doesn't mean I don't feel good about the second part of our eval. The guys and I practiced in the same manner of a scholar reading a thousand books. The time and energy we invested will pay off.

Like simple math. Two plus one equals three.

Van has trouble speaking again, so I give us our final pep talk before we enter the evaluation room. "We just need to do what we know we can," I say. "We know we put so much sweat and blood into this song and dance. We just have to let muscle memory take over."

The members nod, and together we chant, "An Apple a Day!"

Seiya snickers a bit before we head in, probably because he feels clever for coming up with the slogan.

Merlin Kim and the instructors look exactly how they looked a month ago. When I get into position, I adjust the microphone in my hand. I think of my parents, looking down on me from their resting place.

As we sing, the lyrics about finding your dream and pursuing it wholeheartedly, I feel the dream world come take me away. I take a page out of David's book. I let it take me.

The images that come to me are all underwater. It fills me with dread to know that my parents died while seeing the same things— coral, sand, and foam. The other members must be sucked in too, but we keep dancing. We keep delivering vocals that I'd say are about thirty-five percent better than what we can do on a normal day.

I have no idea what the instructors are seeing, whether we changed in front of them. But by the time the song ends, I'm breathing heavily, and the dream world completely pulls back.

A voice laughs in the distance. It scratches my eardrums. I believe in other life forms in the universe—a very different story compared to ghosts—and the voice sounds otherworldly. It says no words this time, but maybe it enjoyed seeing me struggle.

"Why don't we all say it at once?" Merlin Kim says.

A trickle of sweat falls off my brow. I think about probabilities, about all the different things they could say to us—to crush our dreams or make them more real.

"You passed!"

I want to breathe a sigh of relief. But I notice something weird. Or maybe not so weird, considering all the complications and stress he's caused our group so far.

Leo doesn't say it.

In the beginning of our fourth month as a group, Leo Pak calls us into his office again. This time, we don't bring our book.

Someone translates for him, and basically, he wants to see a storyboard from us. Laying out the first several months of our debut. I want to say that it's easy. We've been doing something like a storyboard, writing down our concepts each day.

But the hard part comes when he adds, "You'll need to get the approval of your fellow trainees. Ten of them need to sign off and say it's a good idea."

The next day at lunch, I carry a poster into the room while the other members follow along. We approach a table.

When I take the last step toward the group of trainees, about four girls and three guys, I see their eyes flash a light maroon color. I ignore it. Ghosts don't exist.

"Hi everyone," I say. I agreed that I'd do most of the talking. "We're trying to get our storyboard approved."

Oh. I didn't realize Jason's on the table too. But it didn't seem like he was there in the beginning? Usually, I'd catch him immediately.

Jason and Allen—both indefinitely hate us, with the latter doing most of the damage. But Jason's edge digs into me. "I don't think any of us want to approve of what Apple Hair is doing."

What we're doing? How cryptic.

I set the poster on the table. "We'll make it simple," I say, effectively ignoring Jason and all the other words he probably wants to communicate to us. "We'll let you read it over, and if you like it, sign your name on the bottom."

Our storyboard took our strongest story from Shar's book. I've always been interested in parallel universes or alternate timelines. So, I took that idea and ran with it. Our first couple music videos will introduce us as normal guys in the real world. Slowly, we find that the threads of alternate worlds arrive in our lives, and we pull the strings.

As we discover a new world, we find that much of it reads gray. We need to fill it with color, which means inviting the fans to color it with us.

The first few months of Apple Hair's debut will introduce this world. We want it to be a bit blank, so the fans can fill it in with their imaginations. The world will slowly develop, getting stronger and stronger so that eventually, the line between fantasy and reality blurs.

"So kind of what we're going through now with the dream world?" Corrin had asked me last night. We were the only two awake, talking to the ceiling.

"Yes." I cracked my knuckles, trying to ignore the pain in my back—constantly spreading, like a splotch of paint on a white T-shirt that I can't erase.

"That's smart," Corrin had said.

"Yeah."

As I tried to fall asleep, the pain spread like an ember on paper. Then, David whispered something in his sleep. I found comfort in remembering what it was like to sing on the church stage, when we got a taste of spreading the love of music.

The trainees on the table take a minute to read what we wrote on the poster board. Corrin decorated the board with drawings of the planets and other elements that represent the universe.

I can't read their expressions—like we're all taking an exam, trying to keep all the answers to ourselves. If we were playing soccer, everyone would be running toward the ball from different directions. I wait for the collision, wondering when Jason will say something meant to put us down.

Then, a trainee named Paula speaks. "I don't think you guys will get ten signatures. So, I might as well sign."

Jason snickers, returning to his food. He takes a bite of a chicken tender like Paula personally delivered it for him to chew on.

We move on to the other tables. Some trainees say our idea is too vague. What does a universe that can be colored even mean? Are we lazy by not placing the rules down in this universe?

I also calculated the likelihood that we'd fail in impressing the trainees. Sports and music are my things—and doing good in school. This type of creativity tests my limits, and I can tell the other guys are too exhausted to craft a full-on story.

We get a total of nine signatures. We avoided the last table on purpose, but now Allen looks at us with a smirk. His groupies look up at the same time, like a bunch of birds—following their king.

"Well, I guess we gotta go for it," Seiya says.

I approach the table, opening my mouth to repeat myself for the twelfth time today. Then, something shifts in the corner of my eye. Jason. He puts an arm around Allen, and for a second, they shift into twins, with the same shadow and the same haughty air around them.

"I'll sign," Jason says. "I don't want to overhear your boring story again."

Jason takes the pen from David and writes his name on the bottom in obnoxious loops—it's what we needed, but at the same time I don't want his false approval.

"Let's bring this back to Leo," I tell the other members.

"Wait," Allen says. "If this universe really does end up existing, can I be in it?"

I watch his thick brows. They wave at me like middle fingers. Because I'm tired of talking, I wait for someone else to respond. David responds, which I wasn't expecting.

"If you in an alternate universe are a little less off-putting, then sure."

What David said wasn't that offensive to me, but Allen stands up abruptly. He must take it personally. "Take back your signature," he tells Jason.

Jason has much thinner brows and a more wiry frame. He stands up straighter, like he can feel Allen's influence. "I—"

"No, I have a better idea," Allen says. "Kaden, if you can admit to everyone on this table that you're injured, I'll add my signature too. Eleven signatures—isn't that more than what you need?"

Something lodges in my throat, like I can taste what Van may be going through now. "No," I eventually say.

He hands the pen to Jason. When did he take that from him? It bends in the light, growing and shrinking in intervals. "Cross your name out."

I grab the poster and head toward the door before Jason can make a decision. The other guys surround me, and I'm thankful.

Growing up, I only had acquaintances. I was too busy trying to take care of my little sister to spend time with friends. Getting into Apple Hair may have come with stress and a little bit of absurdity that I wasn't ready for—maybe a lot. At the same time, I have these guys now. They're my friends.

"Come back," Allen calls out. He tries not to yell, probably not wanting to lose his cool in front of everyone in the cafeteria.

We all ignore him. Apple Hair shifts into one. We got what we needed. Now, we just need to see what Leo will say.

Chapter 19

Seiya

Leo appraises the poster board.

He uses his index finger and rubs the ink—like he's trying to see if it's real or something. Man… This guy really gives me the creeps. He's handsome in a way that everyone could forgive him. I definitely don't. My sister would probably say the same thing. I wish she could've seen out of my eyes when he tore a page from our book.

Because he probably doesn't wanna be the bad guy, he nods once and gives us back the poster board. "Pass."

How do I say "dude, I've had enough of you" in Korean? Maybe David knows. Maybe Cory could tell me—but he seems to be pretty close bros with Leo.

After we pass the weird-ass test, we go back to practice. I blink, move, and sleep, until it's time for our month five evaluation. Van whispers something about how we managed to stick together for five months already.

"Hell yeah!" I say. Then we put our hands together, and say together, "An Apple a Day."

The fifth month eval goes surprisingly… normal. No weird thing that Leo adds to our plate. And the other instructors just nod like we're taking a math exam or something. When we pass with an A, I follow the other guys outside and begin to whistle.

"Why don't we check out the rankings?" I say.

"Yeah!" Corrin says immediately. "I want to see if I moved up from last month."

The board puts all the trainees into one group and ranks them based on how well they performed over the past month. I kinda hate it. At the same time, I like to see myself improve. "Well, if we want to talk about probabilities…" Kaden goes on to explain how there's over a ninety percent chance that we all moved up at least one spot.

"I want to scrap with Leo," I say, while we take the elevator to the floor with the board. Scrap—the pidgin term for fighting.

"No fighting," Kaden says, although I'm sure he wants to throw the first punch.

Van makes a gesture that somehow reminds me of a humpback whale. "Wish we could. Five against one."

"He'll probably have all the instructors join him," David says softly. "It seems like he's the one in charge, not CEO Kim."

"Let's fight the CEO too," I say.

The guys laugh, and Corrin clutches his belly—his volume probably going all the way out of the building. I've been learning a lot about manic episodes. It's mad—what Corrin is going through. I wish I could just knock the sickness out of him. I wish I could be like a good older brother to him.

As we approach the ranking board, I realize that the color changed. The edges of the electronic screen were once black and white. Now… the color reminds me of the skin of a Fuji apple.

And our names. Damn. Our names make up the top five.

1. Kaden Reyes
2. Seiya Morimoto

3. Van Le
4. David Cho
5. Corrin Chang

I turn around. "Someone playing a trick on us or something?"

David presses a finger against the screen. "Maybe our evaluation went *really* well?"

"Well…" Van seems to study his name. We were all in the tens and twenties last time. "Maybe we can celebrate."

"Fireworks," I say, randomly.

At night, the trainees gather outside the company. They look up at the sky, their mouths open. I head up to the closest trainee, Paula. "Hey, what's going on?"

She looks away from the sky for one second, giving her about half a second to say, "There's supposed to be some type of show."

I relay the info to the guys. Then, we wait in the middle of the crowd. Some tourists have gathered around here as well.

"Oh shit!" I can't control my mouth when the first firework shoots up from the roof of AWE Entertainment.

The boys and I freeze. The images of the fireworks are the usual ones—circles and stuff. Then, I see a rocket, a mad-looking thing that resembles a Pokémon, and a giant one of Saturn. When the sweat gathers on my temple, I swear again. Kaden looks like he wants to lie down for possibly forever. I grab him and let him support his weight on me.

When the show finishes, the sky still looks like it could turn pink and blue and purple. The trainees and the crowd go off with their applause. Someone in the company must be going loco. I recall my comment about fireworks earlier. Either the ghost is listening like a tiny fly buzzing everywhere, or Leo attached a microphone to one of us.

"Shar's waiting," Van says. "We can talk more at home."

In the van, Shar tells us not to worry. She says to keep writing out our story, and to go ham at practice. We ranked in the top five, so we must be doing something right.

"Seriously, you guys are killing it," Shar says. "I don't know why these strange things keep happening. But just keep writing your story. When so many things are trying to go against you, that means what you're doing is important."

"What if we can't keep this up?" David says. I feel for him. I reach over my shoulder and squeeze his knee.

"Just talk to me," Shar says. "I'll make sure to support you guys. I know you guys want to debut more than anything. I can't do much against all the haunting things. But I'm praying. And every day, I'm right around the bend. I'm here. You have me on your side forever."

As Shar turns into the driveway of the apartment, I get certain on one thing. Shar's a real one.

David invites me to his playground a few days later.

"I've been adding more things," he says. "I think it's a good thing that we can have a little bit of control."

"I like that," I say. "Control."

He scratches his neck as we head out of the apartment past midnight. As we walk together, I feel a strange pull. I can't tell if it's because I like David so much, or if the dream world is pulling us like a cowboy with a lasso.

Maybe a bit of both. By the time we reach the mini garden, David closes his eyes. I feel the dream world wash over me. Here, what I feel the most is the pain of my absent parents. I wish I were closer to them. I wish I didn't rely on my sister so much. Man… I wish a lot of things.

David faces me, swallowing. He must be thinking about something deep within him too—what we can tell to no one.

"It's pretty late," he manages to say. "So we won't stay too long."

I nod. "Yeah, bro."

The garden definitely transformed from last time. The flowers wrap around the whole grass area. A sandbox got filled to the brim. There are two picnic chairs made from solid gold.

"Didn't know you could be so creative," I say. "This is sick."

David grins. I kind of want to kiss him.

"Let's sit?" he says.

As I take the seat across from him, I look up and realize the stars waver a bit, like someone cast a film over them. I think about my friends from high school. "You have more friends than stars," my sister once told me. I guess she was right. I guess I was popular.

"Hey," I say. "Did you have lots of friends in school?"

"A few," David says. "You?"

I start to tell a story about how I knew so many people by name. Then I feel it. The dream world pulling me in and telling me to stay forever. It promises me something. A comfortable life? Trainee life definitely pulls me everywhere. It's exhausting. Maybe it's best to stay here forever with David?

"Don't listen," David says, looking at me intently. "Just keep talking to me."

I realize that I could say a million things. But all those things are not what I actually want to say. I want to confess.

"Do you ever dream of me?"

"You?" David looks at the grass, where a few sunflowers bloom and face the moon, like little soldiers. "Um. Yeah. I dream of you and the other guys too."

"Do you like me?" I say. I can't help blushing. I don't know if he's blushing too. Maybe? Damn, I'm not used to being so awkward.

"What?" he says.

For a hot second, I just stare at him. I decide not to repeat myself. So I talk about something else instead. Our next evaluation—which we know nada about yet.

"I think we should go back," David says.

"Agreed."

He takes out Shar's notebook. Everything becomes a helluva lot easier once we write it down. I don't know what David writes, but probably something about Apple Hair coming down to planet earth.

Earth to Seiya. Do you know how stupid it was to confess?

I come back to the world with David next to me. Chairs gone. Just the grass and the buildings and the stars. Twinkle, twinkle.

"We should—" he starts.

I can't leave like this. I pull him into a hug. More sophisticated people might call it an embrace. I just think of it as *right.* Yup. This feels right. This feels amazing.

He breathes into my shoulder. He stays still. Then he hugs me in return. I think about lazy Sundays at the dorm, seeing him stroll around shirtless. I think about how proud I was when he memorized a dance routine quicker than me—even though they call me the dancer of the group. I swear about a thousand times on the inside. I don't say them aloud. 'Cause he's religious and all—or a person of faith, he likes to call himself.

Soon, we'll enter our sixth month as a group. Something tells me that I need to hold David now. Before the ghost comes back. Before another firework goes off.

This time, I don't think the big mama will be so harmless.

Chapter 20

David

I dream of Seiya holding me, the strength of his arms buoying me up, feeling like he and I could not only debut—we could conquer the world, showing everyone who sees us the power of love and harmony.

In our sixth month as a group, I sit in the front seat of Shar's van and carefully hold the journal she gave us. "We filled it up. I think we need a new one?"

"I'll get you one soon," Shar says. "Anyway, I wanted to talk to you about a dream I had last night?"

"A dream?" Corrin says. He leans back in his seat, eyes flickering—the meds make him sleepier than usual.

"Yeah." Shar takes one hand off the wheel at a stoplight, rubbing her knuckle against her chin. If I really squinted, I could almost make out a golden aura coming off her, undulating in waves against the rainy February morning. "I was sitting in my childhood home. I think I might've been around eight or nine. Anyway, my parents came home from work. We talked for a while… and then they were excited to turn on the television to watch an award show.

"My mother slapped me on the shoulder and said, 'Look, it's your favorite. Apple Hair!'

"I couldn't believe it when I saw all five of you on screen, dressed in tuxedos. You all transformed costumes into these magnificent red and gold pieces. Almost like fire. And then you performed and tore it up on stage."

Silence fills the van for a few seconds, and even though it may be "weird" that Shar had a dream like this, nothing much more can shock us after six months of surprises. I hum and watch the raindrops splatter on the windows, branching out like spiderwebs searching for a home, endlessly lost yet yearning for a final resting place. I guess we are all like those raindrops, trying to find a place that's best for us, a place that will give us solace. Maybe Shar's dream means something more, a good sign that will lead us to where we so desperately want to be.

When we reach the company, I grab an umbrella and wave goodbye to Shar. "Thanks for cheering us up with your dream," I say.

"No problem," Shar says. And then, after making sure we remember our schedule, she drives off and says she'll check back in with us at lunch.

We navigate through the rain and puddles, as the boys probably ruminate on the evaluation we may not be ready for. It's a simple one—one vocal performance and one dance, nothing weird or Leo-esque about it. As we stroll along, I think about my past, going to a youth group and finding meaning in the people there. Youth group always gave me comfort, as I knew that we were all chasing after God in the midst of so much fiery turmoil in our lives. I think of Tony and Blayze, my best friends. They always say how they're praying for me, and I wish for their prayers right now, even as they're only meant for God's ears.

As I enter the building, I pause and shake the rain off my umbrella, watching as the droplets reach with their ghostly hands before falling against the doormat.

The trainees in the lobby immediately recoil as we walk in, as if they shocked themselves with the frigid touch of an icicle, brushing up against their skin. I stare for a second. Apple Hair may be the fire for many weird happenings, but normally the trainees ignore us. Or in the case of Jason and Allen, slowly try to move us toward our downfall.

This feels more like a big shift.

I fall in line with my teammates, heading toward the elevator like usual. Our evaluation starts in thirty minutes, and we want to warm up our voices and limbs. I dream about hearing the fateful "you passed" from CEO Kim, celebrating with the boys in a late-night visit to the convenience store. Although our lives are full to the brim with schedules, we always make time to celebrate in little ways, finding an avenue to fill our constant yearning.

I think about Christmas, how we spent the majority of the day in the practice room, going over last-minute changes to choreography and trying to hit notes that floated so high away from my usual vocal range. We pushed ourselves on that day, and although the day escaped us without the usual presents and carols, we did sit in the lobby of AWE for a while, admiring the ten-foot Christmas tree that reached up to the ceiling with garlands of gold and silver.

Paula stops us on the way to the elevator. Her brows knit together, and she clutches her skirt sewed with the traditional patterns and fabrics of Pohnpei. Her brown eyes reflect a bit of wariness. "I don't normally talk to you guys," she says, and she's right—she usually plays on Jason and Allen's side, supporting them without lending too much of her voice. "We all had a dream."

"A dream?" Seiya stands with his signature slouch—which somehow looks more endearing than lazy.

"Everyone had a dream," Paula says. "A bad dream about you guys. Check your socials."

Because the note in Paula's voice tells me she's serious, I take out my phone and scroll to the first app on the screen.

The trending topics jump out at me.

#AppleHairHawai'i

#Premonition

#BadDreamOrGoodDream

I only have to scroll for ten seconds to figure out that somehow, Apple Hair made the headlines. But it takes me a minute to process the enormity of it all, like trying to swallow a glass of cold water all at once.

Kaden, the smart one, gets it first. "Everyone in Hawai'i had a hazy dream about us. Fifty percent had a good dream, and the other half had a bad dream."

Paula nods. "I guess so. But everyone in AWE woke up after a bad dream about you guys. I talked to the majority of trainees, and they all said the same thing."

"What was your dream like?" I say, somehow believing it quickly. Apple Hair's universe was meant to be kept to ourselves, but somehow it feels like after we finished our book, writing all those stories, the ghost might have had bigger plans.

But why the good dreams? I can only attribute them to God—that people would believe in Apple Hair turning out to be a good force in the world.

A thousand thoughts scatter through my brain, and I almost fall to the floor. Corrin grabs me on one side, while Seiya supports my other side. I almost drop my phone, but Seiya takes it and stuffs it into my pocket, as he often thinks quickly instead of floating around in daydreams like me.

"Millions of people dreaming of us," Seiya mutters. "Kinda sick, if you think about it."

Paula looks at me and swallows, probably just as dizzy as me.

"Well, my dream was a bit vague. I dreamt of a rotten apple. And then I saw your guys' faces, and a teacher from my first high school told me not to trust you guys."

"Was…" It takes me a while to recover my voice, like fishing for something in the middle of a lake. "Were all the bad dreams just as vague?"

"Yeah," Paula says. "From what I could tell."

"And the good dreams?" I say.

Kaden still scrolls on his phone. "Not as clear as Shar's dream. But people are connecting the dots. Something good is supposed to come from a group called Apple Hair. We're getting followers on all our private accounts."

If fainting were an option, I'd grab hold and succumb to it in a heartbeat. But even as the youngest in Apple Hair, I need to be strong. I wipe my hand against my Adam's apple, as if that could tamp the sickness down.

"Maybe this isn't as bad as it seems," I say.

Corrin hums. "People had some good dreams too! That means something."

"I can't believe—" Van loses his voice, and I get a tingle in my jaw.

The tingle turns to an angry wave, cresting over me. Why couldn't God stop Van from losing his voice? Why can't we train in this company like a normal group? For about a minute by the elevator, I hover between pain and death as the presence of the other members draws me back to reality—to facing the music.

And then a realization hits me, tearing me out from denial. This isn't weird—this is part of the Apple Hair universe. This is what we need to face to come out of the clouds, clearing the storm so we could stand on high ground and hold our golden trophy together.

"Let's just get through the eval," I say. "And then we can talk about this."

"Wouldn't news sites all around the world want to talk to us?" Corrin says, eyes darting about. "This is gonna be everything that anyone wants to talk about."

"After," Van says, straightening his posture. We all fall silent, following our leader's signal to transform into our performing mode, to channel the heat of the stars that we want to be.

To me, talking to God means that I shouldn't be afraid to say anything. Since God's always listening, nothing can surprise him. So, I whisper under my breath and think about the little words, floating up—more insignificant than particles of dust. Still, he hears them. He takes them seriously, holding them in his palm. I may not understand everything, but these little whispers help me understand that I'm not the one in control, and I don't have to be.

In front of the instructors, I imagine them as impartial judges. But a little flicker in their brows tells me they've had a dream as well, and the dream was far from pretty.

So, in the middle of my singing performance, I falter. I dodge a note that should be easy for me to hit, and from there the other members also lose the strength in their voices. We finish with a harmony that Diane taught us, but I can barely hit the note for longer than two seconds.

In the dance section, I step on Seiya's foot, and we almost stumble together to the floor like two tangled kittens. Remarkably, we all finish the routine on two feet. Breathing hard, I turn toward the judges and expect their poker faces.

Instead, most have a line between their brows. Leo looks indifferent, while a note of hesitation paints Merlin Kim's voice when he speaks. "I'm afraid that you can't pass this evaluation."

I want to rip out my heart, showing it to the CEO and telling him how many times it beat for this moment, so that the boys and I could pass our six-month evaluation. None of the boys speak, and a small smile flashes across Leo's face before it disappears.

"I normally don't believe in premonitions," CEO Kim continues. "But it's obvious that something is wrong with Apple Hair. Because we haven't reached a firm vote yet with all the executives, we cannot terminate your contracts. We have to hold on to you. But I don't expect you to pass enough evaluations to debut."

Armani, Diane, Cory, and Nancy fall into silence. I realize now the power of emptiness, the power of turning on us, like spinning and finding that the wall of our most sacred room was glass all along.

Outside, Armani meets us and tries to smile. "Off to dance practice," she says.

I wonder what the mystery of her dream was. Will she tell us?

Chapter 21

Van

Armani told us her dream after some hesitation.

She was making a decadent apple pie, and then when it came out of the oven, the crust was gone. *The crust was replaced with tangled strands of hair. And then my whole house caught on fire. The whole house!*

After practice, Shar speeds us home and tells us to double-lock the doors. I stay up late playing *League* and reading a fantasy novel. I lose twice in a row in *League*. Girl, I've been on a losing streak for two weeks now. Anyway, the novel's about a girl who raises dragons in a coffee shop—not the usual sword and sorcery or adventure that I usually read, but hey, I really don't mind escaping to somewhere new.

I feel some of my voice returning, so I hop on a voice call with Nick, my best friend from Saint Louis School.

Nick's voice often cracks. It splits into two when he recalls his dream. "It was so cool, Van! We were hanging out in the library, like we usually always do. And then I saw you change outfits, and then you and your band members serenaded the whole school."

I sigh. I'm glad he had a good dream about us. I focus on playing another game of *League*—this time with Nick, and we defeat the enemy team without even dying once.

"Anyway, this must be destiny," Nick says. His voice comforts me like it usually did when we were hiding away from our other classmates. "It's fate. You guys will definitely debut, and maybe become the most famous group in the world."

The next morning, I down my supplements and prepare myself to wake up the guys. They definitely can put up a fight sometimes when they want another few minutes of rest. When I open my mouth and try to yell out that it's almost nine a.m., a knock on the door rings out, and it doesn't sound like Shar's knock.

I creep out into the kitchen and peek out through the little window that faces the parking lot. Not one, not two, but *at least a dozen reporters stand outside, gathered around the staircase.*

I panic and almost cough out my vitamins. *Ah, that would make for a great picture on the front page.*

Back in the bedroom, I raise my voice while watching Seiya groan in his sleep. "Guys. Guys!"

Corrin leaps from his bed to the floor. His hair matches his wild eyes. "What?"

I swallow a bit. *I'm the leader. I can't go all panicky like that.* "Just. Reporters."

Kaden, who probably can get up the quickest without falling over from dizziness, takes steady strides toward the door. When he comes back, he confirms that I'm not seeing things—a big relief, actually.

"So things are becoming bigger than just us now," David says, using his very-indoor voice. "Bigger than just us and a weird voice. The whole island has either a positive or negative feeling about Apple Hair."

I close the door behind me, like creating a second line of defense. Shar messages us and tells us that she's working on getting to us.

And then, before I can talk more with the guys, *I hear Shar shouting outside.* It must be one against twenty-something at this point. I bet my money on Shar. Sure, she's a kind person, but she can most definitely turn into an angel warrior, like a character in an epic mythology game.

As the noise swells outside, I sit down on the floor. I draw the curtains and think about what this means for the five of us. I force the tightness on my vocal cords to disappear, although it takes as much willpower as getting up in the morning.

"We need to do something," I say.

Kaden sits down beside me. In a few seconds, we fall into our usual huddle, everyone seeming to breathe at the same time. Even in the darkness, it feels like the ghost can't get us. Our sacred space may be pretty modest, but it's ours.

"Well, we have to think about what we can and cannot do," Kaden says. "We *cannot* go out there. But we can think about what to do when the story about us cools down a bit."

"Why can't we go out there?" Corrin says, rubbing a knuckle against his lips.

I punch his shoulder with my left hand. "*We can't.*"

"This is loco," Seiya says. "Hey, I guess the good part about this is that we don't need to go to practice."

Sure enough, David checks his phone and receives a text in our group chat from one of the AWE protocol team members. Our practice is canceled for the day. We breathe a sigh of relief, which seems wrong when our door might get bulldozed down at any second. Do we really desperately need a break that much? Maybe we do.

"I would write something down," Kaden says. "But Shar didn't give us a book yet. Anyway, maybe we can take a break from writing. When we finished writing, this whole thing exploded."

"Agreed," I say.

"Do we have enough food to be holed up in here?" David asks.

I head outside and check the cabinets, trying to ignore the torrent of noise on the other side of the door. We have ten ramen packets, animal crackers, and a box of fruit snacks. In the fridge, I find a carton of turkey cold cuts and six eggs. *Now you know about the pantry of five very busy trainees.*

"We have enough for like, two days," I report back.

"That's good," David says, although his voice reflects the opposite.

"Let's go outside and scrap them," Seiya says.

Corrin laughs, drawing his knees up to his jaw. "That would teach them a lesson."

Before Corrin and Seiya talk about more bad ideas, I tell the team, "This might be a good idea to rest up. Our life basically changed overnight. And…" I fight the temptation to close out my voice, to be comfortable. "We need to prepare for what happens next, whatever that could be."

Kaden busies himself with taking notes on his phone, probably thinking about all the possibilities of our next steps. I bring my gaming laptop on my bunk bed, then realize I can't play anything with so much going on in my head. David and Seiya whisper about the dream world, while Corrin falls asleep again thanks to the side effects of his medication.

By lunch time, I still hear the rumbling outside. I start to cook our ramen—six packets for us to share. When the water bubbles, I pour in the soup packets and the noodles. When was the last time we could take our time, cooking like this?

Eating in the dark, Seiya spills some on the floor of the bedroom, and instead of scolding him, the other guys and I start to laugh. It may be sleep deprivation, or it may be our being locked in the apartment, with the whole island talking about hair and apples.

"I miss my brother," I say, sometime in the night. Reporters still camp outside, but Shar put in a report to the police to order them to stay away.

"Ryan?" Kaden says. "I miss my younger sister."

"You guys are just lucky to have siblings," David says. "Corrin and I had to go at it alone."

"I didn't mind too much," Corrin says.

"Seems like you can talk more now, Van," Seiya says. "I'm happy it's laddat."

I nod. "It seems like I can talk more freely with you guys. With others, I turn into my old self."

"You're old self?" Kaden says.

"I barely talked in school," I say.

Seiya leans against the post of one of the bunk beds. "I had a lot of friends in school," he says. "But I prefer this. This is cool—just having four people I'm closest to. Anyway, I think we're lucky as shit that we found each other."

"It's not luck," David says. "I think it's God."

Before Kaden launches into discussion about the possibility of there actually being a God, I suggest that we clean up our mess from lunch.

Soon enough, it's time to make dinner. *No convenience store? This would've taken a whole intervention before.* Anyway, we make scrambled eggs with turkey. All the guys help with cooking this time, and the whole house doesn't even start burning down.

"My mom, dad, and brother said they had good dreams about me," I say. "What about you guys?"

"Same," David says. "That's what my parents said."

"Do you think there's a reason everyone at AWE had a bad dream?" Kaden says.

I tilt my head from left to right, looking at the steam as the eggs crackle with the oil on the pan. "I thought it was random, but it isn't. I… just want to make Ryan and my parents proud. So that's why I was relieved when they said they saw something positive in the dream world. I wouldn't know what I'd do if they saw me as some evil force or something."

"But the people who had bad dreams aren't necessarily *bad*," David says.

"I know," Kaden says. "I just think the ghost chose them so that they can cause division in us. In Apple Hair, I mean."

By the time midnight rolls around, I manage to fall asleep with the breathing of the other guys acting like a metronome. When I wake up, I make out the same chaos outside. And sirens.

For three days total, we hide away in the apartment and get some much-needed rest. The guys and I talk about everything. I learn David actually resents his parents, although he doesn't tell me all the reasons. I learn about Kaden's addiction, about how Corrin and I aren't very sexual people in contrast. Seiya all but confesses his love for David, although he does interrupt himself by talking about how he idolizes his older sister. *Nice one, Seiya.*

We barely manage to get food inside—a policeman has to deliver the groceries to the front door. And at the end of the third day, when the police are still wrangling those outside, I come up with an idea. "A fan cafe," I say.

"A what?" Corrin says.

"We can make a fan cafe online," I say. "There, everyone can write the stories they want to. Everyone can write down their dreams, even the bad ones. And the five of us can continue whatever canon stories we want. What were we talking about, like, all the time? A place where everyone is a creator, where everyone's imagination has power."

"That's a good idea," Kaden says. "We don't actually need a book. We just need our honest words."

"It'll draw even more attention to us," David says.

"I'm down with it though!" says Seiya.

And so, in the middle of the night, we collaborate and set up a bare bones site. Corrin does most of the work, with his coding background. We all post it on our Apple Hair socials, which we set up last week—mainly to preserve the usernames. We then watch as our new followers find the link.

I open the forum and wait for stories. I wonder what will be the first one the guys and I will see. *Hopefully not a spicy romance between the members. No, thank you.*

Chapter 22

Corrin

Our first story that we post on the fan cafe has to do with finding a blank world. An alternate universe with no color just yet. I suggest to the guys that we should make this first chapter as open as possible. (The epic thing about this fan cafe is that we can make it up as we go along.)

It's just *so cool* that we can start now (as trainees and all). I skip to Shar's van, swinging my arms as high as I can, breathing in the fresh air. A few cop cars surround the area, guarding us from reporters.

"Slow down, bro," Seiya calls out from behind me.

I ignore him. In the shotgun, I give Shar a fist bump. "I've never been more excited to return to practice."

Shar looks *great,* even while fighting for our lives these past few days. "Really? I'm glad. How's your mood been?"

"Better than ever, thanks to three days of rest," I say.

The other guys pile in. I sing a Bruno Mars ballad as we make our way to the company. Shar doesn't tell us how serious our situation is. And I like that. It feels like old times, even though the island must be buzzing about Apple Hair.

"Wait!" For a second, I believe I'm imagining things. Is my mind playing tricks on me again? The AWE lobby looks completely off, all the walls painted gray.

Kaden's brows scrunch together, but the gears must turn in his mind. "A blank world. The ghost must've taken it literally."

Thankfully, the other floors in the company look normal. The trainees avoid us, whispering as we walk past. I try to ignore them. I try to remember the look my mom gave me after she returned from her long shifts as a nurse. *It's great to return home to my favorite person in the world*, she would tell me.

Cory Matthews messages us in our language-class group chat to meet at the pool. (I love the waterpark more than anything, but this was unexpected.)

The pool? "This isn't going to be the typical lesson," I tell the other members.

Sure enough, at the company pool, which takes up half of the fifth floor, Cory Matthews jumps into the deep end and submerges himself with his navy board shorts. He flips his dreadlocks and dons ridiculous goggles—covering half his face.

Oh wow! He probably could've been a professional swimmer if he wasn't a language teacher.

I jump up and down, clapping when Cory takes a lap in what seems like ten seconds. "Very cool, Mr. Matthews!"

Cory heaves himself up to sit on the edge of the pool. "Hey, guys. So, I thought we'd have an individual study session today. I set out your textbooks on the picnic table."

Hey. I won't question it! Ten minutes later into our two-hour class, Kaden grumbles as he flips the page.

"Absolutely ridiculous," Kaden mutters.

Cory Matthews takes yet another lap, drowning out our studying with a bunch of splashing. I look over a grammar rule about the future tense in Korean, confusing myself with the verb endings. I think the water turns a murky purple for about a half second. (But I ignore it, not caring whether my illness acts up or the boys also saw the same.)

I sing on the way to Armani's class, laughing when David corrects Seiya's horrible pronunciation of "strange" in Korean.

Van sidles up to me, smiling and placing an arm on my shoulder. This time, he lets me continue being loud. Kaden scrolls through his phone, probably checking people's comments on our fan cafe.

"All right, guys," Armani says, stretching her legs in her baggy cargo pants. "I tried to get over the dream. I really did! But I can't get that image out of my head. Anyway, I think we should just go over an old routine."

Armani usually stuns with her brightness and energy, but today she gives about half her jazz to being our teacher. I swing around and purposely mess up a step, but she doesn't correct me. Halfway through, she gives us a break for water. I barely sweated at all, so I just take a few sips from Van's hydro flask.

The routine comes from our second month as a group. The guys and I kill the performance! But instead of clapping with vigor like usual, Armani channels her inner golf-clap (underwhelmed?). "Good job," she says.

Diane White may be the passionate and strict coach, but today she brings her bare minimum to the table. She hooks up a laptop to the projector. Then, she has us listen to boy band performances, and she instructs us to try to copy what we hear. I struggle with trying to hit a C in the fifth octave (I know I'm a tenor, but that note feels impossible). Instead of correcting me, Diane just moves on to the next video.

And finally, Nancy Gomez… Oh, I've been thinking a lot about what she told me at David's church. And I realize it's fine! If that's what she believes. But I definitely think my medication is helpful.

Scientists and doctors worked hard to find a medicine to help psychosis. So, it wasn't concocted from the devil or the ghost that haunts us.

She wears a tight red dress and decides to focus today's lesson on makeup. "A part of etiquette is looking good," she says. "Oh, I found this amazing strawberry lip gloss the other day. I'll order it for all of you."

Kaden raises his hand. I can guess his words. "Isn't this kind of illegal?" he asks, trying to be respectful although his knitted brows say otherwise. "Ms. Gomez, you and the others are supposed to be teaching us. That's why we're here."

"I know, I know." Nancy fixes the hem of her dress, and maybe she wants to be on the red carpet right now, where she usually lives. "I just can't get rid of this bad feeling. Anyway, I'm sure I'll get over it. See you guys at church this Sunday?"

Van and I grab some snacks from the break room. I say, "Seems like we're gonna have to take control of our own training."

"Yeah…" He hands me a bag of Doritos.

Before we head back to the other members, I open the bag and take out a cheese-covered chip. I crunch on it. "Hey, Van. Honest and real quick question. Do you also see that I'm gaining weight?"

Van puckers his lips. "It's a side effect."

I nod, taking out another chip. This one looks a bit more coated than the last… I turn it around instead of stuffing it into my mouth. "Van, I kinda hate these meds."

"Because of your weight?" he says. He leans back against the door, as if blocking out someone from coming in and overhearing us. The break room has no windows, but for a second a square space opens up and lets in peering eyes from outside.

I shake my head. Another hallucination? Van must not see it.

"The weight gain is one thing," I say. "I mean, I've always been on the thin side. I guess I could use a bit more weight. Anyway, that's not the main point. I'm always tired, and I keep taking these things." I sigh. I know I had good things to say about medication just now (but the conflict burns in me). "But sometimes it seems like I'm taking poison. Like I'm always behind you and the other guys because of this medicine."

Van nods. "Don't listen to what Nancy says."

"I'm *not*," I say. "This is all from my own thinking. I… think."

Van reaches out and pokes my belly while balancing a crunchy chocolate snack from Japan. "Even with the side effects, you *are* getting better."

I try to smile. "You think so?"

"You're training while also fighting this illness," he says. "No one else could do it. I know you get sleepy, or you see things beyond what the four of us see. But you're doing it. You're still chasing your dream. And I'm really proud of you for that."

"Thanks, Van." I turn back to the Doritos bag, watching as the red morphs into a more comforting pink color. I actually quite like pink!

The next time I take a pill, I'm sitting in the dance studio while the other guys try to figure out a complicated formation, where we fall to the floor like dominos. Like *coordinated* dominos.

I think about my mom. She finally found out about my diagnosis the other day.

"You didn't think you should've told me immediately?" she asked. Her voice was gentle, but I could tell she felt betrayed.

"I wanted to," I said.

"But you didn't," she said.

I responded with silence, pressing my back against the dorm refrigerator. "I'm sorry."

"I know you think I bear quite a lot," she said. "But you're my everything, Corrin. If you told me, I could've helped. Sometimes I think you forget that I'm a nurse."

"I *know* you're a nurse," I said. "It's just, I wanted to figure this out myself. I hope you aren't too mad. I want you to know I'm doing just fine."

"Come visit home soon," she said. "I want to see that for myself."

I made a promise, and then emptiness hit me as I imagined a reporter outside overhearing the conversation. (I'm close to my mom. She's my best friend. But this time, I had to search for what to say. The dream came to mind first—the elephant in the room.)

"Did you dream about us like everyone else?"

She hummed. "Yes. I saw you performing on a glass stage, surrounded by all our friends and family. Dad was there too."

I choked up, and I knew Mom was trying to hide how actually bonkers it was that she shared a collective dream with Hawai'i. "I'll call soon. Promise!"

Chapter 23

Kaden

When April rolls around, I can't deny that I'm not moving at the same speed as the other members. Our instructors do their jobs, teaching us at the hours they're supposed to. I take in their lessons and try to ignore my back—or my spine, rather.

During one of Armani's drills, I count to ten in my head, focusing on the numbers rather than the sharp ache. Perhaps directing my brain to other things will work. I think about my relatives' dreams, the good and miraculous sign that Apple Hair moves in the right direction.

Then I think about the bad dreams, the various premonitions that surround AWE Entertainment. As a believer in only things I can see, it was hard to wrap my head around. But the evidence was too big— when everyone repeats the same fact, I can only deny it for so long.

"All right, boys!" Armani sounds like her usual self, bright and invigorating. "We're gonna go for a big twist in the chorus. Here we go. One, two—"

I give myself the breadth to do it, the same move I've practiced for weeks now. Instead of leaping forward and landing on my feet, I lose balance and fall. My back screams at me for not listening to the warning signs.

The pain magnifies, and soon I lose consciousness. I slip completely away, the buzz of my team members and Armani turning into the slightest noise. And then nothing.

I wake up in the hospital room. A doctor who reminds me of the one I've been avoiding for a while now studies me with a line between his brows. I want to see the other members, just so I can distract myself from what he needs to say.

I turn my head against my scratchy sheets. "Where—"

"Your teammates followed the ambulance," he says. "They're outside in the waiting room. I wanted to give you the news while you're alone."

"Okay." I think about Lora and my grandparents. Now that I'm eighteen, I don't have to call them. I can keep it a secret—just like how Corrin hid his illness from his mom. "Tell me what you came to say."

He talks about surgery. Before I completely tune him out, he says that he talked to my PCP. Apparently, a new development has occurred in the spinal fusion realm. He talks about a safe, effective surgery procedure. Usually, recovery time can extend up to a year.

This surgery will cap the recovery time to three months. He says that the operation has almost zero risk, and the inner part of me latches on to this. Could I really be up and running again, my back less of an issue?

"The point is," he says. "If you continue like this, you can't make it as an idol. Get this operation, take some time for recovery, and you'll be back chasing your dream again."

From the look on his face, I know he must've had a good dream about us. Or if not, he ignored the bad dream—fought against it with what he knows about me already. I know our instructors did that, especially Armani. Even a few trainees, emphasis on a few, like Paula are starting to change their minds.

The members of Apple Hair enter.

"You'll be okay, right?" Corrin says with a thin voice.

I nod, even though the pillow makes my neck stiff. "I'll be just fine."

The four members gather around my bed, still wearing their dance practice clothes. David interlinks his fingers, while Seiya tries to get rid of the line between his brows. Van swallows, and I can already guess his next words.

"You should tell your family."

I nod again, this time giving up when I only succeed in moving a centimeter. "I will. You guys shouldn't worry."

"How can we not worry though?" Corrin says, placing a hand on my bed.

Despite the scariness of the surgery, which I don't want to admit, my heart swells looking at these four guys. Six months, spending every day and second together, turned us into more than just teammates. At this point, we're family.

"I think there's no doubt that the surgery will be a success," I say. "I'll take some time to recover, and you guys will keep practicing. In no time, we'll be back to normal. So by not worrying, you guys will help me out a lot."

Corrin looks like he's going to cry, and Van places a hand on his shoulder. David looks me in the eyes before he turns away, probably lost in worries as well. Seiya says that he'll go get some snacks for us, and I long for his home cooked ramen and boiled eggs. Strange, how my synapses have developed in such a way.

I talk about my form of scoliosis, the rarest sort, the type that needs immediate attention. I gloss over some of the things that I've been experiencing—trouble walking and spasms in my legs, in addition to some bathroom problems.

The surgery is set for the morning. And in turn, my eyes widen. The doctor explains, "Your PCP already scheduled you for the surgery. You were on the waiting list. I thought you were aware?"

"Yes," I stammer out.

Eventually, the guys have to leave—the nurses and security have to force them out, and they manage to steal an hour more past visiting hours. Van told me multiple times to call my family, and since I voted for him to be leader, I listen.

I call Lora first. She knows something's wrong immediately, so I just spill everything at once. "Hey, Lora. You know I've been having back issues, right? Well, I'm going for a minor surgery. There's basically no risk involved, so—"

"What?" Lora peers into her camera, like she could bop her head against mine, like when we were kids. "Why didn't you tell me? Or grandma or grandpa?"

I bet she knows why I didn't tell our grandparents, but I had no excuse to hide from her. "I'm sorry."

She makes me stay on FaceTime for two hours, catching me up on what she's up to at school, the friends she's making and how she competes for the top of the class. She almost cries when I say that she can't see me until after the surgery, and she makes me promise that I'll call her right after. She says that she'll let our grandparents know, but I say that I'll call them too.

Guilt eats away at me long after the call. Could I really have neglected my sister that much?

I'm not in contact with my grandparents on my dad's side, who live on the Big Island, so I just send them a lengthy text explaining the situation. For the grandparents who raised me, I give them a call.

My grandma answers on the second ring. "Grandson," she says, without an inflection of concern. "What's up with you?"

I tell her about falling during practice, and the surgery. She just stays quiet and hums every so often. Then I realize I'm on speaker.

"Come home after," my grandpa says. "Lora misses you. Anyway, you'll be just fine."

After my parents died, my grandparents turned from loving and warm into much colder versions of themselves. Sometimes, I wish they would mourn. I wish they sat down and cried with me and Lora. Instead, they turned hard. I think they resented having to take care of me.

In the morning, I smile when reading the texts from the members. David's one, long and rambly, looks like a novel next to Seiya's "you got this, bro." Corrin fills my screen with emojis, while Van tells me he'll be the first person to help me through recovery.

And by the time the nurses wheel me into the operation room, I don't see the sterile surfaces or the harsh lights. I don't even register the smell of cleaning solution. I just see Lora and the guys, waiting for me on the other side.

The first time the pain seeps through the painkillers, I grit my teeth and refuse to scream. Lora looks at me and knows something's up immediately.

"Hey. Hey!" She slaps my cheek like that would distract me. "Are you okay?"

"I'm okay," I lie.

She shakes her head. "I… I wish Grandma and Grandpa were here."

They found a way to get out of seeing me, but nothing about that surprised me. "It's okay, Lora."

She was here for around five hours, and most of it was spent rambling off about the dream she had about Apple Hair, how she discussed the various dreams with all her classmates. "Do I finally get to meet your teammates?"

"They should be here at any moment," I say.

Two minutes later, Corrin, Seiya, Van, and David rush in with their practice clothes, wiping away their sweat. Lora beams. She impresses them with her knowledge about K-pop history, going on for about ten minutes before I send her a look. She shakes all the guys' hands before leaving, promising she'll be in the front row of our first concert.

"I brought your iPad," Corrin says, handing it to me. I run my hands over the faux leather case, knowing the first thing I want to check.

The fan cafe we set up may not be very active, per say, but it has a few posts. I would think more people would want to discuss their dreams, but maybe they need a jump starter.

"Dude, you should focus on recovering first," Seiya says.

"This will help me recover," I say.

And so, while the guys fuss around me, bringing me food and telling the nurses what I need, I take a deep dive into the cafe. I start a thread, about my own dream for Apple Hair—some of it literal, and some of it about our hopes for what the band could be.

I map out our various stories, expanding on the ones we wrote in Shar's book. As I write and peruse the forum, people begin to respond. They unravel the threads, making their own theories about the guys and the dream world.

The members of the fan cafe also map out a strange occurrence. Their dreams have become more vivid. They can wander in mystical lands for longer, almost like lucid dreaming but even more powerful and real. The creatives of the fan cafe—the writers, painters, and musicians—say that the dream world is helping them foster their imaginations.

The doctor started me on walking the same day of the surgery—I had to use a walking aid, and my steps were slow and very few.

In the second week of my recovery, I can finally walk more than a couple paces. I hold David's hand as he reads me some of the new threads in the fan cafe. After we pace down the hall several times, I find Shar with the rest of the guys in my room.

She hands us a new book. "I don't think you'll need it, now that you have an online space to write down everything. But just in case."

I keep the book overnight and stare at the blank first page. When I write, I imagine a second chapter for Apple Hair. I think about what the guys and I really want. When I'm back in the practice room, I can show this island of dreamers that they can bet against the ghost.

Like I summoned the thing, the lights in my room flicker. Before I hear the voice of doubts, I write loudly, scratching the page. *Tomorrow, I'll be out of here. If not tomorrow, the day after.*

Like my writing has power, the voice recedes.

Chapter 24

Seiya

"Yo. Slow down." After tying my shoe for about half a second, I look up and see Kaden walking briskly toward the company. Like a champ.

"I feel much better," he says, slowing down just a little bit for me.

I keep one hand on his elbow. "Still. You've only been out of the hospital for a week."

"I'm fine," he says.

The other guys follow close behind. We let Kaden set our pace, which is cool. Although the operation may be innovative or whatever, it's still an operation. I keep one hand on Kaden at all times, wondering when we'll play basketball again.

"Shar changed up our schedule today!" Corrin says. "We're going to be doing our very first photoshoot!"

"Photoshoot?" I press my lips together, then strike a pose. "Cool. Sounds right up my alley."

Van chuckles a bit. I watch the line of reporters surround the company building. Since they're barred from stalking us at the dorm, they wait for us here. Hah. There are pukas in their plan. Puka means hole in Hawaiian pidgin. Remember?

No other bystanders, though—people online think it's best to stay away, watch us from afar. Too dangerous, or something. They don't wanna get close bumbai they'll get spooked. Bumbai: later or soon enough.

So, to be honest, I've only been teaching pidgin so far. But I'll tell you a moʻolelo—a Hawaiian story or legend. The creation story with Papa and Wakea. Wakea, the god of the heavens, and Papa, the goddess and mother, are the parents of not only human life, but the plant life that springs up below us. Papa gave birth to a pretty special gourd. Together, they made the earth with the gourd. Pretty sick, right? That's only the real basics. I'll tell you another moʻolelo later.

I hold onto Kaden as we ignore the arms and microphones reaching for us. "We don't have anything to say," Kaden says when a man refuses to budge. Even on unsteady legs, he can still keep it real.

Inside, Kaden finds his groove. I let him go as we all head off to our fittings. The staff members that help us ignore us. Or rather, they do the least in helping us get used to our outfits. The mad thing? Their hands move quickly, and the shadows they cast look twice as big as usual. They complain—away from us but I can still hear—about how they'd rather be helping another group. A group that doesn't haunt them.

In my first outfit of the day, ripped jeans and a faded gray button down, I finally escape from the staff members. Damn. They *really* made it clear they don't want to work with us. Shar's in charge of driving us down to the North Shore. We all nap in the car, and I dream about the space David made outside the apartment.

I also dream of my parents. In my mom's jewelry shop, they ask me about David while sitting on rainclouds. I don't remember what they ask, just the big fat feeling of judgment. Diamonds sparkle in their glass cases. All I can tell my parents is, "You've always let me do whatever I want anyways. Why stop me now?"

Ami barges in, and I distract myself by feeling the love I have for my sister. She gives me a small smile and tells me to be honest.

Even dream-Ami is damn inspiring. When I wake up at the beach, I find us in a remote section of Waimea Bay. Shar parked us all the way in the corner. "Ten more minutes to nap?" I test.

Shar kills the engine. "I wish I could say yes! But Leo just arrived—he's on a tight schedule."

"Why's Leo here?" Kaden says.

"He wanted to oversee your first photoshoot," Shar explains.

Dream-Ami gave me inspiration. I know damn well she wasn't talking just about my parents. If I just can be a bit honest…

Like my sister watches out for me, the photographers at the corner of Waimea Bay pair me with David. I mean. I could be watching the turquoise waves or the way the sky looks against it. I could even stare at the mad flawlessness of the sand. I actually think Ami and I ran down to this spot once?

But nah. I rather stare at David. He wears the same ripped jeans as mine, but his button up stops about an inch too short. I can see part of his stomach. Which shouldn't be *that* shocking since I see him shirtless every day. But something about that just drives me crazy. Just a little bit though.

"Hey, bro," I say.

He smiles, almost shyly, as the photographers tell us which poses to do. Kaden, Corrin, and Van stand off to the side, observing—but I don't think they can hear.

Which is good, because I start off strong in between shots. "Hey, David. I thought… you were close to your parents. But you don't mention them all that much, so what's up with that?"

His brows touch his bangs. With a layer of makeup, he looks like a painting. His jaw goes all tense, and I think he won't answer me. But as we wait for the staff members to set out a few chairs on the sand, he whispers, "A lot of people think I'm close to my parents. But the truth is that I am realizing how toxic they were all my life. They made me question everything, always doubting myself. The only good thing they ever did for me was take me to church."

I nod, wondering if he has more. Maybe he feels shame about sharing this. I take a stab, "Hey, my parents weren't exactly toxic. But I know what it's like to feel so distant from them. I barely said a sentence to them all year. Sometimes they act like I don't exist. Crazy."

He gives me a small smile again. Next to the chairs, we pose by leaning against each other's backs. What the heck were the chairs for?

Be honest, Ami says again. "I don't tell this to everyone," I say. "But I think I'm not normal. Not like Van, Corrin, or Kaden. I mean, I don't *think.* I guess I kinda know at this point."

David looks into my eyes like *he's* staring at a painting this time. "Thanks for telling me. I don't say this to just anyone either, but I'm… not. Either. I mean, my ideal types are Felix from Stray Kids and Taylor Swift."

"Sick." I smile too big, which the photoshoot director immediately calls out. "I mean cool. What do your parents think?"

"They said that they don't care who I end up with," David says. "But that was only after a bunch of comments about how my faith isn't… real."

I put my arm at his waist and pretend like this is all part of the photoshoot. "Hey, same. My parents said they don't care. I kind of wish they did. But I found out." I pause. "I *do* care. It's super, insanely hard to accept myself."

"Really?" David leans into me, and we act like dominoes against the blue and blue background. "I think I've grown more accepting of myself. The religion part of it always gets me, but I guess I don't let my differences question my relationship with God. Does that make sense?"

"That makes sense," I say.

I feel our shoot draw to an end. I guess the director ran out of poses for us. I rush to fit in more words. "Hey, David. I'm glad we can figure out things together. I think I wanted to say that for a long time. That I'm. I mean, I still can't say it, but it feels good to say it. Sorry."

David grins without his teeth, but it feels real and kind of amazing. "It feels good to know I'm not on a team with four typical guys."

I hold his gaze for a second longer than what must be usual. I feel Kaden, Van, and Corrin start to look at us suspiciously. Buggahs.

We take several other unit shots. Corrin, Van, and I go as close to the shore as possible. Kaden and David play with miniature sandcastles. The photoshoot takes longer than I thought. Soon, the sun sinks toward the horizon. Purple appears in the sky. *Sick.*

And then Leo, who hid behind the cameras the whole time, addresses us. Even on the beach, he's dressed in designer jeans and a light blue dress shirt. He speaks in Korean, and I try to understand. No translator or Cory to be seen here.

With the five of our brains, we piece together what he's saying. David's a huge help on this. Basically:

"I'm thinking maybe it's possible for you guys to debut."

"You guys did great in the photoshoot. But you need to stop writing and creating. I can help you. If you stop writing, things will get better."

Because Leo's the person I *least* trust out of everyone at AWE, I can't even force myself to nod. It feels like another warning.

By the time Shar drives us back to the company, my stomach rumbles. I think about ramen and mochi. What I don't wanna do? I don't wanna think about what Leo has up his sleeve. If the ghost really is his friend, maybe he managed to hear what David and I were talking about.

Maybe he'll blast us to bits—put some pukas in us with his powers—come the next evaluation.

Chapter 25

David

Talking with Seiya felt like running with the salt air lightly brushing my skin, culminating with a refreshing dip into the ocean that eased all the sharp pricks in my nerves. Knowing that he trusts me enough to share a secret part of him takes my feeling special to the next dimension. I only wish to share more with him, knowing that there are some things I keep hidden.

What I feel for him—the main wall that I need to climb.

On the seventh month of Apple Hair being a group, I head out to buy Van a strawberry shortcake. He's turning twenty, crossing over the line of "teen," even though we're all adults, technically. A birthday in the group makes me feel nostalgic. Since we were formed in late September, we barely missed Seiya's birthday. Since this is the first birthday we get to celebrate, I want Van to feel more than special today, like we can all dip into the sea together, uncharted and away from the encroaching shore of AWE.

"What a nice… cake." Van's signature sarcasm should annoy me, but his special day carries me into the wind of just enjoying him and the moment.

After a day of practice, we all reek of sweat and fading dreams. We want to reach for debut, but it feels so far away. It feels like being away from God, but I don't know if my pastor would approve of me thinking about it that way. God is ever present. While debut is fading, like the changing tide that never feels certain.

"It's from the best bakery in town," I say.

"Flashing your black card again," Van says.

I nod, wielding the serving knife, watching as the glint distracts me from the main symbol of a birthday. "I'll never stop feeling good about it being my treat."

As Seiya fetches the candles, Kaden and Corrin argue about which one should film and which one should turn down the lights. Corrin ends up filming, and Kaden takes tentative steps to the switch.

"My pyromaniac days are here," Seiya says. "Time to light it up."

"Let's try not to burn the place down," I say.

He grins, holding the matches out to the pink and white candles. As we sing, I manage to forget the words to the birthday song, or at least I lose myself in the nostalgia I mentioned before. The flames on the candles flicker, and the place feels warmer as Van nods along to the song, as he probably pores over all the wishes he has in his head, like the teenage years of his are spinning into one moment of warm reflection.

"Happy birthday!" The four of us yell at the same time, feeling like fate has gripped us and wrapped us around her thread. I know I shouldn't think about fate like that, being that God set us up, putting our group in motion and spinning us until the five of us tangled up like wiry stars.

"Practice tomorrow," Van says with a hint of humor.

"Don't remind me," Kaden says. "Anyway, it's kind of weird how our evaluations are all pushed to the end of the month now. It's part of the contract, so I guess they *have* to test us. But what are we going to do when they basically say we're bound to fail each one?"

All of us echo our worries, like we're tying ourselves around the word *failure*.

Soon, the strawberry shortcake goes in the fridge—or at least two slices of it, looking lonely yet still red and sweet—but not after a debate between Seiya and Van about whether cake belongs in the fridge.

"Time to sleep," Van says. "Thanks, guys."

"I have another present," I whisper to him while the other guys head into the bedroom.

Although I am the one in the group who mingles with the dream world most often, it seems Van shies away from it. Maybe since he lost his voice, he doesn't want anything related to the ghost. I don't want to speak for God in any way, but maybe this world, as tempting as it is, could be the key to our debut?

"I'm not going to let myself be taken away," Van says as we step outside.

Instead of heading to the little park, I lead us a few blocks down to a little library. And by little, I mean the library consists of a little shelf in the middle of the sidewalk, closed off with homemade, teetering glass doors. As I stand and wait, I also wait for Van to change his mind, like the wind or the starlight might open a new door for him.

"Fine," he says. "But don't expect me to do any... world changing."

When the guys realized I have a knack for the dream world, they called me a creator—someone who could bend reality. I think we all have a part of that in us, hidden under years of only brushing against the dream world in our sleep.

The fan cafe also acts as a source of comfort for me, especially when reading that others have been experiencing something similar to the dream world, a cresting wave that spills into the currents of reality. Online, more people, especially everyone within the wide range of artists, are interacting with a hazy otherworld. Even Shar said that she heard the whispers of a voice that sounds like the one we're trying to banish.

"It's scary sometimes," I say, offering comfort. "But I think that it might hold the key to all of AWE's mysteries."

Van pulls his lips to one side, contemplating my offerings. "I think you might be right. Maybe."

"I am," I say, grinning.

Like it heard the playful note in my voice, the temptation sings to me sweetly, and soon our world shifts. The little library exudes an aura like starlight, and Van and I look almost fuzzy next to the shifting light and the darkness which takes on a hue of midnight blue.

"Look in here," I say, opening the library. The wood almost feels soft, the glass like the gelatin of a raindrop cake. When I figured out how the eerie voice worked, catching us off guard with its mysterious warnings, I figured out that the dream world has the power to stop it.

Even now, I feel the ghost reaching for us. I barely hear the words, *Your regret will grow stronger. Until...*

But the voice fades completely when I stretch my hand into the little library. And I pull out... our book. The book that started it all, going from Shar's hands to ours, to the online world where those who dreamed of us can form their own theories and start to imagine a universe where the night isn't dark anymore.

"Why's that here?" Van says. His voice sounds muffled, like what the ghost stole from him intensifies in this fragment of the world. Maybe he took the brunt of the fall for us, the leader assuming responsibility for our catapulting into the Apple Hair universe.

"I found it here," I say. "I don't think it's real. But it shows all of what we wrote on the real pages back at the dorm."

"That's... cool." Van reaches out and takes the book from my hand.

"See?" I say, in a tone that suggests who the birthday boy is out of the two of us. "It has everything we wrote down—all the stories we came up with."

Van purses his lips while flipping through the pages. "I see."

Church bells ring off in the distance. If I were to close my eyes, I'd hear my parents calling out my name, telling me to meet them in the car to go back home. Church was always my safe haven. Driving home with them, knowing that they'd cut me down with another careless word, felt like entering a new world altogether.

Soon, I feel the dream world beckoning me to stay. It says that here, we won't have to face our instructors or the trainees who put targets on our backs. Staying here means being partly in the ghost's realm, but it also means keeping away from harsh reality.

"I think we should go now," Van says.

I don't know what he hears. Maybe instead of church bells, he makes out the voice of his brother, or his parents, his very loving family who gave him their all.

"Let's put the book back," I say. I open the door of the little library, but before we can return the book to its home, a little tendril of shadow tugs it away. It falls on the floor, sweeping out to the middle of the road like a pebble after a rogue wave. I chase after it despite Van's hesitation, because even though it's not completely real, it's still ours.

A lion materializes on the road. It stomps one foot down, baring its teeth. This one's far from an Aslan. Its body seems to be made up of tiny red stars, looking like it could combust into flames at any moment. When it roars, the tiny book disappears. One ripped page lies in its place. The lion fades away, scattered into the wind like autumn leaves.

"Oh." I wish I could say I called on God, like David in his duel with Goliath. Instead, fear melted down my throat and paralyzed me.

I felt like someone who could become a lion's scraps.

"Are you okay?" Van says, stepping up toward me.

Some part of me says, *It's Van's birthday, and you ruined it by bringing him here, giving him the fright of his life.*

Embarrassed, I start to squeak out an apology.

"Don't worry," Van says. He strides forward and picks up the page.

"What is it?" I say, even as I have an inkling, if I could even think past the image of the lion.

"It's the page Leo ripped out," Van says.

I grab the hem of his T-shirt and pull him back to the sidewalk, even with no car in sight and protected by the mysterious time zone of the dream world. "What does it say?"

Van hands me the page. It feels thicker than just a simple page in our journal. The writing, beautiful cursive, takes my breath away with the amount of care put into it—like artwork. In my hands, the page transforms into my worst enemy. And the blind spots of my vision grow like a miasma, taunting me with all the power of its ink.

The words on the page: *1. Apple Hair will realize true loneliness and become overwhelmed by their dreams. They will fall into the fantasy. Debut will always be far away from them.*

2.

3.

The fact that Leo only wrote a few sentences, leaving two points blank, screws fear into me, driving it like a piece of long, cold metal into my heart. I reach deep into my will, calling on God to help me climb back into the real world. I grab Van's hand and watch as we completely fade into the norm of a regular night in Kaka'ako.

"Sorry for bringing you here," I say.

Van shakes his head. "It's a good thing we know what he wrote," Van says. "I—" And then his voice leaves him, like Leo's specter of a lion stole it, perhaps with its roar or one of its red stars, maybe protecting its invisible, vulnerable yet magical cubs.

"We need to talk about this with the other members," I say, not liking what I think I'll hear from everyone.

Chapter 26

Van

I carry five plate lunches from L&L into the AWE break room. Well, it might as well be the Apple Hair room right now. The plush cream couches have our T-shirts and shorts draped over the arm rests. Girl, who said AWE Entertainment would own everything about us? We have this break room. Like… that's something, right?

The break room feels comfortable with its carpet and the walls painted in the same nude color. We lock the door even though we are technically not supposed to—open door policy and all. I imagine Seiya and David sneaking away here and make a face.

"What's wrong?" Seiya says, standing up to grab three of the plates from me. "Garlic ahi smells bad?"

I shake my head. Today's not a good day for talking for me, so I just gesture toward the bag with utensils. Corrin takes that from me.

Kaden, still not knowing the best way for him to sit, settles down into the couch. "So what we know is that Leo wrote down one statement about us," Kaden says. "I wouldn't even call it a story. It's just like one contradiction to what the five of us want."

I appreciate Kaden jumping into the big topic so soon. I guess we only have thirty minutes for lunch… not too long at all to theorize about Leo and his lion. *Leo, you've really done too much, don't you think?*

"We need to understand why he's doing this," David says.

"I bet it's the loneliness part," Seiya says. "He seems like a lonely mother—"

"Oh!" Corrin takes a bite out of his kalbi and accidently drops some rice on the floor. He scoops it up with his hands and gives Seiya an apologetic face.

"I think you're right," Kaden says. "Leo's a lonely pop star. He didn't get a chance to be in a boy band or anything. So, it must be his way of dealing with jealousy."

"He's jealous of us?" Seiya says, drawing his brows together. "That's cray."

The fish from L&L has nothing on my parents' cá kho tộ, but I'd be lying if I said it wasn't delicious. After taking several bites, I find my voice again. "We should just ask him."

"Ask him why he hates us?" Kaden says. "I mean, that could work."

I look at David along with the other guys. "I'm not doing it," he says.

"I think I'd rather punch that dude in the face," Seiya says.

Corrin laughs. "I'd totally pay to watch that!"

Seiya and Corrin high-five, and I try to send them a glare even though it *does* seem tempting to punch Leo Pak. Yeah… that would solve things if he were in a coma for a few months, or maybe indefinitely.

"So what should we do?" Kaden says. "Actually."

As the guys turn to me, I think about Leo's warning at the beach. "Five against one, right?" I manage to say. "We need to do the opposite of what he told us. Keep creating and keep fighting for debut."

Even though I want to say more, I gesture to Kaden when my throat closes up. "Yeah," he says. "I agree. We need to do the opposite. It's not like he owns the company. Merlin Kim may value what he thinks, but in the end, Leo's not the one deciding whether or not we debut. The only thing we can do is prove that we can debut. That means acing the evaluations month after month."

"Even though they aren't giving us a freaking chance?" Seiya says, stuffing a fry smothered with ketchup into his mouth.

"Yeah," David says. "I mean, they're forced to give us a chance. And instructors like Armani seem to be changing their minds bit by bit. It'll take time, I guess."

"Yeah!" Corrin takes a break from chomping on a kalbi bone. "We just gotta do our best. That's all."

With a bit of hope setting fire to my heart—I took a line from David's old poetry account—I eat my fish. I'm just about to try to catch a five-minute nap when the TV turns on. Automatically. More than half a year of being in Apple Hair taught me to almost ignore the magic when it happens, but in the end, I still flinch. Corrin goes pale and clutches my arm. All five of us watch the afternoon news.

"Now, we're here with CEO Merlin Kim," says the newscaster, a Vietnamese woman with too much eyeliner. I think my parents told me we might be related to her, but I don't have time to think about my loving parents. Or my brother—who texts me all the time making sure I'm alive.

"This can't be good," Kaden mutters under his breath.

As the camera zooms into Merlin Kim's face, he gives a tired smile. Maybe the rumors about us had more effect on him than we realized. "Yes, it's an honor to be here and to talk about AWE Entertainment."

"Yes," says the newscaster. "But we wanted to address one thing specifically. Or *group*, I should say. Apple Hair. Do you have any idea about the dreams that everyone in Hawai'i had? Do you want to admit to some of the conspiracies that have been flooding social media?"

"All I have to say is…" Merlin looks older as he touches his chin, the grayness in his hair captured by the camera. "There's nothing the company did to cause this. No magic. No cultish behavior by my employees. Nothing weird going on."

"So, the dream?" the newscaster says, tugging on her pinkish blouse. "There's no explanation for that?"

"Maybe it's something or someone beyond us," Merlin Kim says. "That's the only way I can explain it. Anyway, we all now know that Apple Hair is a group to watch out for."

Seiya grunts. "So, the braddah is just going to use this to make AWE look good?"

David hushes him. I notice that they're holding hands. I guess we all need someone right now. Kaden places a hand on Corrin's shoulder. I lean against the latter, almost like I can't believe what I'm seeing right now. Really… I knew we would make it on the news after the island-wide dream, but a part of me denied it. Acted like the ghost would make the weirdness disappear in the end and we'll just go back to normal.

David mutters a prayer, and I make out the newscaster saying, "We're unconvinced that something fishy isn't going on in AWE." Her voice goes thick like her eyeliner. "There is another question I'd like to pose. People are getting access to a world beyond them—particularly, people who are in line with this boy band. Creatives. Would you like to comment on that, Mr. Kim?"

Our CEO turns stern as a line forms between his brows. "Like I said, my company has no part in that."

The newscaster so much as stifles a growl. "We are still trying to talk to the boys, and my team and I will definitely get to the bottom of this."

"Men…" Kaden says under his breath. "Not boys."

Seiya reaches out for a fist bump, which goes ignored. I almost laugh.

And then, the news flips to the sports section.

I haven't been completely ignorant about what's been going on. Apple Hair has been trending on every social media platform. The conspiracy theorists reach out and pull the threads to make things even more wild. I've been comfortable in my bubble, ignoring all of it.

There has to be an explanation, Ryan texted me recently. *Just keep pressing forward, Van. Take care of yourself, lil' bro.* He also sent me a care package, which included all my favorite snacks that I like to munch on while gaming or reading. He also messaged me to share with my team members.

His very last message? *Have you reached dia in* League *yet? It's taking you long enough.* I smiled when I got that text. I pulled him into playing *League of Legends*, and now he surpassed me in ranking. I still have to put him on the fantasy novels—I think he would enjoy Brandon Sanderson.

"I guess we can't ignore it anymore," David says.

"Yeah." Corrin tries to smile, but he's never been good at faking it. "I think… I don't know. I'm just mad we couldn't catch our nap."

"Same, bro," Seiya says. "I don't think this should change things. Let's keep creating."

"And keep training," Kaden says.

"Yeah." I put all my strength into the word, wondering when the bond around my voice will break.

Hey, ghost? I really kind of hate you right now.

"Hey," Seiya says. He looks at his phone. "CEO just messaged us. Says all our evaluations have been canceled."

Kaden takes the phone and studies the message. "He said he found a loophole in the contract that says the only evaluation required is the final one. For our debut. He's still debating with the others about terminating us."

"So, we have to put all our eggs in this basket?" Corrin squeaks. "Um… I don't like that."

"He probably wants us to fail the final eval, and then hold us until the contract fully expires." David bites on the skin near his knuckle. "It's tricky."

I want to say something very leader-like, like a sage or something. Instead, I stay silent. We all probably think the same thing. We gotta keep going, keep our head above the water of AWE. Before we drown, we'll sing, dance, and create. We owe ourselves that.

I wish there were a vitamin to take for this, to magically cure me of my anxious thoughts. But I guess I don't want to overdose on ashwagandha? For the Apple Hair universe, the next supernova can't be so bad.

Chapter 27

Corrin

If I could describe mania with one word, I'd copy the idols in the industry, BTS. As they said in their hit song, it's "fire." I remember watching that iconic music video for "Fire" for the first time. And now, I think I am living in a twenty-four-hour music video, with no time to pause or even jump to another clip. It's just me, constantly plugging away for the invisible camera (that may or may not be there).

I wish being manic was a bit less intense. Who am I kidding? It might as well be an actual FIRE lit under your feet. Sometimes though, I do feel invincible. I can convince myself that I don't need sleep and that I have an endless amount of energy. If I wanted to, I could probably walk the circumference of the island in the middle of the night (okay, I guess I have to hold my horses there).

Anyway, I wake up one night and feel myself slip a bit further. (Is that even possible, at this point?) Over all this month of May, the heat seeped into the dorm. Maybe that's why the "fire" grew out of control. I kick away my sheets, daring the ghost to threaten me. I don't even glance at the other members. I'm too embarrassed, I guess.

I want to hide this from them. I don't want to ever bring down the group with negativity.

The bitterness of the medication still stings my throat. I've been taking pills regularly, but something fishy's been going on. I wanna be cool as Seiya, as funny and calm as Van. I want Kaden's smarts and David's mood, which has never given him problems like *my* mood.

Anyway, I'm over it!

Calling my mom seems tempting. It's almost as tempting as the dream world itself. I kick that thought away. I just need some air—yeah.

Outside, I play music from my phone. (I wanna hear someone undiscovered, so I let the app choose the songs for me.) A trumpet blares, mixed with dubstep, and I follow the beat down the stairs.

I think about Van's goldfish, who I've never met. What would happen if I had an older brother like Van? What if I didn't take care of a thousand pets in my lifetime, and instead I had a brother?

The four members. Maybe they're my brothers. I skip away from the apartment. I follow my heart and the breeze, letting my feet take me wherever. As I go, my phone buzzes. I wonder if my mom's reaching out to me. She always seems to know everything—single mom powers, I guess. Or *any mom* powers?

I walk, the pit-pat on the concrete pavement making me uneasy. The unease transfers to every part of my body. When the music changes, I imagine myself in the practice room, battling a routine. I picture myself in a full suit of armor, trying to hit the dance moves. I chuckle. Somewhere across the street, a homeless man throws a bottle into a trash can.

The dream world refuses to reach out. Instead, I'm left in the reality of my illness. This seems almost unfair. David can be totally fine while messing with the dream world. This—this difference in my mind is real.

I skip and then walk, and then when that tires me, I run. (I somehow believe running will give me *more* energy.) And for a while, it works. I travel across Kakaʻako, passing two churches and the local H-mart. Then I head in the direction of where the sun will rise. Or at least, where I think it'll rise.

The cold air makes the hair of my arms rise instead. I think about the other guys, who will look for me. Oh well. The island's small, anyways.

I follow my heart, and then I remember something David's pastor said, about the heart being deceptive. I shake my head and run faster. I feel the wind whip at my cheeks, and a spare leaf smacks me in the face. Can a leaf smack someone?

Sweat sticks to my forehead and cheeks, just like in dance practice. I look down and realize I forgot to change. Or… maybe I didn't care about being in my pajamas.

I run and run, until maybe I *do* feel a bit tired. I stop, pausing to rest my hands on my knees. I look at the ground and it starts to swirl. I recognize the voices, that seem to rise from the cracks in the concrete.

You have to keep running.

If you stop now, who knows when your heart will stop too?

I listen to the voices, the ones that are unique to me. The "friends" that I have learned to believe. By now, you'd think I should know better to ignore them. As if I could taste the morning sun, a bitterness sticks to my tongue at the same time the sky begins to hold just a hint of light. My phone tells me an hour passed. An hour of me running.

Eventually, I smell the saltiness. I run for two more seconds and then stop, panting. Now, my pajamas latch onto me like a second skin.

I stumble onto the beach. Here, no one wants to watch the sunrise. I find that a bit funny. Chuckling to myself, I take a seat on a dark green bench. (Is it forest green?)

I laugh as the birds begin to chirp, telling me about how I will be better off quitting Apple Hair. Those ones are easier to ignore, but the ones that say how I'll never debut puts a bitter rock in my stomach.

I'm not crazy. I'm not crazy. I make my voice louder than the other voices.

Eventually, the sun rises and makes everything hazy and a bit dreamlike. Somewhere out in the ocean, I think of a shark eating a small fish. I think about the sun swallowing me. And suddenly, I want the other members here.

I check my phone, which blasted music all the way here. I forgot to charge it. The number two... I only barely register that it's the amount of percent I have left. (Maybe I'm misreading the number too, like I'm misreading everything lately?)

I call Kaden.

His sleepy voice filters through after two rings. "Corrin?"

"Hey, I'm at the beach." I find that a bit funny. I begin to laugh, then stop myself when a couple stares at me—they're walking their golden retriever *really* early.

"Which one?" he says. I already hear him getting up in bed. Someone groans in the background, maybe Seiya.

"I'll send you a picture," I say. "I think it's the waterfront park or something."

"Okay, okay." Kaden jingles some keys. Is he doing what I *think* he's going to do?

As my phone dies, I lie down on the bench and close my eyes. I listen to the breeze, and some sand flies up into my nose. When a little buzzing sensation hops on my skin, I abruptly sit up.

The couple never left. They film me with their phones, and a crowd has gathered. One, two, maybe three dozen people. I try to smile. If Apple Hair really does perform for the world stage later, I can't have this video getting out. Me. Manic breakdown. I laugh when someone points at me, even though all the other members would act differently.

"He's part of that group," one girl says.

And this time, I wish the ghost were here to drown them out. I know that this very real crowd judges me in real time. I don't feel like one fifth of Apple Hair. Right now, I'm the schizophrenic guy who probably had a role in the bad dreams. And the hopeful dreams? Ugh—I can't focus on that right now.

When the glare of their eyes makes me jump in my skin, I watch the road. Sure enough, Seiya's car races down toward the nearby parking lot! I jump up, and the crowd flinches. They give me a little pathway—in case I want to bolt like a dog.

Kaden, in *his* pajamas, comes running my way. He limps on the last few steps. He glares at the people surrounding me, shouting out in one breath, "Everyone, move it!"

He takes my hand, and together we head to Seiya's car.

"You're driving," I say, as the people behind me murmur louder and louder.

"I don't have my license for nothing," he says. "Why did you run off like that? That scared me. Really."

"I don't know…" I knead my hands together. Suddenly, all the energy I had leaves me. "Maybe this isn't a good idea."

"What's not a good idea?" Kaden says.

"Staying in a group," I say, the words itching my throat.

Kaden's silent at that. I don't dare to glance at him.

"It's okay," he says. "You'll get better. I've read about many cases like this. The first month or two is the hardest, but then you'll begin to stabilize. Your body's getting used to the medication, but it will have an effect. Trust me."

Suddenly, all my doubts come out (as if in a burst of rage, my mind heats up and I go full-blown-panic-attack). "Yeah, but what if

Nancy's right? What if the medicine is actually evil? What if my whole body is being controlled by something else? Like… I don't know. Like someone playing my body like a video game?"

Kaden juts a hand in front of me. "Squeeze my palm."

I gulp. Sure, my mind tells me that Kaden may be an alien, or maybe my mother who dressed up in a really good makeup and costume combination. She would need a really good prosthetic to achieve Kaden's nose bridge.

But it's him. Kaden, our reliable team member. I go ahead and squeeze his palm.

He takes his hand back. "See? You are in control of your body. In fact, when you look back at this moment of mania, you'll remember these confusing emotions and see them in a new perspective. Then, you'll be so happy about being stabilized."

He sounds so sure of himself (I mean, he always does, but still), so I believe him. I don't bring it up again—the possibility of disbanding.

We're silent again. But honestly! I feel a bit better, except I can't get alien-Kaden out of my head—though now, it's more funny than terrifying.

Chapter 28

Kaden

I hobble over to the little library. If Seiya and David gave into the temptation of the dream world, I can do the same.

Like with my addiction, each time I give in, it gets a little easier to justify falling. Studies show watching pornography can alter the brain, can even affect your gray matter and your ability to make choices. It can even affect your mental health and lead to sexual dysfunctions.

Come to think of it, this choice is different. Sure, the dream world is addicting, dopamine-rush inducing. But could serotonin also be involved? After all, serotonin tells you that you've "had enough" of something, leaving you with pleasantness and a satisfied state of mind. I would have to conduct more experiments.

But my choice now is an intentional one. Coming to this library right before we head to AWE might be a bad idea, but a part of my brain justifies it.

I reach into the shelf as the dream world brings me under water.

When my parents died while snorkeling, it took me through all stages of grief. But what no one told me was that it wouldn't be linear. I'd deny what happened for one full day and was angry for the next full week. Denial would come again, and then depression which lasted so long I thought it was a natural part of my life. Just when I thought I'd accepted it, I would bargain again. Maybe the ghost has been in my life for longer than I thought.

Under water, I must remind myself to breathe. Coral forms on my periphery, and schools of fish swirl around my head.

I ignore it all and find Leo's page. He wrote the second line.

2. Apple Hair will grow apart, and the hours they spent together will be in vain. The best option for them would be to quit. Quitting will be the reasonable thing to do. The path toward normalcy.

I try to crush the page in my hands. Instead, it stays whole and unmarked by the time I open my fist again. I close the library door after stuffing the paper deep inside. Corrin's words about quitting have been in my mind since he said them, and they come back now. The drive from the beach back to the dorm room.

Although we're in no position to celebrate any more birthdays, Corrin's nineteenth rises in my memory. We bought him an entire Oreo cheesecake from the Cheesecake Factory, even though he's lactose intolerant. We all ate, and no one brought up Corrin almost getting mobbed just a week before.

The interest in Apple Hair turned to all forms of speculation, confusion, and outrage. I try to ignore it. But even my *grandparents* contacted me asking if everything's okay. If my grandparents started to care, this whole mess of dreams transformed into something bigger than what the other guys or I can handle.

Shar says something about the atmosphere in the company changing for the better. Her words, which usually give me hope, barely register.

During dance practice, I can't join my team members. I stand off to the side, following along with their hand motions. The disconnect from the rest of the group affects me. I keep seeing the empty space in our formations.

I raise my hand. "Armani? Back's acting up again. I think I need a bathroom break."

"No problem," she says. A second later, she goes back to call out the beats for the other guys.

Instead of heading toward the bathroom, I head straight for the elevator, trying not to limp. I guess I didn't lie. My spine still throbs, the muscles around it tender. When I press the button for one of the office floors, I imagine Van shaking his head in disapproval. We always act as a group, but this may need to be a lone mission.

I walk steadily toward Leo's office, where he called us to meet him so long ago. Drawing my hand back, I knock twice.

He answers in a second, like he already stood near the door. He looks like a model and like the star that he was. He raises his brow, but surely, he expected me.

"Hi," I say, closing the door behind me. "I wanted to talk to you about something. Why are you writing those things in our journal? What's the point of it?"

He shakes his head and retreats behind his desk. I realize "retreat" might be the wrong word because he looks powerful behind the dark wood and his cup of pens—this may be where he wrote down those sentences. Those *actual* sentences on our lives, as if he could decide our fates for us.

"Why?" I say again.

"You know already," he says. His English sounds just fine. Maybe he's pretending about not knowing the language.

And maybe we were right, about the loneliness. Could there be a hint of jealousy involved? I plant my feet against his carpet, staring him down. If fear's in me, it mixes with the determination to protect my group.

"Stop," I say.

He shakes his head. He opens a binder, taking out a page—our journal's page. He sets it on his desk. "Try."

I most certainly want to punch him as he swerves around me and leaves me in his office. In his absence, I taste the presence of the ghost, like a layer of charcoal over my tongue. I head straight to the page and grab one of his too-expensive pens.

I see the two points that he wrote and try to cross out the first one. Even though the pen scratches the page, nothing happens. I try another pen, then another. As I try for the fifth time, the ache in my back magnifies, like I just finished a complex dance routine. I open yet another pen, a gold fountain edition, and try to cross out the second line.

When the tip touches the page, it summons a blast of wind. It carries me over the desk, like I suddenly gained the ability to levitate. In one inglorious maneuver, I flip over the desk and collide with my back against the door.

Even though the surgery was "seamless" according to my surgeon, it still hurts no matter what I tell the guys. As I crumple over on the floor of Leo's office, I groan and wonder how hard it'll be to deny the existence of ghosts now. A smoky scent drifts underneath the door, and I wonder if I somehow set the whole building on fire. I close my eyes for a second, almost passing out. The pain reminds me of an electrical current, spreading with zero effort.

Someone knocks. Leo? I turn about an inch before the door opens. Van's face, not Leo's.

"What happened?" he says.

I laugh a little bit. How will I tell him I tried to cross out a sentence and got blasted across the room? This can't be real.

"Nothing," I say. "Let's go back to practice."

"You were taking long," Van says. "I had a feeling you didn't go to the bathroom. I heard your groan from the hallway." He holds my forearm as I wobble back to the elevator.

Back in Armani's lesson, I stay on the sidelines again, following along with my hands. As I try to make myself useful through memorization, the mirror flashes and shows me glimpses of Leo's office. He sits behind his desk and holds his golden fountain pen. He steeples his hands as if Apple Hair's downfall is imminent after just a sip of a coffee and an hour of contemplation.

In the recording booth, the guys and I arrive a few minutes early. Diane's usually here, but she probably wants to spend the least possible time on us.

I sit on a high chair, trying to ignore the temptation to lie down. The other guys begin to ask questions about what I did in the middle of dance practice. Quickly, I recite the line Leo wrote and brush over the fact that I went flying across his office.

"Oh my gosh!" Corrin says. "You gotta be more careful."

"It's fine," I say.

And in the silence, I think about the question we were all too afraid to ask.

"We should think of all the options," I say. "All the variables. I know we didn't want to ask ourselves this, but we should at least bring it up. What would happen if we were to disband?"

David, who usually takes his time to answer, grunts. "By bringing that up and making it an option, we're already getting close to giving up."

Corrin taps his fingers on his forearms. He improved from the time he ran away to the beach, but he must remember what he told me in Shar's car. "It's getting hard. I don't know if it will ever feel easy—all this constant training. And Leo, of course."

Seiya places a hand on David's back when the latter looks close to shouting. "Guys. No harm in bringing it up, yeah? *Every* group goes through the feeling of wanting to quit."

"And not every group is haunted by forces unknown to them," I say. "It gives us all the more reason to quit."

"There's a reason why God gave everyone on the island that dream," David says.

"Not all of us believe in God," I say. "There's not a divine behind everything."

"How can you say he doesn't exist after all that's happened?" David says. "If anything, the ghost should prove to you that other powers exist."

"I don't want to have a theological debate with you right now," I say.

Van raises a hand. He coughs, fighting the curse. "Guys… I know I'm the leader. I know I should have a big say."

"Yeah?" Seiya says, when Van struggles with the next sentence.

"But," he says. "We should vote. In situations like this, we all should have equal say."

"Sure," I say. "We can vote. Everyone who wants to quit, raise your hand."

In the end, no one raises their hand. I snort, almost breaking out into laughter. "I guess that answers things. See? No harm in bringing it up."

Diane enters two seconds later, holding a stack of sheet music. She hands out about a dozen pages to each member. "Big day today," she says. "We're learning some original music to identify your style." She cuts us each with the razors in her eyes. I imagine dying in this room, pummeled by Diane's sharp remarks. My back throbs.

I don't second-guess myself often, but perhaps I should've raised my hand?

Chapter 29

Seiya

This Leo dude's got to *chill.* This guy reminds me of a basketball with pukas—not just one, but ten. Basically, it means he's an insult to what a producer should be.

When I was a kid, I used to play with fire. My parents didn't care at all how I spent my time, so I went outside and lit matches. I burned leaves, and then bigger things. I can't fully explain the feeling I got from it. Let's just say seeing things incinerated in front of me made me feel like a badass character in an anime.

My older sister Ami eventually told me to stop. But still, I lit things up. I would describe this love for fire as "lit" itself, but I don't want an eye roll from Kaden.

When we need to go grocery shopping on a Friday night, I walk with David to the nearest store. And I don't mention that I want to buy matches.

"Kaden's birthday's coming up," I say.

David grunts, looking like he wants to punch the air or the nearest tree. "Yeah?"

"So?" I say. "We should celebrate it. Like we did with Van and Corrin. Like they'll do for us too."

"I don't want to celebrate his birthday," David says, sounding like he's much younger than eighteen.

I reach out to fluff out a flat section of his hair—it's the part he sleeps on, and he's always messing with it in front of the mirror. He shoves my hand away. All right?

At the grocery store, no one recognizes us, probably because we wear matching black beanies and baggy outfits. We look like thieves in my favorite game of all time, *MapleStory*. I imagine sipping an extra large boba and playing all Friday night. Man. Simpler times.

"So why don't you wanna celebrate the dude's birthday?" I say, plopping a box of cereal into our cart.

David's cheeks look almost pink when he leads us over to the next aisle. "He suggested that we quit. That's not cool."

"I mean, we were all thinking it," I say.

"Seiya!" He almost hisses my name.

"Anyway, we all voted against it. I don't know why you're so angry."

"Going back home isn't an option for me," he says. Somewhere in the next aisle, a baby starts to cry. The parents coo and call the baby's name. Jeremy? Jerome?

"It's not exactly a great option for me either," I say. "But if there's so much suffering and shit…"

"We knew there would be suffering," David says, his knuckles going pale over the cart.

"We didn't know Corrin would have a breakdown," I say. "Or that Kaden would go for back surgery, or that Van would freaking lose his voice."

"Still." David shakes his head, pulling at the end of his beanie.

"We didn't know we'd come across Leo or his lion ghost either," I say.

"God put us here for a reason," David says. "It sounds cheesy, but it's true. Don't you believe in God too?"

I recall the services where we attended with David, and the times I'd go on Christmas and Easter. "Kind of."

"There's no such thing," he says. "Kind of believing."

"Doesn't it go against your… I don't know." I feel like a basketball's in my throat now. "Your whole identity? Everything you shared with me?"

"We don't know what God thinks about you and me," David says. "Well, I guess we do. We know that he still loves us."

I hum, then I steer our shopping cart in the direction of the bakery. Really lucky day—because there's an ube cake right on display, Kaden's favorite. "How lucky," I think aloud.

David grabs the cart and steers in the opposite direction. A group of highschoolers must recognize us, because they stop a few paces away and whisper.

"Don't say that you don't wanna buy a cake!" I rush over to pick up the ube cake. I bring it back to the cart and put it right in the center. Grinning to myself, I almost forget about our kind of fight.

David sneers at it, as if about to comment on the food coloring in the frosting. "I'm not celebrating. Go ahead and buy it, though."

"What's your deal?" I say. "I thought we all agreed that we're family."

"That's what I thought too, until Kaden brought up that we should just quit. Like it's so easy."

I can tell people in the store eavesdrop on us. Shit, it's like there are eyes all over, and I'm not talking about security cameras. "It's like… da kine. It's like parents bringing up divorce when really, they would never do that."

"I wish my parents would separate," David says.

Bruh. Maybe I picked the wrong thing to compare. "After we sing happy birthday, everything will be all right again."

"No, it won't," David says. "It won't erase what Kaden said."

After his last word, the lights in the supermarket go dim. Shit. Not now—not when it's me and David and we're trying to sort some crap out.

A plastic bag goes flying. Right over my and David's head. Empty? I don't know. But then, the voice which I haven't heard in a while sounds ultra-clear.

I see that I was right all along. Apple Hair was always meant to split apart.

The gravelly voice reminds me of when a fire goes out. The coals going dead. When it speaks, the store spins a hundred degrees. Customers scream as bags, groceries, and carts go flying.

I watch as the ube cake soars above David's head. My bro looks stunned as it falls to the ground. The cover opens, and the purple splats all over the floor. Like a smacked fly.

I almost laugh, but then the invisible tornado goes ham. More groceries go flying, including everything in our cart. I hold onto David. He holds onto me. We forget about our argument. Or at least, I know that *I* forget everything we just said.

"This is more than subtle," David says. He trembles, so I hold him closer and say something about this being normal. Like we just expect to walk into the grocery store and see crap flying.

"Are you okay?" I say, when the invisible storm settles down. A bag of cat food litters the entire aisle with little kibbles. A boy who must be eight or nine lies face-down on the floor. As the screaming settles, a young mom picks up her child and books it straight for the exit. Everyone does.

I thought Apple Hair would be a good thing in people's lives. Now it's like we're a curse.

I hold a trembling David for a little while longer, then I pull back. My emotions must be high or something, because I just let it all out. "I wanted to tell you this," I say. "Maybe it's real bad timing. But I like you, a lot."

A line between David's brows softens before hardening again. "Why are you saying this now?"

"What?" I say, wondering if I'm hearing correctly. Hey, maybe the ghost really messed with my ears.

"I don't want to talk about this," he says. He rams the cart straight for the cat food, rolling over some ube frosting.

"Why not?" I say. "There was never a good time!"

Miraculously, David keeps shopping. We get our necessities again, and the employees begin to clean up the massive mess. By the time we check out, the store looks almost normal if not for the cheerios and Doritos on the floor.

Outside, we carry the four bags of groceries. Two for him, two for me. My voice catches a bunch, but I say it again. "I like you. And it seems like more than that sometimes."

David goes quiet. Maybe he thinks of his parents, who would have a million things to say about this right now. "Maybe Kaden is right," he says. "Maybe we should quit."

"Are you worried that it would mess with the group or something?" I say.

David looks weighed down, even though I know he could carry three times the amount. Dance practice limbs and all. "Exactly," he says. "We can't have us holding hands when we're worried about the group falling apart."

"I don't think I can ignore it any longer," I say. "What I'm feeling."

For a second, I think he'll drop his bags and hug me. Instead, he keeps his eyes straight ahead. "Let's just not talk about this now."

As we walk, I think about the tornado coming over the whole road. Cars flying and everything going crazy. "Are you seriously thinking of quitting now?" I say. "So randomly?"

"I'm not sure we can even be in a group," he says. "If you and I have… this going on."

"This?" I say. "Hey, it's more than that. We can make it work. Who cares that it's not conventional? For a typical boy band, I mean."

He closes his eyes, setting down one bag on the floor. He presses a hand against his right eye. I think he might cry. Then he shudders and pulls it away. He speaks to the ground. "I can't do this right now, Seiya. Sorry for being a… diva."

I try to smile. Put on my easy grin—the one that made me so popular in school. When I think about quitting, though, it completely poofs away. Incinerated.

"Why don't we just wait to see what Leo writes next?" David says suddenly.

I wait, and he hefts one bag over his shoulder. Our apartment floats into view. Our home. It once seemed permanent. But now I tell myself—it's ours at least for now?

Chapter 30

David

3. *In a final effort to escape the dream world, Apple Hair will try to harness their magic. In the end, they will fail. They will find pain in the dream world. They'll split and never reunite.*

After the guys and I read the final "act" in Leo's story, we exit the AWE library and try to return to work. In Armani's class, we work on our formations, finding the little details that make or break a group looking clean and fresh, as Armani often preaches. Diane teaches us how to harness the power of our mixed voice, and Cory pushes us to practice more intermediate conversations in Korean. Even Nancy seemingly puts away her bad dream, teaching us how to ace an interview and be in control while filming a vlog.

But even though our instructors change their minds a bit about us, Leo's three curses on us affect me more than I'd dare to admit. So, in July, the tenth month following Apple Hair's inception, I feel our group shifting into the valley of the shadow of death.

Corrin barely holds on, constantly adjusting his meds and seeing his psychiatrist, but the delusions and hallucinations still haunt him, giving him pain through tendrils and the threat of a watery grave. Every time Kaden tries to rejoin dance practice, he comes close to injuring himself and has to sit out, and the frustration radiates off him stronger than any of his physical pain.

Van, despite all his efforts to regain his voice, sinks further into himself. He still tries as the leader to bring us together, but sometimes he seems to be reading an imaginary, gigantic book, covering his face and putting his nose between the pages.

Seiya and I—ever since our fight at the grocery store, we've been avoiding each other, or at least that describes my attitude toward him. I can't bear liking him at the moment, when our group's falling apart at the seams, losing ourselves to the valley.

I try to think about the many words of wisdom my pastors blessed me with, but every time I try to apply something, I think about how they never had to face Leo Pak and his evanescent lion. I dread seeing the lion again, dread every time the ghost talks to us—one line here and there, further sinking its teeth into our flesh, running its claws across our throats.

I try to have conversations with my members, but the July heat makes us angry and unapproachable. There are many times we pick up food from 7-Eleven, devour our meals in separate corners of the dorm room, and head to sleep one by one.

The worst part is that I *know* we've been through so much. We lasted ten months battling unseen forces, and now we're going to let Leo and his three statements about us rule us and define our world? We can do better. We're Apple Hair, the group that entered the mind of everyone on the island, lighting fire to the barriers, dipping into the ocean of the unknown. We're strong, brave, and glittering through the plain and worn-out pages.

Except when we're not.

For the people who gained interest in us, along with the reporters and the fans who started to crowd our online cafe, the shininess and mystery of our group slowly begin to fade. We still receive comments, people sharing their theories, but people moved on. The ones who unlocked a new form of dreaming share that they have reached a lull in their creativity, coming under the weight of writer's block and general dryness in their imaginative lives, as if entering a desert without an oasis. Even if people on the island know who we are and have a general interest or fear about us, they don't crowd outside AWE or try to find us at the dorm anymore.

Maybe we *will* fail at finding our magic. Maybe we'll fall, past the point of no return, and God won't be able to help us out of the valley.

I keep praying, and I keep asking for strength. I think about returning home to my parents, who tried to snuff out my spirit every day with their words and glances, staining me like a squid's ink on a white cotton T-shirt. I can't return to that. I take deep breaths, go through our practices that last most of the day, and return home to do it all over again. July may be the pain that took us by the neck, but we'll make it through.

My vain hopes fade to the background whenever one of the guys insinuates that we should quit, without actually saying it aloud. No matter, I *will* get to the mountaintop. Apple Hair will find a way out of the path we're on, a detour out of the thicket of vines and thorns.

It isn't until I find Seiya crying on the staircase of our apartment complex, trying to wipe the tears away quickly as if they would make him less of a fearless and brilliant person, that I press my back against the door, closing my eyes and trying to mellow out my pain. I want to put my arm around him, but it feels like I'm not welcome to do that anymore. I breathe in, feeling the burn in my nostrils, the fresh wind carrying a voice that sounds familiar now.

I did try to warn you, after all.

August brings the back-to-school spirit. Maybe the change in seasons makes me heady for something more, like picking out an outfit for

the first day, or cutting your hair so your friends don't look at you and call you a mess.

Van gathers us all in the library at AWE. "We need to do something," he says.

The guys and I stay silent, like the ghost stole our ability to speak as well. I clear my throat, and I find it as difficult as wading through quicksand. "I think we need to try something else besides writing."

"Like what?" Seiya says. His eyes flash tender before turning hard again, and I miss the days he'd make fun of us for anything.

Corrin and Kaden share a glance. "We need to do the opposite of what Leo said," Kaden says.

Corrin nods, rubbing at his eyes. "Yeah…"

"So." I place my fist into my palm, savoring its satisfying noise. "First, we need to stay together. Second, we need to find our magic, whatever that means? And lastly, we need to find healing in the dream world."

"Healing in the dream world?" Van says.

"Yeah," I say. "There's a reason we have access to it. It's part of our story, and we need to find something there. No matter how scary it is, or the temptation of staying there forever."

We decide to head to the zoo on Sunday.

While Shar drives us there, she listens to all our theories about the dream world, why everyone saw us in their dreams, and the horror that is Leo Pak. She continues to be a steady ear, an angel who continues to protect us, even though she could leave and manage another group with less poisonous enemies. She must feel the slump as well, but she remains cheery as she drops us off at the zoo. She tells us to take our time, repeating that she's confident we'll find out the answer, like a shiny object within a forest of weeds.

"Let's head to the lion," I say. "I know we'll find something there."

At the lion exhibit, I allow myself to close my eyes. I feel the dream world tug on my sleeves, and I know the guys feel it as well.

"Here we go?" Van says.

About nine seconds later, I open my eyes again and see the zoo covered in mist. Half the mist looks like shadow, while the other half reflects a dusty blue.

Like we guessed, the lion in the exhibit shifts into Leo's lion. A specter made out of red stars, roaring at being awakened. I hold my ground, even as the thing approaches the boundary and looks close to breaking the glass or jumping over the enclosure entirely.

"Let's go," I say, and I find that my voice floats down from the heavens somewhere, joining the mist in a symphony of senses.

I take out my piece of paper. The guys do too. We all wrote down our favorite stories about Apple Hair, the ones that paint us as heroes and make us wielders of light and hope.

As I read my story, I take hold of this world, grabbing the reins instead of letting it control me. And I realize, we are more than our dreams and more than this world. We can make what we can of this other dimension, even with the church bells ringing and reminding me of all the toxic words that defined my past, making me feel small and like God didn't love me.

As we read, I listen to the other stories that the guys decided on. Some are more like fanfiction, while others frame us as warriors, magicians, kings, and vagabonds.

The lion steps backwards. The red stars that make up its body grow translucent. Its roar fades away too, as if sucked away by the power of our words, banished by our string of syllables.

When I finish my story, I wait for the guys to do the same, savoring every second of our creativity, the possibilities of our universe. Corrin finishes off with a happy-ending scene, and then the church bells fade.

For the first time, the dream world doesn't seem so scary. I plant my feet, imagining myself as belonging here. And the guys' expressions change as well, as they watch the two mists mix and then fade in color, as the lion freezes at the back of its enclosure, succumbing.

Healing can take many meanings, but God gave us this opportunity to read out our stories, like a band of affirmations that will counter every one of Leo's statements.

July, I will take you and make you mine. August, I'm ready to face you as well. Maybe we aren't all there yet, and there's a lot of healing that needs to take place first, but this was a first step toward the mountain top.

"I think it worked," Van says.

"Now we just need to do the same thing in AWE," I say.

"Read to a giant lion?" Corrin says.

"Maybe," I say. "Or maybe just take this magic all the way to debut. We're almost there."

Chapter 31

Van

I realize it hasn't been that long since I was a child.

But when I was *really* a child, my family and I went to the Punahou Carnival. Yes, Kaden's alma mater. The carnival's more than famous here in O'ahu. There, we ate malasadas and gyros until our bellies were full. We stopped by the used bookstore as well. That's where I was introduced to my love for reading.

Actually, crowds scared me even then. I wanted to be alone, playing a game on my computer. Ryan teased me and said I didn't know how to have fun. I was like, *I'll show you.*

At one of the games, I stepped forward. "I'm playing," I had said.

My parents said I didn't have to. They probably sensed my nerves. They know me so well. Ryan raised a brow and gestured for me to go ahead.

The game was to throw a ping pong ball into a cup, where dozens of goldfish swam around languidly. I lost the first few times, throwing it all the way over, or too short. Then, I threw the perfect ball, and it landed into one of the cups.

"You know, this is cruel to the goldfish," Ryan said as he held the plastic bag of our new pet.

"Yeah, but I won." I was proud of myself for taking a step out of my bubble.

"You can name it," he said.

I named the goldfish Hero, and it's still alive, thanks to the care of me, my parents, and my brother. Hero being alive means a lot. It shows the love of my family can even go so far to keep a carnival fish healthy and happy. Honestly, I wasn't expecting the little guy to last... *Sorry, Hero.*

It's weird, telling myself that I not only need to make my parents and brother proud. I need to make my goldfish proud.

In my dream, the guys sleep on futons scattered across the forest floor. I guess some things don't change, even in the dream world. Girl, we are running sleep deprivation to the max. *Dream world, please devour us...*

I sit up on my own futon, knowing that I should expect the unexpected. Isn't that kind of the thing in the dream world? I've noticed my normal dreams, while sleeping, have changed and been colored in. Like a true alternate universe. Do I dread falling asleep now? I wouldn't say so. I mean, I do feel rested even after the kaleidoscope dreams.

This one feels different, though. The guys are all sleeping like we're still in the dorm. Their snores might as well be real. Over my head, the stars shoot across the blanketed sky in slow motion. A vibration in the canopy tells me I'm not alone.

I want to wake up one of the guys. Wouldn't it be better not to explore this forest alone? It's like a magic forest, from one of the many fantasy games I've played. I try to squint to make out the spaces between the trees, but all I get is the murky unknown.

It's weird, how I can already guess how the other guys would react. Kaden would immediately start thinking of a plan. David would take a minute or two to be lost in the environment. Seiya and Corrin would probably start joking around. Me? I'm not cut out for this, honestly…

Maybe I should fall back down and go to sleep again. That would really confuse whoever's the god of these dreams. Instead, I stay standing. I imagine myself taking the watch for my group, a leader slash sentry.

Not to be the bearer of bad news or anything, but I don't think I can tell myself I'll go back to sleep. When I wake up in the dorm, will I feel rested after *this one*? I can't say for sure. The dream world has its own set of rules, constantly confusing and surprising me.

I look down and realize I've been sleeping with a dagger. My clothes, leather and some type of cloth, hug my body and make me warm. Oh, Ryan… if only you can see me now, like one of the characters we used to play as.

I whirl around as a twig snaps—like the perfect start to a horror movie. Or maybe a thriller. The guys murmur in their sleep and roll around. Seiya drools. Gross.

It's only… Merlin Kim.

He enters the clearing wearing wizard robes, dark gray mixed with navy blue. He holds a large wooden staff with a crystal attached on top, and a beard extends his face. His hair, gray—almost silver— stands out under the moonlight. I squint, making sure it's really him.

"CEO Kim?" I say.

"Wow." He turns in a full circle, as if marveling at the clearing. "Who knew I'd see Apple Hair here? You know, I've been wandering for quite a while, looking for someone to talk to. Van Le, good to see you here." He gives me a customary *bow*, and I just stare—too shocked to respond.

"Do you… um." I cough, thankful that the grip over my voice has loosened. "Are you the same CEO Kim that we know?"

"Of course," he says. "I meant to tell you that my dreams have been much richer since you five entered the company. And that Leo. Something's up, and something bad. I want to say I regret bringing him to Hawai'i, but I can't cancel his contract so easily. He has power, too. And connections."

"Oh." I look down, expecting one of the guys to wake up. Somewhere in the distance, an owl hoots twice. "Have you changed your mind about us?"

"Actually, yes." He raises his staff, watching as the midnight-blue jewel catches the moonlight. "I may have had a bad premonition, but that doesn't automatically mean that you or your group is bad."

"So, you're going to start letting us do evaluations again?" I say, unable to hide the hope, a tiny crack in my voice. *Seriously, Van? Play your cards better.*

"Not exactly," he says. "Executives are going back and forth. And although I see you guys as worthy of support, not everyone does. Actually, I don't know how to convince the whole company that you guys have potential. A magical potential."

A rock settles into my stomach. "Please, CEO Kim. Give us one more chance." *I couldn't sound more desperate if I tried…*

He grins. "I'm going to need a bit more convincing."

I consider going on my knees. Too much, probably? "I…" I look down at the four guys I've spent almost a year with. They're counting on me to speak up. This time, *I* put the reign on my voice. I call myself the master of my words. "CEO Kim, we've been working so hard. We put the hours in. We have the talent and the heart. It's only right that we get the chance to debut. Apple Hair entered everyone's dream for a reason, and it could be the reason of helping everyone heal through music." I pause, letting the words flow naturally. "We want to create our own universe. Not because we want to feel powerful or on top of the world, but because we want everyone to know what it's like to be safe and happy while making their own stories."

Merlin Kim considers my words. Suddenly, he raises his staff. The jewel glows a bright turquoise. The sky rumbles. A *lightning bolt* flashes, right onto Merlin's staff. The forest explodes with sounds of every possible animal, until a calmness settles on everyone. *I am* so *not cut out for this. Where is my paladin-fit shield when I need it?* The guys still sleep. Maybe we *really* need just one day to knock ourselves out for twenty-four hours.

"I like that, Van," he says. "Because you impressed me, I'll give you one chance. If you and the members can put on a *magical* performance, using everything that you've learned up until now, I'll bring you back up on my list to consider to debut."

"Really?" *Wow, now's not the time for my voice to squeak like that.* "But what does a magical performance mean?"

"That's something for you and the guys to figure out," Merlin Kim says. He turns around, lifting his now-glowing staff. "Anyway, I have more of the forest to explore. I'll see you all tomorrow."

I stand in my silence for a while, breathing harder than usual. A magical performance? *How in the world are we going to do that?*

Chapter 32

Corrin

After what must be my thirtieth visit to the psychiatrist (I've not really been counting), I get a medication that's supposed to help me "even more." That's the simplified version, by the way! The complicated version is that after months of symptoms, I've been given the label of schizophrenia, a mark on me that I won't be able to shake.

The first night I take the meds, I imagine my life before getting sick and after. There are not many pretty images in my head. In fact, most of my thoughts revolve around my "downfall." Dramatic, I know! I've never wanted to stroke my cat, Cosmos, more than now. She would know how to comfort me, even though her main goal is an extra treat.

But slowly, I do get better. The medication helps, and that's how I know Nancy Gomez was spewing nonsense at David's church. I'm not as sleepy, I can think without interruption, and even though my weight does stay on, I feel like I can keep up in practice.

"It's amazing," I tell my mom on the phone. "Maybe I should get into medicine. Like studying it."

"Maybe you should," Mom said, audibly relieved.

I'm in such a good mood that I skip away from the guys during our practice break, rather than taking a nap like the rest of them (tempting… but I'm on a mission).

I've a feeling that I need to write another part of our story, which at this point has branched out into multiple universes and timelines. One thing that has remained constant? Our focus on everyone in the world running on imagination. The magic of our world is based on creativity. For instance, one of my stories is about a cat cafe where the patrons paint while stroking the cats. At the same time, the cats participate in the art by mixing colors. Unique, right? Seiya said otherwise.

I take a blank page with me, promising to write down everything later on our online fan cafe. I've been perusing (yes, perusing) the cafe often, and I've been loving the unexplainable ways that the forum members have been taking control of their dreams, literally and figuratively. Sure, the fan cafe has slowed down, but I've been doing my best to keep it alive.

Searching for a quiet place, I pass some sneering trainees. I try not to sneer back. *Very* hard for me not to do.

The trainees, so annoying and all-over-the-place-negative, make it hard to focus. I take the elevator to a random floor. When the doors open, I realize I haven't been on this floor before. This floor, dedicated to office workers, isn't normally on the list for trainees.

Oh well. I skip down the hallway and enter a room with an open door. A miracle! No one's in here. I shut the door behind me and sit down on a beanbag, which stands out like a literal red thumb in the corner of the room.

I rest my blank page on my knee, holding my trusty pen close. What should I write?

I blink three times, and slowly the room changes. First, the air wavers. Weird? Second, the floor turns a differing shade of brown. (It reminds me of the fur of my dog, Jasper.) And then, most shocking of all—all my trainers materialize around the center table.

Armani Bera, Nancy Brown, Cory Matthews, and Diane White sit around and nurse what *looks* like iced lattes. I open my mouth, starting to apologize.

A few words tumble out of my mouth. But they don't react. Sip, sip.

When they don't notice me, I realize I may be invisible. Or maybe I'm seeing things! This definitely messes with my mind more—thanks AWE Entertainment!

No matter, I know this deals with the ghost rather than my own mental health. The other guys would see the same scene.

Nancy Gomez starts off strong with a "I just don't trust them. And I trust my intuition."

"They're working really, *really* hard though," Armani says. "How can they be evil when they want something so pure?"

Cory purses his lips. "They *are* trying extra hard in language class."

"We are…" I mumble, before covering my mouth with my palm. But they don't hear me. In the periphery of my vision, a grayness swirls around like the innards of a cauldron and tells me that the instructors and I may be in separate dimensions right now.

"I'd say we give them a chance," Diane says. "They can truly take the world by storm, following up with that dream."

"That's the thing," Nancy says. "Why are we trusting a bunch of young guys who may be practicing mind control or something?"

"That's a little extreme," Armani says, brows scrunching up.

"There's no way those boys are capable of mind control," Diane says.

I refuse to pump a fist, even as the harsh vocal coach gives us a compliment along with a dig. I sit down, extra-still on the bean bag, watching the instructors give their two cents. By the end of another two minutes, Nancy manages to bring Cory to her side.

"I guess Nancy does have a point," Cory says. "I just don't know. Why do we have to worry about this when Merlin should have it under control?"

"He obviously doesn't have things under control," Armani says. "He's struggling with the bad press. And Leo isn't doing much help besides trying to target the guys. I feel bad for them. They're so young…"

"What Leo's doing is wrong," Cory agrees. "But he could be aware of some type of truth. He could see things that we don't."

"What, like a ghost hunter?" Diane looks like she wants to punch something with her voice.

Another minute passes, and then I know what I must write. Like a story, but more like an affirmation. Something that will counter the three things Leo wrote down on our page.

I click my pen and scribble, trying not to shake as I write down the words (difficult, being a guy prone to shaking).

And a seed of hope was planted within Apple Hair's instructors. They began to believe in the universe that Apple Hair made, a creatively explosive one. And their doubts faded away.

After writing, I expect some big explosion in the room. Instead, Nancy leans back and gestures into the air. "Fine. I don't think it's fair to judge them so harshly."

"But let's remain cautious?" Cory says.

And just like that, the four instructors disappear.

Whoa, that was trippy. I stand up and bring my page with me. I'll type what I scribbled on the page into the fan cafe, but I think I should keep this a secret. Not because the boys won't believe me, but because the guys have enough pasta on their plates.

Later that day, we finish up our practice in the movie room. It's called the movie room, but basically, it's a projector set up between twenty chairs. Armani wanted us to watch the various performances of idols who made their mark on the world.

On the twentieth performance, Seiya pauses the movie—just when the guy idol on screen jump-kicks the camera.

And something strikes me. "Hey, I have an idea," I say.

"Yeah?" Seiya says, almost like he coordinated this with me.

In the darkness of the movie room, I guess I still am afraid. But the excitement sticks with me more. "We should do our magic performance at a university. *The* university. UH Mānoa."

Van looks confused. "Why?" he manages.

"Because," I say. "Didn't we all say we wanted to go to college and have the experience on campus?"

"Yeah…" David leans in, like he'll totally get me.

"People in college are around the same age as us," I say. "They're going through the same struggles. Okay, maybe not the exact same. I'm sure they don't see ghosts.

"But still, we should perform on campus. Right in the center, you know where the big tree is by the gym? If we want to create something magical, we're going to need the right crowd. That means people who are really in tune with the island. Not just some tourists at Waikiki."

Silence fills the room, and the voice almost strikes. *That's the most—*

Van raises his hand, bringing silence again—but a comforting one. "Good idea. I'm all in."

Kaden hums. "That's actually really smart, Corrin. I'm jealous that I didn't think of it earlier. I think the college crowd will definitely appreciate Apple Hair. Isn't going to college like trying to find your own little universe after all?"

In the quiet of the movie room, we brainstorm and go over the details. We confirm the site—campus center, along with some of the props we need. But the main thing is polishing up our dance and vocals. We'll need to execute them flawlessly, all live and no tricks.

"Of course we need to invite everyone," Kaden says. "All the instructors, Merlin. Even Leo."

At the mention of his name, the room chills. I imagine a lion forming in the corner.

But luckily (!) it doesn't.

We brainstorm until Shar texts us—she's busy with some admin things, so Seiya will drive us back tonight. Even in the midnight hours, I learned that I can definitely count on these boys. (Maybe not with making healthy food choices, though. But I guess that's a given.)

"Let's continue to plan," Van says. "We got one shot at this."

"One shot, braddahs!" Seiya says.

I smile. When I follow the guys to the van, I imagine the seed of hope growing (and growing and growing).

Chapter 33

Kaden

I take the bait despite my knowledge about the dream world, what it can do and how it can hook you. Going against my intuition isn't like me, but I've been bent many times since late September of last year.

I enter the realm in the middle of the day. More specifically, while I lie down on my stomach after a particularly arduous dance practice.

The room I'm using, the last one down the hall, I chose because of its distance from everyone. The isolation. Since the surgery, I've had flare ups sometimes which feel like needles digging into my spine. I've looked up many explanations on why this happens, and the lack of clear answers made me stop looking altogether.

As I lie down on the floor, a sweet melody draws me away. I know I can refuse, but I let it take me. Sometimes, the easy thing to do just makes the most sense. However, the consequences don't escape my mind.

I no longer lie down on the floor. Rather, I lie on a beach towel, the warmth of the sand seeping through. The sun's rays eliminate the needles in my back. When I raise my head a bit, I see my family's favorite beach in the past. White Plains.

Although the dream world can trick my senses, it's rare when I'll be transported to a new place altogether. To a new time.

I hear my sister in the background. And then, when I already feel overwhelmed, my parents speak. First my dad, then my mom. Do I remember my parents well? No. But I know my dad was an accomplished professor, publishing his findings about medicine and the brain. My mother was an equally smart professor—although for her, raising me and Lora took priority.

They speak happily. I can't make out the words, but they must sit behind me on beach chairs, just like they used to. Perhaps they are debating. Perhaps they comment on something incredulous my father's supervisor said. Has his publication been approved? In a prestigious academic journal, no less?

I keep my gaze forward. If I turn around and see them, I won't be able to come back to reality. I dig my elbows into the beach towel, focusing on the grip of the displaced sand.

I fear the ocean, of course. But the more time I spend here, I begin to appreciate it. Perhaps I'll take Seiya up on the opportunity to teach me to surf. With my senses and fears subdued, I turn into a different person with less inhibitions. I must find something to ground me. But what? What in this vision is real?

As my parents and Lora continue to speak, I think about the first few years after I lost them. Lora was very young, and my distant grandparents made it hard to process my own feelings. When Lora grew up, I remember trying to cheer her up but failing miserably.

At the time of my parents' death, I was only five. Lora was two but held onto the sense that something was deeply wrong.

As we grew older, my attempts never stopped to put a smile on Lora's face. But the years were empty, and my grandparents grew even less present, if that was even possible. I needed them, but they made the choice to shut down. Perhaps it started as an emotion, but the continuation of their disappearance was an intentional one.

Eventually, I turned to the Internet, then to explicit content. No one was aware, and I buried my struggles deep inside. In Punahou, although I aced every test and led many groups, I was searching for something more. I decided that it was something that only music could give me.

And I tried my best to be composed in front of my sister, even when things were falling apart internally. With my pride, I never truly admitted to myself that I was falling apart. Because I wanted my peers and mentors to think of someone capable and levelheaded when they heard the name "Kaden Reyes."

If I turn around, I can see them again. The dream version of them, at least. The sun's rays, so real, and the wind that carries salt into my nostrils tell me that they'll be as close to how I remember them as possible.

Instead, I keep my gaze forward. If I lose myself to the temptation, I might never return to Apple Hair.

The ghost chooses this moment to speak. *Kaden.* The way it says my name tastes nasty, how I would imagine dirty slime would taste. *Why don't you just turn around? They want to see you—they miss you as well.*

I'd rather lose half my brain than listen to the ghost, so I stay stubborn. I search my pocket for something to write on. A piece of paper and a pen, which I always carry with me now. Being prepared doesn't have to be complicated sometimes.

When my parents laugh, a rich sound like a melody, I almost turn around. To see them again, smiling, at one of their favorite places in the world, would mean more than a new spine.

But I put the paper near my chin. With trembling hands, I begin to write. *Apple Hair…*

Why do you always have to think of the group? the ghost says. *Just stay here. Just be comfortable. I know you want to rest in the arms of your parents once more. Here, your physical limitations will never give you problems again. Your injury will be healed, and you'll have Mom and Dad.*

I scribble—*found their way back to each other. In fact, their creativity was founded on the real world, despite the temptation to lose themselves to fantasy.*

Slowly, the edges of the beach fade back to the corner room. I breathe in the salt one more time, savoring the way the sun eliminates all discomfort in my back. My parents' voices go last, along with Lora's giggling.

The corner room seems so dull. I run my fingers on the carpet. The itchiness is welcome, along with the dust motes swirling past my eyes. So normal and comforting that I wouldn't mind counting each mote.

I crawl. I stand up, ignoring the needles piercing the soles of my feet. Sure, my back throbs. But I ignore it. I head straight outside, afraid of what I'll find with the other members. Something tells me the ghost wants to act against the guys at the same time. I count my steps toward the studio, where we're supposed to go for another two-hour session with Armani.

Instead of finding Armani, I find Allen and his crew. Jason and Paula also stand in the midst. "Why is this fair?" Allen says, waving his hands around.

Van looks like he wants to retreat. But he stands firm. "It's just a performance."

"Why do you five get to perform at a university?" Allen pushes. "It's unfair for all the other groups and trainees. It's special treatment. Again."

I push through and join the other four. "What's the problem?" I say.

"The problem's the same as always," Allen says, making a sour face. "Apple Hair sneaking up on everyone again. If not a super freaky dream, then something that will put them on a pedestal."

Seiya places an arm around David's shoulder, and Corrin looks toward me. He worries his lip. I open my mouth, imagining my parents. Not my dream world parents, but the ones who taught me to speak up when necessary. Yes, I remember that at least—how to say the word "No."

"Hey," I say. "No one's stopping you from performing as well. Why don't you bring this up with CEO Kim? You can have your own sets with your own teams. Just don't interfere with the performance that we're planning."

Allen looks like a tortoise about to charge. "Performing as well? Like some kind of random concert?"

"Why not?" I say.

Allen's groupies exchange glances. I bet they wanted us to cancel it altogether, but now I posed a challenge. If they don't perform, that'll be their fault for missing out. I stand beside my members, forming a makeshift wall.

Jason puts a hand on Allen's shoulder. "Maybe we can perform too," he says.

Paula raises her voice. "Right. We'll ask CEO Kim if we can also perform, and I don't think he'll be against it."

Corrin smiles without his teeth. "Glad it's settled!"

One by one, the trainees leave the room. Their footsteps remind me of scuttling crabs, and of course they have to shoot daggers with their eyes. Jason and Allen go last, along with Paula who sticks around just a second longer. "Not all the trainees are against you anymore," she almost whispers.

I click my tongue. "I find that hard to believe." For some reason, I can't keep my eyes off her. Her prettiness reminds me of glaring into the sun. She wears a monochromatic dusty mauve color on her cheeks, lips, and eyelids.

"Really," she says. "Take me for example. I don't think you guys have bad intentions."

"Thanks," Van says.

Seiya adds, "Yah, that's a big help, Paula."

"I'm looking forward to sharing the stage," David says.

When she leaves, Armani sticks her head through the doorway. "Did I interrupt something?"

I smile, almost excited for practice—back in the real world, with these guys. I can't turn my back on my new family, not when we have a magical performance in the works. Yes, perhaps I changed my stance on the term magical.

Chapter 34

Seiya

"So, we don't actually have any magic," I say. "How are we gonna create a magical performance? We gotta figure out something, bumbai we'll start looking like fools on stage."

Kaden ponders this in the dance practice studio. "We have an hour before vocal class. Why don't we go somewhere else? This place reeks."

Corrin lifts his arm sheepishly. "Sorry."

Kaden cracks a grin. "Not you."

On the way out, David flips through the pages of our original book—the one from when Shar got us Jollibee. Damn. It's been a while. We have other books now, and our fan cafe, but we always go back to the one that started it all.

"What's your favorite thing we wrote in there?" I ask him.

He tilts his head from side to side, but otherwise ignores me. That buggah. I guess we haven't made up from the grocery store shitstorm.

In the elevator, Van presses the button to the penthouse floor. We go to the indoor garden, and we sit on the stone benches between the gardenias and hibiscus. The sweetness makes me forget about the sweat of the practice room, and the sunlight through the greenhouselike space invigorates me. With David and Van on one bench, and me, Kaden, and Corrin on the other, we face each other. Almost like we're hiding within the flowers, just like a rogue in *MapleStory*.

"It's not like we're wizards," I say, like we've never stopped talking. "We can't summon anything to the stage."

"Magical can have many meanings," Kaden says. "CEO Kim didn't specify."

"He didn't," Van agrees.

"How about we just dress up like magicians?" Corrin says. He laughs. "We can make it the theme of our show. We can get wizard hats. Robes! Basically, the whole getup."

"How are we going to dance in robes though?" Kaden says, knitting his brows.

"Maybe just the hat," Corrin says.

I snicker at that. "Epic."

After twenty minutes of talking nonsense, I raise a finger in the air, swirling it around. Like I actually have a wand or some shit. "We can do what we do best. Introduce people to the dream world."

David clenches his fist. "Is that even possible?"

"We already did it once," I say. "Giving everyone a dream. Some people are really going hard in their own dreams. For those who aren't, we can fire them up again."

"I thought we knew that it's the ghost who causes a stir," David says.

"We are still a part of it," I shoot back.

Kaden stands up, staring in the direction of the sea. "It could work. It will be a really big risk though. We have no idea if it will actually manifest, not even a percentage to go by. Do we really want to bet everything on a feeling? A hope?"

"We can write a major part of our story on stage," Corrin says. "That will really get the crowd going!"

David flips through his book again. "I know." He gets that really sexy smile. "We haven't properly introduced our fans to the world yet. It's always been the five of us as characters. We need to let our fans into the universe."

"Properly," Kaden repeats. "I can see that happening. That means we have to find a name for our fans."

"They're already calling themselves AHs online," David says.

"Aws?" Van says, squinting.

"No, like our acronym," Kaden says. "Maybe we should write them into the narrative in the intermission. Between our—three or four songs?"

"Looking more like three," Van says. "We want to perform originals, and we don't have very many."

After talking for the rest of the hour, we decide to welcome our fans into the universe on stage. We don't know exactly how it will look like, but we bet on the dream world appearing and really freaking out Merlin Kim. Or at least convincing him that we are pretty dang magical.

Shit. By the end of the hour, I'm ready to go home. But we have a combined session with Diane and Armani to hammer down the songs for the showcase. About thirty minutes in, I feel woozy. I still nail my rap part though, if only to impress David.

"Three songs," Diane says. "You guys are going to have to perform way more than three if you do hold a concert one day. You can't be running out of stamina from the get-go. Use your technique and *sing!*"

Armani looks a bit taken aback, but she uses a calmer voice to say, "Just remember you'll have a small break between the first two songs. Then, an intermission. You can save up your energy for the last song. The finale. You got this, guys!"

Corrin wiggles his brows at me. I guess he really did convince them of something? I couldn't understand how he turned invisible though.

By the end of the session, sweat drips off me, and I feel disgusting. I'm sure the guys don't want to see me faint in the middle of the room, so I go outside. I feel David's eyes on me, weirdly. We all know we need to make up. But dude. How?

Ami calls me the second I step out of the room. "Are you free?" she says.

"Where—"

"I'm in the company!" she says. "Can't I surprise my brother every once in a while?"

Panicking, like the ghost can find her or some shit, I run down to the lobby. The lobby was redecorated lately to match the August season. When I squint, I can make out what looks like apple trees imprinted into the walls in gold and silver outline.

"You look spiffy as always," I say, breathing hard.

She smacks my shoulder. "And you're a mess."

We sit down at the cafe at the same level, and I order myself an iced caramel latte and a hot soy latte for her. "I'm happy you finally get to visit, sis."

"Yeah, this place is pretty impressive." She grins at me, like I have something to share.

I skirt around like a little devil. "How's college?"

"Same as always," she says. "How's the intense trainee life?"

"It's… getting complicated."

Ami takes one sip of her drink, flipping her hair in the way I knew since she was seven years old. "Is it the dream thing? I'm thinking it could've been a collective hallucination. Or something more spiritual."

"Oh, that's definitely a huge thing," I say. "But I was thinking, ugh. Something more related to one of my members."

"You like him?" Ami says.

Suddenly, my drink feels like a boulder in my hands. "How—"

"You never told me anything," she says, simply.

I take the bait, knowing my sister well. She knows everything. No cap—everything. "Well, I do like one of the members. I'm sorry I never told you."

I expect her to smack me in the face with an "I knew it!" Instead, she just smiles at me and tugs at her subtle cat eyeliner. "Thanks for telling me. Finally. But I think if you had a fight, you just need to talk it out. Or take him on a date away from the company."

"Good advice," I say. "Thanks, Ami."

Ami has always been my lifeline. When my parents busied themselves and only cared about each other and their careers, she was always the one to check up. We're more than cool. She's the only family I can count on completely. She briefly mentions about how our mom is expanding her jewelry business.

"I know," Ami says. "I want to make that face too."

As we sip on our drinks, I know I have to make it to my next practice session. Cory and Nancy are teaming up for a lesson on how to carry ourselves on stage—when we're *not* singing and dancing. What a mad concept.

"It was a short time," Ami says, regretfully. Then she reaches out and takes both my hands. "Seiya. Really, thanks for telling me. I know I downplayed it, but it means a lot. We always trusted each other with these things."

I squeeze her hands back. "Sis. I got you too, always."

"Is it David?" she asks with a smirk.

I roll my eyes and groan, starting to get up. "Wha—Never mind. Just come to our performance at UH."

"I'll be there," she says.

And I know, unlike my parents, she makes promises and keeps them. I know she'll be there, right as we start getting turnt in the dream world.

Chapter 35

David

pple Hair is no stranger to the all-nighter. But we prefer to get enough sleep, especially keeping in mind Corrin's lack of it, which led to his spiral, which he often compares to an abyss, something the other members and I know mostly nothing about.

A day before the performance at UH Mānoa, which CEO Kim is calling the "amalgam of youth and school spirit," I take a swig of half a bottle of water, savoring the sweet relief it brings to my mouth and throat, cooling me down from the bones outward and kissing my skin.

In the practice room, we are hammering down the details of our dance and vocals. Diane, Armani, and the other instructors have already gone home for the day—tired enough as it is to help so many groups prepare for what will be a two-hour long event.

When I head to the cafeteria to steal more bottles of water for us, I hear the voice on my periphery. *You will never… You will never…*

I don't let it finish. I leave the cafeteria and watch as the lights flash twice overhead, like they can read my mind and echo my flightiness. I navigate back to the dance practice room, where other trainees have infiltrated.

"We have this room for two hours," Allen says. "Why don't you guys practice in the library or something?"

"Why don't we!" Kaden says, throwing his hands in the air.

Five minutes later, we find ourselves in the library. We tried the other dance practice rooms, but they blacked out whenever we entered. We refuse to let AWE overtake us and our desire to rock the stage tomorrow, so we'll continue to practice between the bookshelves, losing ourselves in the scent of the pages.

"Just one more night." Corrin pants, putting his hands on his knees.

Seiya's Bluetooth speaker sounds just as good as the surround-sound speakers in the studio, and the acoustics are great to hear ourselves harmonize. About an hour into our all-nighter, Shar drops off pho. Van almost screams in delight when he finds that it came from his favorite place downtown. We slurp on noodles, savoring the rich broth and aromatics, both of which go down better than any medicine—like home, exploration, and the color of comfort.

"We'll try calling on the dream world at around four a.m.," I say. "Let's try not to lose ourselves in it."

"Bros," Seiya says. "Why don't we let Van fall asleep? He might run into wizard Merlin again."

Kaden laughs, probably from the lack of sleep. "We've seen enough of wizard Merlin."

Corrin straightens up, stretching his arms over his head. "I'm ready to impress whatever version of Merlin shows up tomorrow. Fighting!"

Fighting, adapted from the Korean phrase 화이팅, otherwise pronounced "hwaiting," is said as a call, an echo of the soul, to keep drawing on that fighting spirit. Don't we all have that within us? A motivation, no, something stronger that tells us that we need to keep going, that we need to grasp our dreams within our teeth, before we can swallow it like warm honey.

Sure, "fighting" has been adapted for English speakers, but the word was always part of me, when I used to look up sporting events on my phone, back when I was interested in the Korean volleyball team. I longed and dreamed for a day where I could say "fighting" without a hint of sarcasm, with all my soul, to make myself believe that I can achieve the dream that God gave me.

"Fighting," I whisper back. This time, I feel myself believing it— I feel it drawn from my spirit, as if a bucket dipped into the well far down where I thought I was empty and had no energy left to spare.

Against our minds, the ghost pushes. I know it wants to bite, drawing blood if it can. Still, the five of us together form a sort of rampart against it. We constantly push back. We won't let it win.

The books in the library seem to expand, because the shelves begin to creak. We ignore them and start our dance again. Our first two songs have hard-hitting choreography, and we'll finish with a ballad that draws the hearts of the audience together, like strings between paper cranes.

I stare at Seiya too many times, studying the line of his brow or jaw. We haven't yet made up, but I still can't deny my feelings for him, growing stronger than a spark or ember, more like a fire that has overtaken my lungs and heart. I want to touch him, if only to draw back his bangs and pat down the sweat on his forehead.

"One more time," I tell the boys, when we've made another mistake in the choreography. I was supposed to fall in front with Seiya and Van, but instead I stayed still and ruined the formation.

"We still need a nap before," Kaden says. "Or we're going to absolutely flounder on the stage."

"Agreed," Van says. "We'll stop once we run through it without any mistakes."

On the twelfth time, I sense the victory ahead, like tasting a metallic tang in the air. We run through our two songs with choreo, slaying the ballad afterwards. "It's time to call on our dreams."

Corrin snickers. "That sounds funny."

"Yeah," Van says, cracking a grin.

We hold hands, closing our eyes and trying to write the story in our minds. We agreed on one line that we'll write down together tomorrow—*With the help of AH, Apple Hair found a true friend in their travels throughout time and space.*

I sense the dream world hovering on the periphery of my senses, wanting us to enter, to take hold of sweet temptation and bite into its fruit. When I open my eyes, a force like a hammer descends straight onto my forehead. I break holding hands with Corrin and Kaden. I fall, along with the rest of them.

And I dream. Or really, I know I'm lying down, but the memories come to me unbidden. I taste them like ground up metal, or what I imagine mercury to taste like.

I see my parents. Mom and Dad, dressed impeccably during one of our holiday parties. At our table, before anyone else had arrived, my mom said, "David, are you sure you're a real Christian? I don't sense the genuineness in you."

"I had the same thought," my father said.

As I struggled to answer, our family started to trickle in. I couldn't speak, knowing their criticalness would last longer than the sun would burn. Their comments about my faith haunted me longer and with more fervor than the AWE ghost ever had.

"You may be going to church," my dad said at home, as he flipped through a magazine. "But you aren't doing enough. You aren't serving."

"I just got back from a missions trip," I said.

"Yeah, but wasn't that out of your own selfishness?"

Sometime within that same year, I helped my mom bring back the groceries from her car. "We accept you fully, you know, but you can't just expect to live the way you are and call yourself a believer."

"What do you mean?" I said.

"A personal relationship with God looks like something your father and I have with him," she says. "You have to follow our lead."

"How am I supposed to—"

"Just watch, learn. Try to copy. David, I don't want you to end up in hell."

The fear of hell haunts me as I lie fainted in the library. It draws me to-and-fro the dream world, grabbing at my skin like a troll with inky veins and shark-like teeth. I always imagined what it'd feel like to be in hell, to finally prove my parents right that I didn't belong in heaven. That I'm just an insignificant, horrible person.

As I try to find my way back to AWE, I hear Seiya whisper.

I think about the guys. The love they showed me. The love they always give, no matter how down they feel. They have shown me that the relationship I had with my parents was toxic, like always being stuck in the fumes. They showed me what truth is, the unbelievable acceptance that I've tried so hard to find all these years. A sparkling diamond within the fields of dust.

I awake. In the dark of the library, only one light remains near the door. Everyone else passed out too. Seiya has me in his arms, cradling me to his chest. I stay still, letting us sleep. Our forms resemble shadows, living and breathing. I know the guys fight their own memories, the experience that the shadowy ghost drew on to threaten our group, our existence.

Tomorrow, our debut will hang in the balance. I promise myself to draw on the strength the members have given me, pulling as hard as I can on the magic. The universe we have deserves to be shared, to be experienced. Merlin, the instructors, even Leo will see the truth.

A breath escapes me, and I shake as I release it slowly through my parted lips. If I'm not careful, I could slowly succumb to the cold, even with the strong anchor of Seiya's arms. Sure, maybe I could use another run-on sentence to describe my feelings, like my fate could be pulled left and right and perhaps even torn in two. But I decide on a short promise to myself—about everyone seeing the blinding truth.

I bet my life on it.

Chapter 36

Van

Being alone may have been comfortable to me, always, but when I stand in the wings of AWE's stage in the middle of campus center… I find a different sort of comfort. One that includes waiting to give a performance in front of a thousand people. The comfort tells me that I'm at the right place, that becoming a performer was the path I needed to take.

My parents and Ryan, also in the crowd, motivate me. I knew if they could, they would've brought Hero too. Yes, a goldfish in the crowd. Who would question it?

I draw the members together. "All we wanted was to debut," I tell them. My voice comes out strong, thanks to my thousands of times resisting the curse—like lifting a dumbbell, easier each time. "And this is our chance. I know when we got together, we never imagined we would face anything supernatural… but I think we're capable. Not to be wizards or anything, but to continue creating. We have three songs and a shot to really make our universe real. Let's do our best. Yeah?"

"Yeah!" Corrin answers. Seiya follows up with a "Yessir" that could probably be heard in a two-hundred-foot radius.

"Well said," Kaden says.

David mutters something. Probably his agreement.

We put our hands together, huddling close as Allen's group goes out on stage. His boy band, coming after Paula and Jason's co-ed group, will be the last group before the Apple Hair finale.

Allen and his boys sing a rock song. Or shout, rather? They travel across the stage in wide steps that remind me of elephants. They *do* show a massive amount of energy though, and the crowd cheers for them with delight.

UH Mānoa's campus center, full to the brim with a standing audience, holds the crowd all throughout the staircase to the food court, spilling in every direction to the various classroom buildings. The stage, right in the center by the famous tree, also has a giant screen that lets everyone see more clearly. I watch Allen's face as he pants during the closing of his group's song. *Give me a break, Allen. You know you're just panting for attention, and* of course *you'd take the role as the ending fairy.*

Ending fairy. It's the last team member that people will see after watching a K-pop group perform on a music show. Usually, the fairy will hit the camera with some sort of pose. I half expect Allen to give a little wink, but he sticks to the whole panting gig.

Merlin Kim comes out on stage, dressed in a red aloha shirt and designer jeans. He says, "Now, I want to welcome a group that's been making the headlines. Whether you saw them in your dreams or on their fan cafe, please join me in welcoming Apple Hair!"

The thunderous applause mixes with a foreboding in the background. The sky, filling in with a bit of gray, reminds me that the ghost is always watching. Girl, can't that thing leave us alone for a second?

I ascend the stage first, dressed in a bright pastel outfit—light blue jeans and a pink T-shirt. My members, dressed similarly, stand out bright against the black stage. I raise my microphone. "Hey everyone, we're Apple Hair!" My voice comes out a bit wobbly, but I steady it while thinking about what's at stake.

The members all introduce themselves, leaving me last.

"And I'm Van Le. Today we've prepared three songs for you. Are you ready to get lit?"

It was Seiya's idea to include the last line. I refuse to cringe at myself.

"Yes!" the crowd yells. Some people whistle, while others bark like dogs or make noises that I can't quite describe besides the *excitement*.

I take the center position for our first song. "Spring in Fall" was composed by all five of us, a bright pop song with a fast choreography that feels like running.

"*We were always meant to be in spring,*" I sing, making sure my voice comes out steady. "*Now we're fall, fall, falling.*"

The song describes a breakup, but also the possibility of finding a new season, a new start. I hope Leo's watching. Watching us kill the stage, that is. I don't know if he feels jealous or resentful, but I hope he's a bit pissed as well.

The choreography of the first song should tire me, but I remember the hours toiling over our routines with Armani. It feels natural. I put more energy into it, changing the vibe from *practice* to *something that people want to see, to admire.*

Hopefully Diane's watching too. My voice doesn't crack as I switch registers to falsetto.

Soon enough, the first song finishes. The sky looks like it's going to rain. *Thanks again, ghost.* I sense a pressure in the air, pushing down on me. The voice whispers, but I ignore it, not even bothering to make out the words that want us to fail, to crumble in front of the audience.

We head right into the second song, "Pink Beaches," a pop and hip-hop track that features a rap from Seiya in the second verse. He completely takes control, transforming into the image of swag. I'd be jealous, but he's part of our group. A part of me. I don't have to be jealous.

My voice floats up and away, talking about the fantasy of living on a pink beach with your lover for eternity. The song was composed by all five, again, with Corrin's strumming on the guitar and David's dreamy harmonies. In one part of the choreo, Kaden reaches for me, and we spin in opposite directions, representing splitting from the harmful reality of life.

And then it's time. As I pant, I recover quite quickly and speak into the mic. "We would like to introduce you all to something. Our universe."

The cheers don't die. They turn into something bright and unwavering, like a fire spreading throughout a parched forest.

As requested, Nancy Gomez wheels out a whiteboard to the stage. The cheers reach a new peak for her. She passes us all Expo markers, and the crowd's noises change to curious.

"Let's write this together," Seiya says. "Leggo!"

We each take turns, writing the sentence that will hopefully change everything. *With the help of AH, Apple Hair found a true friend in their travels throughout time and space. Together, they called their universe MEORI.*

Meori is the romanization of the Korean word for "head" or "hair." It was our idea to name our universe as something that represented our tie to K-pop. It was a last-minute decision, but we decided that MEORI would be fundamentally different from the dream world we first encountered—there will be no element of temptation, of entrapment.

The crowd *oohs* and *ahs*.

Then, the sky shifts to a darker gray, and I know we must battle the ghost.

"Let's all enter the universe together, shall we?" Kaden says.

As Apple Hair stares at the sentence, I feel a tug. A whisper finds its way into my eardrums. *Give up now. Come to the dream world and escape. Don't ever come back to this cruel reality.*

I watch the other members, who may be hearing the same thing, or something different. I share a nod with the four of them.

We put our hands together, bringing up our mics to our faces with trembling hands. In one voice, we counteract the ghost with the power of five. "Welcome to MEORI, AHs!"

The crowd shifts, looking up to the sky. They mumble, as if not hearing us at first.

Then, the sun breaks through the clouds. I hear Shar cheering in the background, as if she summoned the sunlight herself. I hear my parents and Ryan.

And the dream world wraps the audience in its hold, just for a few seconds. The air turns bright and sparkly. The crowd gasps, reaching out and touching the air as if they can feel the change.

Leo's lion, standing at the top of the cafeteria building, roars once and then fades into little pieces of scattering red. The crowd doesn't hear it.

They reach out, as if popping bubbles in the air. After ten seconds, the sky returns to a neutral blue. The cheering mixes with wonderment and shock. The thousands in the crowd all felt it, the feeling of entering another world.

I know we succeeded, but it's time for our final song.

I sit on the edge of the stage with the other members, as the opening piano arrangement to "Broken Art" sounds out.

"Broken Art," a heart-wrenching ballad, goes out to everyone chasing a dream that feels unattainable. My voice almost breaks on the bridge, when we do a run over the minor key.

As the last note fades out from David, I watch the crowd. I don't see our instructors or my family, but the faces of new fans tell me we did it. We proved ourselves with a magical performance.

If Merlin Kim has anything to say… ah, I just *know* he'll have to give us a chance after this.

Chapter 37

Corrin

Merlin Kim caves, no choice but to give us a shot. A final evaluation—he promises us that. Yes! I want to jump on the roof and shout at the top of my lungs. I want to throw a massive-red-rubber-ball at Leo's face and watch him attempt to dodge. Wouldn't that be hilariously epic? I can hardly imagine Leo's face. It would be a memorable moment in MEORI. Not just our canvas now, but our world!

Of course, I don't voice this image to the guys. (They would definitely call me the kid of the group. Again.) Instead, I keep it to myself while we push forward. *Toward the finish line*, as my mom had texted me. *It's like your longest night shift ever is coming to an end, Corrin.*

We don't know what the final evaluation will look like, but it can't be much harder than what we just did. (An epic UH Mānoa performance will go down in the books, I know that for sure.)

One Thursday night, the day after David's birthday (we got red velvet cake), I find word about a new hire in AWE. Not just any new hire, but a counselor!

Before I got sick, this news wouldn't even register. I'd probably ignore it and go about my day. Maybe I'd make a lackadaisical comment about the said counselor. But now that I see a psychiatrist, this kind of excites me in a weird way.

"Hey guys," I say. "Let's see the new counselor together. I booked us a session, like a family therapy type of thing. Aren't I the best? It's at midnight!"

"And why is a counselor seeing people at midnight?" says Kaden.

"I don't know…" I say. "I didn't question it."

"I guess we can go," Van says, without the telltale strain in his voice we learned to ignore for so long. I guess we shattered the ghost slash lion thing? I haven't seen Leo in ages, but I know he probably will make an appearance soon, popping up out of nowhere. That handsome guy-slash-ass could have something up his sleeve.

"Let's go," David says. Nineteen looks pretty good on him. I can't get his smiling face out of my head, when we sang him happy birthday in the dorm. When he blew out the candles, I felt the most normal that I've been in ages. That's saying a lot!

There were bags under our eyes then. Just like now. But I'm hardly tired when thinking about a good therapy session with the guys. I mean, my psychiatrist does a good enough job, but exploring deeper issues? Hm. Maybe I shouldn't have invited *everyone in my group* for the first session?

"Glad you think of us as family, dude," Seiya says, putting his arm around me. He smells after our practice, but I don't really mind that much. I probably have nose blindness to myself (definitely a thing, especially in our apartment where Febreze can only do so much).

We head a few floors up, to a nondescript room in the corner. When we open it, I find complete darkness. So dark that the light from the hall doesn't even pierce it.

No windows or anything. I mutter to myself, "Maybe we got the wrong place…"

"No, this is the right place."

I freeze. The person within sounds just like—

Leo Pak. If Leo Pak could speak English. I turn around in confusion and a bit of fear—my teammates freeze like statues as well. Should we run? Is this Leo's massive grand plan to destroy us?

"Come in," the person says.

I share a nod with the members, knowing we wanted to confront Leo, the five of us finally settling the ripped page. I lead the guys inside, and Van closes the door behind us. My eyes don't adjust. Still, I see absolutely nothing.

"There's a couch if you turn right and go to the back of the wall," the person says.

I obey, still testing that voice. It can't be Leo—I think this person might be an extension of him, or maybe his brother? I can't be sure, so I ask, "Who are you? What's your name?"

"That doesn't matter," the counselor says. "We're here for a session for the five of you, are we not? I can't hardly waste your time by talking about myself."

"Okay…" And because it was my big idea to go to therapy together, I add, "We'd like to start, then."

"Tell me what you're going through," he says. "What's been good? What's been bad? And what's been challenging or confusing?"

I clear my throat, trying to figure out if it's David or Van who rustles beside me. "Well earlier, a bit after the beginning of our formation, I was diagnosed with schizophrenia. Not a good thing, by the way. It's actually been really hard. Not just for me, but for everyone. I felt like I was holding us down sometimes. Okay, maybe not sometimes. All the time."

"That can be difficult," says the voice. I realize there's no change in the air, no crossing of his leg or arms. "Living with a chronic illness while trying to chase a debut as a pop star."

"Yeah…" I try to think of the other things I wanted to say, but they feel so unreachable. Now that we're with this strange guy. How are we even supposed to find the door when we're done here?

"Tell me more," he says. "Maybe another member wants to chip in?"

"This would fall into the bad category too, also challenging and confusing, but we often felt guilty," Kaden says. At my left. "Corrin was the only one going through these stressors, and we couldn't do anything. We were so busy, so we didn't comfort him or take care of him the way we should have."

"That's not true," I mutter.

"It is," Kaden says. "With my back problem, at least I can sit out on dancing to focus on recovery. But Corrin had it different. It was much harder for him."

"Do the rest of you feel guilty?" the man says.

"Yeah," David and Seiya echo. "Yes," Van says a beat later.

"Well, it isn't anyone's fault," he says.

Okay. This dude definitely isn't Leo! No matter how much he sounds like him. His voice, less cold, reads more neutral (and almost indifferent). I might actually start liking this man!

"I think it's just good that I'm stable now," I say. "So no one has to feel guilty anymore."

"The medicine *is* helping," Van says.

"As it does most times," the counselor says. "Corrin, I want to ask you. What else has been good?"

What is good for me? "There is so much more!" I say. "I mean, I'm living the dream. I feel closer than ever to reaching my goals, and I love being in a group and working together. And all my pets are doing well back home."

The counselor gives a soft affirmative hum. "Good, Corrin. Does anyone else want to chime in? Maybe Seiya or David?"

I hear some whispering beside me. Eventually, Seiya gives a little grunt. "Yeah, Mister Counselor. I just wanted to make a comment to add more good to the table. We seem to be past the petty fights, so yeah. We are much more like an actual family. 'Ohana."

David's voice follows, light as a leaf in the breeze. "Yes. And maybe this is a personal thing, but Corrin's opening up more to me. We talk often about Christianity and how he has a curiosity about what I believe. I've been praying hard for a moment like that."

"Yes!" I say. "I mean, I'm still an agnostic, but I'm more open now. I think going to church and singing with the worship team was pretty life changing! It changed me. I felt like I was a part of something bigger."

The counselor keeps still. No notetaking or anything. (Should I be worried for our lives now? I guess not, because the atmosphere feels pretty safe in my books.) The counselor says, after a beat more, "Now that you are almost on the path to debut. Do you think you can last as a superstar with your condition?"

I want to take back what I said about him. His question is *a bit cutting* to say the least. "I think so. There are many singers who struggle with mental health issues."

"Some of them don't end up in a very good place after fame," he says.

Suddenly, the darkness of the room turns heavy. And somehow, *darker*. (I almost reach out and grab one of my teammates' hands, but I resist at the last moment.) But I think the change has to do more with me, not the Leo-type-person.

"I think since I have so much support," I say, "I'll turn out just fine."

"I see," the doppelgänger says.

Van jumps in. "The training is the hardest part. If you survive this, Corrin, you can survive whatever comes after."

"Amen brother," Seiya says. Kaden and David also mutter an agreement.

"I see," the man says again. "I think you have already figured out so much on your own. Did you really need to see me?"

I laugh a bit when the counselor chuckles, a sound that rings *so* much like Leo (!) that I freak myself out a bit.

"I'm glad you have four good people as your support system," he says. "Is there anything else you'd like to ask me?"

"Why did you ask me that?" I say.

"Well, I wanted you to convince me that you could make it as a debuted idol," he says. "Now that I'm counseling people like you, I want to make sure you can handle the lifestyle."

"Makes sense," Kaden says, in a way that tells me he kind of wants to punch the person across from us.

"I'm sure I can," I say.

"You convinced me," he answers.

I guess I did. After talking a bit more about the struggle of waking up and trying to find more time to relax with the guys, I finish the session with, "Thanks, I learned a lot! And processing things with you confirmed that I'm really on the right path."

"Well, I look forward to the next session," he says. "Find me anytime."

I stand up and try to find my way to the door. Eventually, Kaden grabs my hand, and David opens the door for us. When I turn back, I still can't make out the guy's face. I rush out of the room, because we have an hour-long session until one-thirty a.m. More dancing, I think.

My first experience with family therapy? Not bad! I think I'd do it again.

Chapter 38

Kaden

"The final evaluation?" Merlin says. He twirls a pen with his left hand, and for a second, he looks like the wizard Van must've seen in his dream. "It's going on as we speak. You will know whether you pass by the end of October."

"How do we know what we're being graded on?" I say. "Shouldn't there be some sort of performance? Or something else?"

"You're just going to have to do your best for another month," CEO Kim says. "And your result will come naturally."

The other guys nod, but I can't let it go. "But—"

"You put on a great performance at UH," CEO Kim says. "You proved that you could craft a spectacular performance. To flesh out the beginnings of a lush world. MEORI? It might just be the opening for you all. Your portal.

"And you made sense of all the dreams I've been experiencing. Could this be the world that you created? We don't have the answers now perhaps. But just do your best. You—Apple Hair—changed us as a company forever, so we're going to do something a little different as your final test."

I end up nodding.

There's a science to guessing C on a multiple-choice exam. I'll just have to make the best guess in this circumstance, no matter how much I want to think about what I need to prepare for. It infuriates me, sure. But there are plenty of things I've tried to control this year that ended up falling out of my grip.

On Seiya's birthday, Merlin Kim approves some time off. We end dance practice by noon, and a nervous Van drives us to Wet 'n' Wild. He has his license. Although he barely uses it, he wanted to have Seiya relax and not have to dodge any reckless drivers.

"Time off on a day that's not Sunday?" Seiya says. "That shit's unheard of."

"Yeah," I say. I want to ask the guys, yet again, what they think we're being graded on. But I know they're sick of me asking, and being a broken record just isn't my style. There are other questions too—more important ones. "We have something to clear up. MEORI and the original dream world that we encountered. They're different, did we not decide? We should be very clear not to promote the unnamed dream world to our fans, or they may fall into the temptation of it too."

"Oh, I have a great name for it," Seiya says. "And since our righteous David is here, I won't swear. But it's something that rhymes with Mind-Luck."

"You can't be serious," I say, while Corrin laughs without reserve, the bright sound filling Seiya's car.

"Let's just call it the dream world," David says. "We don't want to give it any more power than it has. I think that we should just keep the ghost, dream world, and the voice in its own category. Something that we shouldn't think about."

"We must think about it," I say. "If we are to counteract it, and to prepare ourselves for the future."

"Leo," Van suggests. "He's a huge part of it. Why don't we just call it that?"

"Leo?" I ask. "Wouldn't that get confusing?" Sensing an argument brewing, I decide to reel my opinion in. "Let's have Seiya decide."

"Hmmm," Seiya says, as if he's contemplating the existence of life over the course of eleven seconds. "Leo it is. But not in all caps. Just Leo, so we don't give it the same strength as MEORI. Makes sense, huh?"

Even though I want to challenge and revise, I give in. "Sure. We should be able to guess whether we are talking about the actual producer or the world, just by context."

"Let's not think about assignments right now!" Corrin half exclaims and half groans.

I ruminate on my thoughts as David and Corrin debate about whether Corrin's pets would be able to be memorialized into a mobile game in the future. Van turns up the music of Seiya's song of choice, the latest rap song that made the *Hot 100*.

Wet 'n' Wild in September still retains enough heat to feel like an oven when I step barefoot toward the first attraction, the lazy river. *Relax, Kaden. It's just water, and statistically no one has ever died on the lazy river.*

Could I be wrong, however? Perhaps someone has actually died in the lazy river, and I didn't have the time or the bravery to look it up. It's not like me to assume. Also, it's not like me to try to ignore a worry. Here today, I jump in after the team members encourage me—a little impatiently, though I don't blame them. About a dozen kids are smacking against my team members with tubes that are thrice their size.

For a long time, I sit on my tube and just let the current take me. I almost laugh. Sure, the terror of the water was a hard beast to face. But now that I feel the safety of the river, I can reassess. This feels like heaven, to be outdoors like this, not having to worry about executing a perfect dance move or high note.

I test my back, stretching it out. Sure, a slight ache still bothers me. But other than that, I can move like before. The dancing proved it too, and this day out spurs on thoughts about a new physical reality for me. The doctor was right. Who would have guessed that? I should have known to trust someone devoted to healing peoples' bodies.

"Let's try something more intense after this!" Corrin says, after popping up in the middle of his tube like a weasel. Droplets spray me, and he flips his soaking mop of hair.

"Okay," I say, not thinking too much about it.

The Orange Twister, an attraction built just last month, should surprise me. I mean, apples and oranges should never go together, and I suspect that "Leo"—the Leo that accompanies the ghost, the dream world, and the voice—has something to do with it.

But I also know our dreams and writing changed our real world, like ink on a page that cannot be removed.

I climb the steps. And sure enough, anxiety sets in.

The Orange Twister was built by professionals, I remind myself. It starts about fifty feet above the ground. It includes a massive funnel, a slide that almost lies perpendicular to the ground, and rushing water that reminds me of the most fearsome wave.

And even though we're not on the beach, I'm reminded about how my parents died. Drowning under the Orange Twister sounds like the most horrible possible way to go. And even though the water park isn't the beach, it still resembles it quite a bit.

"I'll go down last," I say, trying not to squeak with my voice.

"All five of us can go at once," Van says, grabbing a massive red tube in the shape of a seashell.

"Okay," I say.

"Not like you not to know that, Kaden," David teases, resting a hand on my shoulder.

"You must be scared," Corrin says, smiling too brightly for

someone about to drop fifty feet.

"Pfft. No."

Seiya helps Van heave the tube to the line.

Before we actually commit, David checks in with me. "Are you sure you're okay, Kaden? We know about your phobia, and we can always do a less scary one."

"No worries if you can't, brah," Seiya says.

Van nods at me with a reassuring steadiness in his eyes. Corrin nods too, although he smiles, still with anticipation.

I nod. "We can do it. I'm not afraid."

Perhaps I learned that speaking a story will make it true. I convince myself, not just my team members.

At the top of the Orange Twister, one person waits their turn. Or rather, one person and his groupies. Allen. We didn't see him while standing in line earlier. In fact, where was he the whole time we were waiting? I recall the first strange happenings in the AWE building. I know that history always repeats itself.

"We decided to take some time off too," he says before anyone can ask what he's doing here. "See you at the bottom!"

And he takes off. Leaving us as the next to go.

When I first found out about my back, the logician in me told me that I would need to pay more attention to it. The second part of me said it'll turn out to be no big deal. We all know where that led to in the end.

Even though the Orange Twister was built a month ago and there's been no accidents, I still tremble when thinking about falling and injuring my back. That combines with the fear of water that I've had ever since my parents drowned. Together, I think I'd slip out of the tube solely out of nerves.

"You can do it," Van says.

"Yeah, bro," says Seiya.

And for the birthday boy, I sit on the tube and await the employee to push us down, who looks strangely a bit like my little sister. If she saw me now, she'd be proud. I imagine her smiling face. I imagine the day when I will see her graduate from high school.

And we're off.

As we spin and slide into the center of the funnel, I scream at the highest pitch I possibly could make. I didn't know I could reach a note that high? Could this be a new method for expanding vocal range?

My center of gravity whirls completely off. I don't know which way's up or down. With the four other guys screaming as well, we make a note of dissonance that feels like everything will explode around us.

We drop. Flying in the air, I imagine letting go and splattering against the sidewalk. Instead, I hold on. Five seconds or more pass before we hit the bottom. The tube completely submerges, and I flail around until David grabs me. We swim to the edge of the pool, and my eyes must expand to frisbees.

Allen's there. Laughing. "Surprised you guys made it down."

Because I'd rather die than look scared in front of Allen, I make it out of the pool. I drip in not just relief and exuberance, but with newfound courage.

"I want to challenge you to a dance contest, Kaden," Allen says, crossing his arms. "Or are you too much of a grandpa for that now?"

"A dance contest?" I perk up. Allen's a good dancer, but not as good as me. "Like a dance off? You're on."

Turns out, Allen's been planning this stunt for quite a while. A male trainee around my age fetches a sound system, which includes a huge jukebox that most likely weighs more than half of him. We debate on a song, settling for a surprise song shuffled for fairness.

By the wave simulating pool, I stand with the water still soaking my hair and swim trunks. Even though only a few people watch, with so much water-park distraction and the whole spontaneous nature of things, I still want to beat Allen.

As the song plays from one of Allen's teammates' phones, I lose myself in its enchanting, almost trance-like beat. Allen goes first. He moves to the beat, sure. But I catch his sloppy lines. His little moments of unease. He stops, then points at me.

Even with the ghostly ache threatening to come alive in my back, I go. I freestyle just like how I know Seiya can do so well. The water flips off my hair, over my bare chest. And I know I got this.

No more fear can touch me. I know I can win.

Chapter 39

Seiya

Life turns to hard mode during the end of October. No cap, we must get a few hours of sleep each day the first part of the week. By the end of the week, I get about three hours in the last three days.

The training intensifies, and I know it's all part of Merlin Kim's grandmaster plan to assess whether we have our shit together. That's his whole kuleana—the Hawaiian word for responsibility. But there's a whole other meaning behind that word. It's a blessing to be carrying out your kuleana. You should always remember that, OK? Same for me and the guys. Our kuleana right now is to pour our all into being trainees.

"Step it up, guys!" Armani says, as we perform our tenth time in a row. A cameraman in the room records our every movement. Every time I stumble, I imagine our chance of debut ripping up like a damn sheet of paper.

"Good job, good job," Armani says as we close with our ending pose. *Are you okay, Armani my dude?* No lie, she looks a bit frazzled too. Then she winks, saying, "It's the last day of October. You guys are almost there. I don't want to get emotional right now on you all. Just know that I am rooting for you. After all, I don't teach just anyone, and I don't brag to my strict and sometimes unreasonable parents for no reason. Guys! You are so, so close."

In Cory Matthews' class, he plops the five of us in front of the room to do a group presentation in Korean. Wait for it—in front of the other trainees.

It takes me a few seconds to load up, but I say, trying not to slur my words together, "Learning Korean has been one of the greatest privileges I've had thanks to AWE. There's nothing like slowly learning and getting a mastery over something that was once so foreign to me."

Man. I might as well be writing an essay on stage. David completes our presentation with a long "thank-you" and a note, "We hope to debut very soon, so watch out for us."

Jason and Allen raise their eyebrows. Paula gives us a silent thumbs up. A blackout knocks the crap out of the entire classroom for about four seconds, before the lights come back on and Cory tries to take hold of the antsy trainees. Man. Leo really can't let us catch a break, huh?

In Diane's class, we perform enough warm-ups to probably warm the earth, again with the camera following us around. I spit the hardest I ever had, making sure I enunciate on every word of my rap. Yeah, I have improved in rap in more than any other area of my training. I guess I'm a little proud about that. Even my voice changed. I used to have this mad little wisp at the end of my words. Now, I spit with a steady tone.

By the end of the fifth time through the song, Diane raises her hand. "That's enough. Good luck."

Then, Nancy takes us through a mock interview. She asks me, looking straight into my soul, "What do you think about dance challenges?"

"Dance challenges?" I say, trying to find out where the trick lies. "I think they're great. They really help songs trend. Sometimes though, I wish it was about the song and not just trying to rake in the views. Ya know?"

"Interesting," Nancy says, moving on to the next member.

I think I messed it up for all of us, but Van gives me a shaka. Damn. Have I really not explained the shaka yet? It's a sign where you put your three fingers in the middle down. Then you extend your thumb and pinky. It basically means "hang loose" or that things are all good. Fine, dandy, and great.

But hey. If the leader likes it, I'll take it.

At the end of the day, or early morning, Shar finds us in the lobby. "Hey," she says. "Company wants to give you guys a surprise."

"Surprise?" Kaden asks, as if braddah Leo could strike again.

"It's a good one, don't worry!" Shar says. "You'll be staying at a beach house in Hau'ula for two days. No cameras, no schedule. Think of it as a reward for you guys."

We head back to the dorm quickly to pack our essentials. Gotta get that good cologne for me. The company sends a nondescript all-black van to take us. Man, Merlin really is more than loaded. The guy could probably take us around in this all the time. It smells like cotton and a bit like how the Leo world smells? Strange thought, I know, I know. But the world smells a lot like a fat-ass dopamine boost. Sweet, and just a lil' spicy.

In the van, I fall asleep with a thought. It turns into a resolution. I gotta tell the guys something pretty important.

Hau'ula's beach waves "hi" to us as we drag ourselves and our backpacks inside. Without even saying anything to each other, we find our ways into the rooms and collapse. I share a room with Corrin and Kaden, and both of them knock out first. I stay up a bit, reflecting deeply. Yeah, yeah, you probably see right through me. Staying up means like ten seconds thinking about what to say. Then I tell myself just to wing it.

Shar finds us in the living room with a mage costume the next day. Like an actual mage in an RPG. "Hey, guys," she says. "I figured we didn't get to celebrate Halloween yesterday."

"You should've got us all matching ones!" Corrin says.

We all agree that we want to do nothing but sleep, stare at the beach, and sleep some more. Oh, and eat. A silent private chef who looks like Tom Holland cooks us killer loco mocos for lunch, and we don't talk about the evaluation. We leave it behind us, even though the result will come up in the next few days.

The private chef whips up beef stew for dinner, and then he leaves. We get a text reminder from Shar to relax and do nothing else.

In the middle of dinner, I stand up, putting my hands on the edge of the dining table. "I have a confession," I say.

"Save it," Kaden says, but in a tone that tells me to go on anyways.

"I like guys," I say. "So, you might call me gay. Or something. Yeah."

The whole table goes quiet, and then Corrin laughs and claps. "We know. *Anybody else* have something to share?"

"I'm bi," David says. "If you want to call me that…"

"Great," Kaden says. "Are you two dating?"

Van holds up his hands. "Wait. We just want to say we love and accept you." And because he can't keep a straight face, he bursts out into laughter. The whole room turns into a circus for a hot second. We don't recover for about ten minutes. By the end of it, all my nerves have gone away. Damn. Was it really that easy?

I mean, it wasn't easy. It felt like a chain got a hold of my throat. David was mega cool about it, though. He said the words with a bit of hesitance. But could I have spurred him on? Me?

"No, we do though," Corrin says.

"Yeah," says Kaden.

"Sick." Suddenly, the relief feels like an ice packet against my hot head.

At midnight, I follow David outside, and we walk along the shore. No sign of the ghost. The voice only popped up in the periphery every so often, throughout October. I think Leo's biding his time or some crap.

I watch the shore and try to come up with something poetic like David. Nada.

"That went better than I thought it would," I say.

"I knew they'd accept us," David says.

Us. We have to be getting somewhere, right? "Do you forgive me for that day in the grocery store?"

"I should be the one to say sorry," he says. "And I do like you. A lot."

We stare at each other for a long time as the shore creeps up, almost tickling our toes. I reach out and grab his hand, remembering the day I first saw him. He put a weird feeling in my chest, like someone was just tearing it up in there.

"I might just—love you," I say.

"I love you too," he says, so easily.

And we lean against each other in the moonlight. When my lips find his cheek, I think about my friends in high school who would urge me on and tell me what a wimp I am.

Then, he smiles. His blush is visible even in the moonlight, or maybe I'm imagining things?

No matter, I imagine a stage where we can be together. Performing for a long, long-ass time. I feel his breath. I get almost high. When I clutch his hand, I think about having self-control for a whole year.

It's a MEORI type thing. It's a vibe.

This was really, really worth the wait.

Chapter 40

David

The magic of a first kiss spurs me on, and I bask in it throughout our stay at the beach house, living in it, breathing it, and memorizing the notes of it like a perfume down to its last drops. When it's time for us to return to Honolulu, I feel a certainty that can only come from God. I trust him with all my pulsing heart, even though uncertainty raged at us with a vengeance much like a poisonous fog, threatening to close all our throats completely and pluck every single good thing we planted into the ground of our trainee life.

We don't know what we were being graded on throughout the month of October, but it was certainly the month we worked the hardest. We sweated so hard we almost bled, and we rehearsed until we knew nothing more, just our reflections in the mirror and our voices combining into a harmony that grew more beautiful each day.

Merlin Kim meets us in his home in Hawai'i Kai—that's how I know it's serious, and the chill on my arm almost feels ghostly, although I know we've stayed clear of the full force of Leo for quite a while, as if creating a calm through our combined imaginations.

CEO Kim's house, a three-story masterpiece, greets us with a limestone-colored exterior and pillars that remind me of a long-lost palace. CEO Kim finds us in his front yard, where the smell of the beach, only a few minutes away by walking, ripples through my nostrils.

"Welcome to my abode," he says. "Or after I met you guys, should I call it the wizard's den?"

"You could." Kaden's brows scrunch together, and I know he wants to say something else, possibly about how ridiculous that would be. I've learned to appreciate his honesty, though I know our difference is so great, as I would rather hold my tongue nine times out of ten.

I follow after Van, feeling Seiya's stare on my neck, almost like the weight of a feather, barely noticeable but still there. It took everything within me not to return the kiss. But I know a slow pace would do me good, give me time to fully figure out my identity, pulling out the tangled thread and weaving it into a whole new piece of multicolored fabric.

Merlin Kim's house may be monotone from the outside, but the inside comes alive with jewel tones, with copious amounts of rugs and fancy plush couches, like the gems have totally overtaken the haystack. I sit on a couch big enough for all the members of Apple Hair, which just so happens to be apple-red. Merlin takes a seat on a sapphire armchair, facing us directly. From behind him, the sunlight casts him into a shadow, but not with the spirit of the lion.

"So, I know you have questions," CEO Kim says. "Truth is, you've been meticulously recorded for the whole month of October. I'm sure you noticed. My team and I have pored over your videos, assessing multiple factors that will decide whether you're able to debut or not.

"It was a very tough grading system. The rubric the execs and I created was ruthless, sparing little room for error. It wasn't just dance and vocals, but also your teamwork and individual personalities. My close team of about a dozen have finished grading, and we have the results in this envelope."

From his left, he reveals a small envelope, camouflaged in the same sapphire blue as the chair. I know it couldn't have come from nowhere, but it certainly seems that way, as if he fully encapsulated the idea of a wizard who can wander through forests instead of succumbing to dreams that are dictated in his subconscious.

Slowly, intentionally, with the stillness of a marble statue set in concrete, he hands it to Van, reaching across to bridge the gap. I tremble when thinking about what's inside, the yes or no that will decide our futures, that will either carve us apart or bind us with invisible yet unbreakable shining thread.

Beside me, I reach out and grab Seiya's hand. He squeezes once. I think about the year I spent with my team members, which was so hard sometimes it felt like we would fall into an endless pit, constantly rolling about with the uncertain force of gravity. Seiya said he loves me. Sure, I know that is different from how he loves the other members, but he still loves them. He treats them and holds them up in love, just like I do for my four new brothers—that will never change, and we can never be severed completely no matter what happens.

"Go ahead and open it when you're ready," CEO Kim says. "You can take your time. Or not. Whatever you choose."

Van looks like he wants to hand the envelope to someone else, but he scratches his Adam's apple and bears the weight, just like he bore the curse that lifted in October.

I think about returning to my parents, living under the same roof where I felt like my faith wasn't real and I'd end up in an inescapable hell, literally. The combined toxicity of that blinded me, telling me that happiness, always out of reach, would stay that way, a mirrorball forever forging into the distance where I could see it but never quite touch its reflective surface. If I go back…

Unceremoniously, Van rips the envelope open, revealing a small golden card within.

I peek over and read the cursive black letters, spelling out— "Congratulations, Apple Hair. Prepare for your debut in the first quarter of next year."

A tiny spark leaps off the golden card, almost singing my eyebrows off.

And then Seiya yells, "Hell yeah!"

We embrace so tightly my arms might fall off, but being crushed by these guys might just be the most comforting and exhilarating sensation on earth. In the background, Merlin Kim chuckles. He stands up and puts a hand on our shoulders, alternating between the five of us, standing over us like a true forest wizard who finally found what he was looking for in all four corners of a hidden domain.

"Congratulations." he says. "To tell you the truth, I was already convinced after your performance at UH. I've never seen anything like it. And maybe I am convinced that magic exists now?"

"Thank you," I say.

He brushes it off with a grin and dad-like waving motion with his arms. "I didn't do anything but vote yes."

Merlin Kim, as the sun traverses the sky, tells us that we will continue with a few months of training in South Korea. The AWE branch in Seoul will take good care of us, giving us unlimited space to learn all we can about K-pop, the ins and outs of what it means to truly create a masterful performance, to dive into the hearts of an audience with as much prowess as we can muster. Upon returning to Hawaiʻi, we will finalize our debut EP and first music video.

We all give Merlin Kim a hug. And when I close my eyes, I see him once again as the lost wizard, wandering the forest and discovering the unlimited possibility of dreaming. Merlin, without a doubt, shot up to the sky like a lighthouse, like the soul that was just looking for a reason to support us.

Shar drops us off at the airport in the next week, and she gives us each an individual bone crushing hug that could probably fuse two pieces of metal together, forging them into a new element altogether. I check once again for my passport, feeling the contours of my bag to make sure everything's there. Unfortunately, I can't be like Seiya who checked his things a total of one time, as if seeing things in his bag in a single glance was enough for him.

"Don't worry," Seiya says. "You got everything. Trust."

I follow the guys to print out our boarding passes. The whole time, I blink hard and question whether I'm truly dreaming, wandering the world we created, MEORI. Fans have started to write out what MEORI means to them, and the members and I have created the lore in our fan cafe.

In MEORI, the magic system is based on creativity. Imagination is your limit, and the ecosystem is run by the freedom to craft projects. A microphone that can amplify your voice for a mile without hurting anyone's eardrums. A glimmering piece of metal that you wear around your neck to enhance your writing abilities, crushing any creative block through its invisible waves.

Although "anything is possible" might be a cliche for a storyworld, I truly believe it for MEORI. The members and I will start out in this storyworld with separate lives, but we will come together to create a boy band focused on healing and expression, a group that everyone who enters the world can look up to, to collaborate with.

Corrin spent a lot of time focusing on the new animals in MEORI, while Van started a history of its literature. Kaden's working out the history and the nitty gritty politics of this new world. While Seiya has been focused on sports and music. I have tried to flesh out the beautiful landscapes, similar to the plains and fields and mountains of our world, except imbued with special colors that were inspired by my more tender moments in the original dream world. After all, I don't think what I created outside our apartment in Kakaʻako was all that bad, but rather an extension of us—a part of us that was still learning to open our wings of possibility.

To put it simply, the fan cafe is thriving again. Or should I say bursting with something entirely new, a vibrancy that was unmatched before our debut was confirmed? There is still much to explore with this different avenue of dreaming, going beyond lucid and bleeding out into our real world. But it's more than comforting to have a small island of new dreamers to discover with, even if they aren't fully aware of the entrapments and razor-sharp steel threads of Leo.

And then we head to the security screening. A bit more anxiety rushes through me, but my heart quickly replaces it with pure excitement for seeing South Korea. I went three years ago, and at that time I was solely focused on living out my faith as a Christian. I still am, with four other guys I could share my testimony with. Wasn't this year a huge part of my testimony as well?—watering new seeds, making sure new roots were planted into solid ground, safe from the winds and waves and jealousy.

The happiness of the week, like I was floating within a cumulus cloud, comes crashing down when I realize who stands ahead of us in the line. Leo. No mistaking it, the producer holds a designer backpack, with his hair styled like an idol on the way to a weekly music show. His clothes fit him effortlessly, as if made to fall across the lines of his body like art pieces off a custom frame.

"Do you guys see him too?" I say.

He turns around, flashing us a little grin. In it, I sense a hint of the lion, a bit of lightning in his dark brown eyes, another challenge in his flawless posture and platinum earrings. If I were playing a mobile game, this would be my second encounter with the final boss, where the playing field has been completely flipped over and dusted with ashes.

I turn to the boys. Instead of panicking, we share a little nod. We fought him before, and we can do it again. Maybe in Seoul, we'll face more ghosts. A different lion.

But we did it. We're going to debut, setting the world aflame with our dream. Our dream of creating our universe came true, and the plane will take us to expand that world, until the legacy of Apple Hair will hopefully lead everyone to feel love. Just like how I know God loves me, I love him and these guys. Not just team members.

Family.

Acknowledgments

I sound like David, but I couldn't have done this without Jesus' help!

To my family members, thank you for supporting my dream—even in the times when I was discouraged. Shout out to my friends who always push me to write just a little more, to push out one more chapter or project.

Thank you to BTS, TXT, One Direction, and all the boy bands and K-pop artists who inspired Apple Hair. You are brilliant and talented.

Thank you to my editor Raven. You are a superstar! My proofreader, Brandee, you really gave me the confidence to finish. To Polgarus Studio, thank you for your wonderful formatting. I can't forget about my cover artist, Nisa, who absolutely slayed with the design. The boys look so good and dreamy.

Reader, thank you for reading this whole adventure. May you continue to attend all the concerts of your dreams. I promise you the boys will be back. Van, Corrin, Kaden, Seiya, and David want to give you a big thanks too!

About the Author

Airen Ho was born to two loving parents but somehow became ravenous for a good, loving protagonist. He loves everything to do with boy bands and gaming. He also has a passion for makeup and beauty.

Airen lives with multiple cats under the bright sunshine. He can be found writing, reading, or trying to increase his vocal range.

Follow him on socials:
TikTok & Instagram: @ahairen
Wattpad and Substack: @airenho
Facebook: @AppleHairStory

Subscribe to the official Apple Hair newsletter at www.applehairstory.com. I will be sharing behind-the-scenes, AUs, and exclusives from the five members!

If you enjoyed this book, please leave a review on Amazon, Goodreads, or both (which would be awesome)! Thank you so much, reader. Please look forward to Apple Hair's debut.